SHIPPING ONLY

Glimpse of a Stranger

JOE DAVID BROWN

• • • • • • • •

William Morrow & Company, Inc.
New York   1968

Published simultaneously in Canada
by George J. McLeod Limited, Toronto.

Printed and bound in the United States of America
by American Book-Stratford Press, Inc.

Typographical design by Sidney Feinberg

Library of Congress Catalog Card Number 68-14809

FOR Frances Phillips
Edith Haggard
John Willey
(In the order of their appearance)

PART
1

ONE . . .

. . . and I remember only one bitter winter morning a distraught middle-aged man appeared in the streets of the town. he wore neither an overcoat nor a tie and his blue suit was rumpled and sour with vomit and whiskey. the man's long raw face had been battered by booze and despair, but there was some pride in him yet. he had gone into a public toilet somewhere and tried to make himself presentable. lint from a paper towel clung to the graying stubble of his beard and he had plastered down his thinning hair with water. he had the lurching walk of a drunkard and his hands shook and fluttered and jumped as if they were wild things trying to escape. as he met people, the man would stumble toward them anxiously, saying, "I am lost and I wonder if . . ."

most people would look at the man coldly and brush past him without a word. but occasionally someone would stop and listen with an unresponsive and wary face. there was a frightening intensity about the man then. he would clasp his shaking hands and bare his long yellow teeth in a grimace meant to be a smile. and he would lean forward and speak with eager hoarse gasps which made his words difficult to follow because they would rise and fall and collide, " 's . . . awfly . . . decent . . . ofyoutotakethe trouble. I . . . can't . . . seemtofindmy . . . hotel."

"What's the name of it?"

"That's . . . justthetrouble," the man would say, trying to control his darting hands. "I don't know. 'S a bigplace . . . a . . . very . . . bigplace . . . ontheedgeoftown."

"There ain't no hotels on the edge of town far's I know."

"Oh yes. Oh, yesyes," the man would protest, leaning closer and baring his teeth even more to show he meant no offense. "It's . . . ontheedgeoftown . . . I'm certaincertain." he would rise teeteringly on his tiptoes and jab frantically toward the east, as if to show that if only he could see over the buildings he could point to the very place.

"Well, I been livin' here all my life and I ain't never heard of no hotel on the edge of town. The only hotels in town far's I know are the Windsor . . . the Towers . . ."

during this recitation, the man would lean forward with his eyes fixed desperately on the speaker's lips, and he would raise a trembling hand and make a frantic beckoning motion as if to say, go on, please, go on. but no one ever said the name of the right hotel and the man's grimace would become more strained and he would straighten up and sigh. then he would lean forward again and, if possible, his manner was even more beseeching than before. "The . . . owner . . . of . . . this hotel . . . isalittleman . . . a tinylittleman . . . no . . . bigger . . . than this." and he would hold his hand not much more than three feet from the ground.

everybody would walk away then. some people would laugh, and some would look frightened, and others would look annoyed. but they all would walk away. and the man would look stricken and call pleadingly after them, " 'sfact . . . wait . . . honest . . . 'sfact." he would take one or two unsteady steps as if to overtake them and say, "All of my clothes are still out there. Here . . . looklook," and desperately he would yank at his shirt cuff and pull it out of his sleeve, as if his dirty shirt was proof that everything he said was true.

sometimes someone would ask, "Why don't you go to the police?" the man's eager manner would change then and his raised lip would come down over his teeth. "I did . . . andthey toldme . . ." he shrugged and waved his trembling hand in a contemptuous gesture, and it was obvious the police had no time to waste on the man. indeed, once during the day, when a small knot of curious people gathered around the man at the entrance to the biggest building in town, a policeman on the corner saw the gathering and came over to investigate. he was a big man with a stupid, sullen face and he moved ponderously as a bear in his fleece-lined boots and heavy blue overcoat which had a hood attached. he stood at the edge of the crowd listening to the man and, without a word, shouldered his way forward and placed his big mittened hand under the man's elbow and began hustling him away. from some place, the man mustered up an impressive dignity. he glared angrily and his voice was almost commanding, "What's the meaning of this, officer? What are you trying to do?" the policeman stopped and stared at the man sullenly for a long time, then he dropped his hand and said, "Don't go blockin' this entrance," and walked away. the man gave an angry shrug as if to straighten his wrinkled jacket and called mockingly after the policeman, "I won't do that, officer. Oh, I certainly won't do that!" he walked away muttering and leaned dejectedly against the building for a long time before he started approaching people again.

all that day and until far into the night, the man wandered up and down the town, talking to anyone who would stop. once you had heard his story, you could stand at a distance and follow it by watching the man's gestures. the eager lurch forward with clasped hands . . . the teetering on tiptoes and the frantic jabs toward the east . . . the leaning forward again with the pleading beckoning motion, and finally the gesture about three feet above the ground . . . followed by the passer-by's departure.

the man was not in the streets the next morning. late in the afternoon his frozen body was found curled up in a paper carton in the alley behind a drug store. and the man's death grin was exactly the same as his beseeching smile had been in real life.

once he was dead the police took a great interest in the man. in only a few hours they learned that he had been a Chicago attorney with a promising career until he became a drunkard. only three days before his wife had brought him to Hilltop. a fancy rest home six miles east of town which catered to rich drunks and drug addicts. he had been drunk when he arrived. as soon as he was shown to his room he had climbed out a window and come to town and drunk until his money ran out. the owner of Hilltop was a man named Foster who had lost both his legs in the first world war. he disdained artificial limbs and walked on leather pads fitted to his stumps. he was not quite four feet tall.

when people in the town read about the dead lawyer, they shook their heads and made clucking noises. "Of course . . . of course," they said. "That's what the poor sick man meant. How stupid we were." but, of course, it was too late then because the stranger was dead. he had been hopelessly lost among all those people. and nobody had offered him a seat by the fire, a drink, a kind word, or had even really cared that he was lost . . .

He told Cynthia about the lost man while they lay between pink silk sheets in the house in Chelsea. He was drunk, very drunk; but not too drunk to know it, so he spoke slowly and carefully, and he was surprised and pleased to discover that his voice sounded exactly like his father's had when his father preached on a Sunday.

When he had finished, Cynthia rolled over and raised herself on her elbows and studied him with that amused, rapt look she had when he said things she didn't quite understand. Cynthia was famous for her cool beauty, but as he looked at her tousled hair, her half-closed eyes, and her heavy creamy breasts hanging ripely against the pink sheets, he suddenly decided she looked as wanton as. . . as . . . yes, as wanton as Aholah. He said, "Thy name is Aholah and thy have bruised the breasts of thy virginity . . ."

"Never mind my virginity, you drunken Holy Roller," Cynthia said. "What's the meaning of that parable?"

"What parable?"

"The parable you spake about the lawyer."

"Oh." He wrinkled his forehead with drunken concentration, and when he remembered, suddenly, all his anguish and despair became so unbearable that he found himself unable to hide it. He forgot to speak like his father, and his voice was ragged as he said, "I am as lost as that poor man. Every day I wander around . . . looking . . . looking into strange faces . . . searching for someone who will help me. Every time I turn a corner . . . open a door . . . walk into a room . . . I pray I will find somebody waiting there who can help me."

Cynthia threw herself on her back and laughed her big, full actress's contralto laugh until the bed shook. "You are really drunk, lover," she said, delightedly. "Oh, Lord—are you ever skunk drunk!"

Surprisingly, he felt himself begin to cry. Even as drunk as he was, he knew he was behaving like a fool. But he shook with great drunken hiccuping sobs. "Yes, I am drunk," he sobbed. "I am very drunk, but it doesn't matter. Because tomorrow I will be sober—but I still will be lost. I am hopelessly lost and I am afraid . . . I am so afraid that nobody will help me, and I never will be found again."

TWO...

He awakened slowly, reluctantly, refusing to make the slightest effort to return to consciousness. And even after he was fully awake, he still lay there in complete surrender. It was always worse first thing in the morning before he had a chance to muster his defenses; a heavy, suffocating agony, almost like an actual physical pain, tightening his guts and making him want to clench his teeth. *Oh, God, he thought, must I live another day. I want to die . . . why can't I just die?*

He lay very still, trying to keep his body relaxed and his breathing even, wanting desperately to escape again into oblivion. Then, ever so faintly, he heard the rumble of traffic on the King's Road, the quick impatient toot of a perky little horn. The sound widened the boundaries of his despair. The agony almost became panicky fear. *I won't get up! Oh, God, I can't get up.* Blunderingly, clumsily, he tried to escape.

. . . the sound of the sparrows nesting under the back eaves was the sound he heard first. he lay there, half asleep and cozy, with the old Star of Bethlehem quilt pulled over his head, listening to their squabbling, and when there was a soft bump he knew one of the older birds had arrived with food even before the little ones began their excited peep-peeping. he never let on that he was awake when she came in, always playing a sort of game by singing Let the Blessed Sunshine In . . . Let the Blessed Sunshine In, and when she pushed back the curtains with a rattling sound, and the sunshine came pouring in, he would bury his head deeper in the covers and give a loud groan,

14 . . .

and she would give a little laugh and say, "Paul. Paul, dear . . . son."

—But it was no use. Or was it? He heaved a deep shuddering sigh, as if drawing together all his strength and courage, and unwillingly opened his eyes. The heavy curtains always kept the room in total darkness. Stretching out his hand, he felt the other side of the bed. Cynthia was not there, so he knew it was well after noon. The agony was still there; it was always there. But he said, "Stop it! Stop it!" half aloud and angrily, and tried to forget it.

Still not moving his head, he reached out to the bedside table with a practiced hand and snapped on the lamp and found a cigarette and the heavy silver lighter. He took a couple of slow thoughtful puffs on his cigarette before he returned the lighter to the table and sat up to take stock of himself. Except for a slight cottony taste in his mouth, he felt well enough. He had not the slightest remorse because he had been drunk; it never occurred to him that he should have. He knew that he drank too much, but he knew also that liquor was not one of his problems. Usually he avoided making the point even to himself, but the truth was he had some vague conviction that it was only because he went on a spree periodically that he had escaped ulcers and a psychiatrist's couch.

He had only a dim, disjointed recollection of his crying jag. As he sat smoking his cigarette, he brooded on it gingerly for a while. Then, without much effort, he pushed it to the back of his mind. He supposed he had looked and acted like a fool, but that didn't bother him too much. But it did bother him that for the first time, he had openly revealed his deep and malignant despair. He preferred to keep it a secret, partly because he detested self-pity, but mostly because he was ashamed; he felt so weak and frightened because it lurked there, threatening to—but he reached out and jabbed out his cigarette, and resolutely shoved that out of mind, too. He wouldn't mention anything that he had said. Whether she took him seriously or not, Cynthia probably wouldn't either. One of the things that had kept them together so long was that they never held post-mortems on drinking bouts or quarrels. He gave the silk sheets an automatic disdainful kick, swung his feet to the floor, and stood up.

He was a tall man, six feet, three inches. In his clothes he looked thin almost to the point of gauntness, but as he stood naked it was apparent that he had ample flesh, perhaps he even had some to spare across his broad back and wide shoulders and heavy upper arms. He crossed the room and opened the door to Cynthia's black-and-gold bathroom. She had not left it long before; it was heavy with the pleasant, musky odor of her steaming body, her cologne, and her tiny Turkish cigarettes. He automatically stopped and peered into the brightly lit gilt mirror above her wash basin, and when he saw that he had only a slight puffiness under his eyes, he felt even better. He crossed to another door, walked through his dressing room, and went into his own bath.

Less than twenty minutes later, he was shaved, showered and dressed, and standing casual inspection before the full-length mirror in his dressing room. He centered his tie, and turned and began to walk away, but, then, as was almost habitual of late, he came back and somberly studied himself in the mirror. As a boy and an adolescent, he had often done this; looking deep into his eyes, studying his features and trying on his expressions one by one, trying to fathom the mystery of what he was and what he would be. But, in those days, it seemed almost all his questions began with *Will you—Will you be rich? Will you be famous? Will you go to Africa? To Paris? Fly the ocean? Have nerve enough to kiss Mary Lou Bass?* Asking whatever his juvenile fancy and imagination made seem dreadfully important.

Now, in his middle years, the question he asked of his mirror was simply *Why?* Why had living become so joyless, almost intolerable? Why, especially, when he had gained as much fame as he desired, when for years he had had more money than he needed? Was it simply that the years had brought a realization that neither was important? No, it was more than that. He stood there, a tall, graying man, and measured his reflection with a melancholy eye. Even though he wore one of his Anderson & Sheppard suits, and everything else he wore, from underwear to pocket handkerchief, was European in origin, he knew he looked unmistakably American. Once he had been proud of this characteristic, and insofar as anything still gave him pride, perhaps he still was. He had been both amused and pleased when *Time* in a cover story it did when he had three hits running simultaneously said: "Derrick-tall Paul Fraser looks like a cowboy who went to Oxford." There were things about him which did fulfill the stereotype of a cowboy: his height and rawbone slimness, an air and a look of ruggedness, a certain deliberateness in speech and movement, and even an unmanageable forelock of crisp blond hair and eyes that were a trifle bluer than most blue eyes. But all these things were a legacy from his Scots-Irish forebears. Life had molded him, and tempered him, until he was far too urbane for a cowboy, and, even aside from his height, there was an individuality about him which was too subtle to define but which caused him to be noticed. "No matter where Paul goes," Cynthia once said, "people always wonder what the hell he's doing there."

But he did not dwell on any of these things as he studied himself in the mirror, for he was not a markedly vain man. And this was not so much a virtue as good luck. From earliest childhood, he had been accustomed to being found both agreeable and attractive by most people. He accepted the fact as naturally as he accepted the color of his eyes. So what vanity or conceit he may have been born with had long ago been jettisoned as being both unnecessary and not worth the burden it imposed. His concern now was not with what his appearance revealed; he was trying to determine what it concealed. He pitilessly studied his graying hair, now almost silver-white at his temples, the two deepening furrows in his cheeks, the tracery of fine wrinkles around his eyes. *You're not getting any younger, boy.* Could it be just age? Was this awful depression, this agonizing sense of unworthiness, caused by something so biochemically simple as the male climacteric? But, no, he had pondered this possibility before; and always he had dismissed it, just as he dismissed it now. It was silly. His glands were not packing up on him. True, his blood did not course as hotly as it once did, his eye could not be snared so easily. But sex had never been a problem, thank God; it was sufficient unto the day—yes, it was beautifully sufficient.

The hard truth was, for a man of forty-six, who drank too much and kept irregular hours, he was in far better physical trim than he had any right to be. No matter how much they poked him and thumped him, and made him submit to their stupid little indignities, the doctors had never been able to find a single thing wrong with him.

He looked straight into the eyes of the solemn man facing him. *Why do I want to die?* And he heard the answer as clearly as if it were spoken aloud. *Because you've had it, fellow. You don't give a good damn what happens today, or tomorrow, or next year. You've just simply goddamned well had it up to here. You're a big, fat failure.* And because he believed it was true, it was true—crushingly, unequivocally true. He gave a deep sigh, and with dread, turned to face another day.

By English standards it was a beautiful day. Light from a feeble mid-day sun was filtering through the tall windows of the dining room and reflecting off the jumble of silver on the sideboard, the polished surface of the mahogany table, and Cynthia's too golden hair. She was wearing the tomato-red dressing gown he had picked out at Patou's, and, as always, she was as silken and scented and glossy as if she was awaiting a curtain call. Discarded pages from the morning papers were scattered at her feet. When he entered, she excitedly brandished the page she was reading. "Paul, darling, do listen to this. It's the *goddamnedest* thing!" Then while Alice, the bashful little Irish maid, brought his juice and coffee, Cynthia dramatically read the account of an incident that had taken place in the South of France. A couple who owned a large Alsatian dog were having some friends in for cocktails when suddenly, and for no obvious reason, the usually well-behaved dog went over to a woman guest, sank its teeth to the bone in her arm, and refused to let go. When all efforts to pry the dog's jaws apart failed, its owner was forced to kill it by smashing in its skull with a heavy metal ashtray.

"Now isn't that the goddamnedest thing!" Cynthia said.

He nodded, and when Cynthia continued to look at him so expectantly, he said, "Yes. Yes, it certainly is." He was thinking how typical it was of Cynthia to go for months making no comment at all on news stories about death, disaster, impending nuclear doom, and all varieties of human woes, and then suddenly becoming all worked up over a story of a deranged dog biting a woman. It didn't annoy him; it simply was—well, it simply was typical of Cynthia. If he had any feeling at all, it probably was amusement. Maybe even admiration. It was one of the reasons Cynthia was such a superb actress. More than any actress he had ever known, she lived on imagination and emotion. He studied Cynthia, so eager and vibrant, so elegant and shiny in her $650 red *peignoir*. Cynthia was a delight. Sometimes when he watched her making one of her grand entrances, sweeping out so regally, smiling with just the proper blending of graciousness and condescension, even he found it hard to believe she was the uninhibited, unpredictable, badly educated little Bronx girl who shared his bed. The little Bronx girl was wonderful, too; but she didn't exist outside their bedroom. She was merely the manikin on which Cynthia hung her roles, including that of a brilliant and famous actress which she played all the time. Cynthia wasn't content to have second-hand knowledge of any emotion. She had a hungry, amoral compulsion to test everything, dig her fingers into it, fondle it, taste it. She wasn't merely being giddy about the episode of the dog. It was a challenge; a situation too unique to have been imagined, so it wasn't in Cynthia's emotional repertoire. He knew she would ponder and puzzle and shudder over it until she had decided exactly how she would feel and behave if a large dog came up to her at a cocktail party and sank its teeth into her arm.

"... damnedest thing!" Cynthia was saying. "What do you suppose ever made him do it, lover?"

"Him? What makes you think it was a him?"

Cynthia looked at the story again. "All right," she said. "What made her or him or it do it?"

He shrugged. "Maybe it just went crazy. A good dog should have enough sense to have a mental breakdown."

"I wonder," she said. "I'll have to remember to ask Arlie. He'll know." Arlie was her analyst. "Have you ever been bitten by a dog, lover?" she asked.

"Hundreds of times," he said.

"Oh, do be serious."

"I am," he said. He thought about it for a while. "When I was a boy," he said, "there was a single dog that bit me that many times. It was ..." But then Mrs. Purdy, the housekeeper, came into the room, and Cynthia held up the paper. "Mrs. Purdy, do listen to this. It's ..."

Alice poured him another cup of coffee, and while Cynthia and Mrs. Purdy talked about the dog and household problems, he sipped it thoughtfully.

... every afternoon when he pushed his bike up the steep hill on underwood avenue he would say a little prayer that the dog wouldn't be there, but when he reached the top of the hill it always was, skulking on the lawn of the white house with the green awnings and the chinaberry tree growing near the front stoop. he would stand there, rolling up the paper and catching his breath and never taking his eyes off the dog. then he would get on his bike and hitch up his paper bag and take a deep breath and pedal down the hill as fast as he could, with the wind whistling past his ears and the tires humming on the sidewalk and going bump ... bump ... bump ... as they passed over the cracks. the dog was always waiting and it would creep forward, crouching low with his belly almost on the ground, and his ears laid back on his head. when he raised his hand to throw the paper, the dog would give a little wiggle and come running across the lawn as fast as he could and then there would be a black-and-tan snarling fury at his feet and he would kick out at the dog and try to keep his balance while the heavy paper bag thumped him against the side and the dog would nip him through his black stockings right above his high shoes . . . nip him . . . nip him . . . nip him. and one day he lost his balance and fell, and he was gripped with a cold fear when he found himself on the ground, and instinctively he raised his arms and covered his face and head and crouched there, waiting for the dog to bite him. but nothing happened and after a while he looked up, and the dog was sitting there grinning, with his tongue hanging out and making whimpering noises as if to say, "Well, get up and let's go do it again." wonderingly, he put out his hand and the dog came to him immediately and licked his fingers and frisked around his feet and then he petted the dog hard and said, "Good boy! . . . good boy! Why you're a nice dog. We're friends—aren't we, boy . . . aren't we, boy!" but when he picked up his bike and got on it, the dog crouched low and when he started off it dashed forward and once again there was a snarling tan-and-black fury about his feet . . . nipping . . . nipping . . . nipping. but it didn't hurt much; hardly at all, in fact, because now he knew the dog was just playing . . .

He sat thinking about the paper boy for a long time. He did not realize Mrs. Purdy had left until Cynthia placed her hand on his. Apparently she had been watching him for some time, and she had a look of tender amusement. "What are you thinking about, lover?"

Because he knew it would please her, he told the truth, "I was thinking about how the world sang when I was a boy."

She didn't change expression. "How do you mean 'sang'?"

"Well, it's hard to describe, but when I was a kid there was a sort of soft and continuous humming—a kind of joyous leit-motiv about me all the time, particularly when I was alone.

I don't remember ever thinking it was particularly remarkable. I guess I thought everybody else heard it, too."

"When did it stop?"

"I don't know." He thought a moment. "Maybe it didn't. Maybe I just stopped listening. Or maybe it stopped when I lost my innocence."

She laughed. "You never lost it, lover."

"Oh, yes, I did," he said. "But maybe I did keep it longer than most kids."

"I never had any," she said.

"Of course, you did. It's standard equipment, like the sucking instinct and a fear of falling. It's a protective cocoon we all have. I've never decided, though, whether we break out of it or the outside world breaks in. Anyway, we lose it."

"And that's when we spread our big beautiful wings and fly away?"

"Good Lord, no," he said. "That's when we stand naked and vulnerable and squirming. We have a hard time until we grow another protective covering to last us all our lives. And what kind we develop depends on a lot of things—how sensitive we are, how easily we bleed, how much we get cuffed around."

"I wouldn't know about that, darling, I had a very sheltered upbringing. The only singing I ever heard was when a drunken Irishman upstairs came home and sang down the dumbwaiter."

For the first time all morning, he smiled. "What did he sing?"

"Oh, *Danny Boy, Did Your Mother Come From Ireland*— the goddamned works."

"What was his name?"

"O'Hara. John Michael O'Hara."

"Why did he sing down the dumbwaiter?"

"Because it was like a sound chamber, I guess."

"He must have been a fine fellow."

"He was a worthless son-of-a-bitch," she said. "He used to beat up his wife and kids before every performance."

"Oh," he said. He thought about it. He said, "Well, he couldn't have been all bad if he sang down a dumbwaiter." He finished his coffee, sighed and stood up. "Must go. The hand of the diligent maketh wealth."

She rose and came to him and put both her arms around his waist. "You'll be backstage?"

"Yes," he said, "I'll see you at intermission."

"Nate and Dolly are having supper with us. I thought we'd go to that Moroccan place where the eunuch dances with the drum."

He felt annoyed. "He's *not* a eunuch, Cynthia. He's just a poor little colored homo."

"Well, whatever his problems, darling, Nate and Dolly will enjoy him."

"Do we have to eat there?" He disliked the Moroccan place, especially the food.

"Not if you'd rather not," she said.

"I'll book a table somewhere," he said. He stooped and kissed her good-bye.

As he walked through the hall, he pondered, as he had a thousand times, on the force of Cynthia's kiss. She simply had never learned that kisses could be perfunctory, polite or merely affectionate. Each time she kissed, it was as if she were welcoming home a lover from a long war. Once when he mentioned it to her, she said, "Well, for God's sake, a kiss is a kiss. You either kiss or you shake hands." During rehearsals, he always watched fascinated when Cynthia played a love scene with an actor for the first time. After they felt the hot blast of that kiss, there was always the glazed, unbelieving look, then the little smirk, the preening of the moustache, followed by a cocky assurance. Fairly often there was some awkwardness later, until, presumably, Cynthia set them straight that a kiss was merely a kiss. He was not certain she convinced them all. He had not been faithful to Cynthia; really didn't know whether she had been faithful to him. He knew she would tell him if he asked. It was unbelievable how much he liked

Cynthia; sometimes he adored her, just as sometimes he felt like strangling her. But he didn't love her. Not really love her. He was glad he didn't because loving somebody as unpredictable and unrestrained as Cynthia would be a misery. To be married to her would be a calamity. She was already famous when they met, her name a household word, because after making a name on the New York stage, she had spent five years in Hollywood grinding out pictures. Neither of them could remember the first time they met, nor which one started the sly and shifty maneuvering that eventually led to a weekend together. But he never would forget the sunshiny morning five years ago when they sat together in his automobile outside her hotel in New York.

"Well, where do we go?" he asked.

She grinned at him. "Why, Atlantic City. Where else?"

So they went to Atlantic City for the first time in their lives and demanded the bridal suite at the biggest, flossiest hotel on the boardwalk. Within a few hours the lobby was full of reporters and they had to take the telephones off the hooks. They didn't dare go outside. But they managed. Yes, they managed very well. There was a huge round bed as white and as hideously ornate as the bottom tier of a hundred-dollar wedding cake. And even the first time they made love, it was amazingly, unexpectedly perfect. All weekend, they made love and laughed and tossed about happily and took perfumed bubble baths together and ate cheese cake and milk at midnight.

He delivered Cynthia back to her hotel early Monday morning. She slid out of the car with a small smile and a casual wave. He had not been in his own apartment more than a half hour when the doorbell chimed, and when he opened the door, to his delight, Cynthia stood there. Theatrical as always, she had three or four hats piled on her head, her arms loaded with furs, and she was carrying a large brass birdcage containing a white cockatoo. She grinned at him. "May I come in and visit?"

He smiled and stepped aside. "You're always welcome," he

said. Was she still? He didn't even have to pause to think about it to realize she was.

As he emerged from the house, Harold, his cockney driver, was leaning against the front fender of the Bentley. Harold came to attention and gave him a deferential little salute. "Good day, sir," he said. "Pleasant day today, sir."

"Yes, it is," he said. He paused a moment, looking up and down the quiet street. Then he looked at his watch. It was a few minutes of two. "Well, follow along, Harold," he said.

"Right-o, sir,"

As he walked up the street, he studied the dingy brick fronts of the houses. They had fascinated him ever since he learned that they had been built in 1713 as workers' cottages, and there had been a terrible scandal because the builder had been accused of using shoddy materials and profiteering. Now almost 250 years later the houses were still solid, under protection of the National Trust as historic monuments, and had become some of the most expensive residential real estate in London. Solid, all right. That was the word he always thought about in connection with England and the English. He had always admired the English, particularly since the war when he had been stationed in London and saw their matter-of-fact, almost ridiculous heroism during the blitz. Looking back, he found it difficult to understand why he had hesitated when Cynthia first brought up the idea of his taking over the London production of his play. The play was a hit and Cynthia was an even bigger success than she had been in New York. After five months he had learned to love the civilized, well-ordered routine of London, and if he was eaten with unhappiness, well . . . He paused thoughtfully and took out a small notebook and a gold pencil. In the personal shorthand which was a holdover from the days when he was a young reporter, he wrote: *f I mus b unhapy eres no btr pl tan London.* He could drop the line in a bit of dialogue sometime. With the right twist, changing the town to suit the location, it should be good for a laugh.

He waited at the corner of the King's Road for a double-decker bus to swish past, and crossed the street to a small tobacconist shop. He made his daily purchase of 25 cigarettes and asked Mr. Thompson, the horse-toothed proprietor, about his gallstones. He also listened while Mr. Thompson told him about his sister's son who was recovering from an operation for a double hernia. After he left the shop, he paused outside to light one of his cigarettes and stood there a few moments feeling the warmth of the wan sun, and thinking that was another thing about London. It reminded him of how it had been when he was a boy and tradesmen always had time to chat with their customers because they were friends and neighbors. *". . . Essie looked mighty pretty on Sunday, Mr. Sadler." "Yeh, well, Essie takes after the Wellses, them was my grandma's people. You must remember ole grandma Wells. All the Wellses was fairskinned, well set-up people." "Seems Essie's seein' a lot of the Hankins boy?" "Yeh, well, Roy's a good boy . . . good worker, too, Roy . . . reckon Essie could do a lot worse. Couldn't think more of Roy if he was one of m'own. That'll come to forty cents, miz Shelton. Now what else can I do you for?"* He walked up the King's Road, past the butcher's and greengrocer's, stepping around the meandering housewives with their string bags and prams, studiously ignoring the bizarrely dressed young swingers parading the street in twos or threes or gathered in clusters outside the garishly decorated Mod shops. For perhaps a week after he arrived in London, he had been amused by the deadpan little girls with their miniskirts and their kewpie-doll twiggy eye makeup, the slouchy young men festooned with brass buttons and wearing their hair teased up like fright-wigs. But now he had discovered how phony they were—their preening self-consciousness robbing them of any charm; always keeping their pimply buttermilk-colored faces flat and impassive—but darting their eyes around covertly to see what attention they were attracting. It gave him a mild satisfaction to pretend he did not see them.

Outside the fishmonger's he paused momentarily to look at

a basket filled with eels, then crossed the street where a curb-side barrow boy was hoarsely hawking apples, and turned in at a florist shop. Ruth Anglesly, the rather pretty upper-class Scotswoman who owned the shop, smiled when she saw him and made a motion for him to keep quiet. She raised her voice. "Oh, Renee, Mr. Fraser is here for his buttonhole." Almost immediately, Renee, the big lumpy girl who was her helper, burst from the back of the shop with a red carnation in one hand, grinning excitedly. "I saw one of your films over the weekend, Mr. Fraser," she said. "One you wrote and directed."

He smiled and bent forward for Renee to put the flower in his lapel. "What was it called?"

"*Love in a Canoe*—with Derek Hunter and Joan de Witt," she said.

"Good Lord," he said, surprised. "Is that still playing around? Where did you see it?"

"At a cinema in Bidborough," Renee said. She giggled. "Oh, it was cool," Renee said. "Especially the part where she pushed him in the water and held him under with a paddle."

He smiled at Renee without quite seeing her. He remembered the scene. Yes, he remembered it very well. He remembered how big, slow-witted Derek had been afraid of water and how he had refused to admit it. He had made Derek put on a bathing suit and all one weary afternoon he had rehearsed him on the set which was built in the pond in the back lot. But no matter how hard he tried, no matter how much he stretched his lips in a forced grin, Derek couldn't hide the panic he felt everytime he went under water and came up sputtering. He couldn't recall the clever line Derek was supposed to say, but finally they changed it to, "Hey! I can't swim!" With the look of genuine fright on Derek's big dumb handsome face, it made the whole scene.

He was thinking about *Love in a Canoe* as he left the shop. Despite its assinine title, it was a pretty fair picture. He had brought it in at about 800 thousand, which was about right in those days, and it had grossed 3 million 2 and . . . He broke off with an angry grunt. What in hell was wrong with him? It was a lousy picture—terrible, like most of the pictures he had done. He thought about it and sighed deeply. Did he really have any integrity left as far as his work was concerned? He certainly no longer had any illusions about the literary value of his plays. But that bitter truth had come slowly, gradually, too. In the old days he had been hurt and puzzled almost every season because some jerk who needed a bath and a barber and a psychiatrist was called a genius because he scrawled some obscene and badly organized junk that kept a curtain up for three acts. Sure, they had called him the Boy Wonder of Broadway, but that was because he had so many hits in succession—not because any one of them was ever considered really important. Maybe it still wasn't too late . . . maybe he should write something murky and incestuous that stank of decaying magnolia blossoms and . . . Oh, for God's sake, that was silly . . . stupid. He couldn't write that kind of play, and he didn't want to. Anyway, what happened to all the geniuses who sputtered for a season? Most of them were long since forgotten, but he had gone on and on. Yes, he supposed he had husbanded his small talent like a good and faithful servant—if it was a talent. After his first two plays were successful he had felt slightly guilty, wondered when somebody would discover his secret. But even when he told it to anybody who would listen, it didn't seem to make any difference. Maybe it wasn't as simple as it seemed. Maybe it was sort of Godgiven, or, anyway . . . Goddirected. When he came back to the city room that day he certainly didn't have the slightest idea what he was going to write. He simply spread his notes out beside him and, almost without thinking about it, began to transcribe what the mayor had said, word for word, phrase for phrase, putting in all the ers and ahs and the twisted syntax and the tortured phraseology, and as he wrote he began to laugh to himself and he knew it was wonderful. It helped because the paper was fighting the mayor, it helped a lot; but it was good, anyway. When it appeared and everybody came around to tell him how wonderful it was and he got a bonus, he felt marvelous. It worked once so he tried it again and again, and before he knew it he was the hottest writer on the paper and people were calling him a humorist . . . all because he had discovered that when he wrote down with painstaking correctness everything people said and did they were funnier than a stageful of chimpanzees. They were God's jest. But if it hadn't been for Sam, dear, sweet Sam . . . He felt a small cold pang as he always did, when he remembered Sam was dead.

. . . he was sitting behind the desk in that untidy old office with the brass cuspidor on the floor and the faded and fly-specked photographs and handbills covering the walls, and as always, he had his short legs spread to support his big belly and the legs of his pants were hitched up exposing his cheap socks and his alabaster shins and there was a musing, searching look on his big ugly compassionate jewish face, and he reached out and tapped the paper on his desk with his pudgy hand and he said, "I been reading what yuh been writing, kid, and I think yuh got sump'in. Yuh think you could do a play, nuthing fancy, just sump'in, about some people, maybe some nice geezer about to do sump'in crooked and a nice dame trying to keep him from doing it. Yuh know the kinda thing I mean." "Well, I . . . I could sure try, Mr. Aaron," he said, overwhelmed. "Well, why don'cha give it a try and bring it around and let me read it?" "All right, Mr. Aaron . . . all right," he said, and he got up and shook Sam's pudgy hand and started for the door and Sam said, "Kid," and he turned and Sam said, "Yuh got any money?" and he stammered, "Why . . . why, sure, Mr. Aaron . . . sure," and Sam got up and reached in his pocket and took out the biggest roll of bills he had ever seen and peeled off two bills and waddled over and handed them to him and said, "Don't ever say that, kid, always say you don't have enough," and then he laughed for the first time, his big infectious belly laugh and Sam handed him the bills and he almost gasped because they were both hundreds and somehow he thanked Sam and bolted through the door and ran down *the steps and as he walked through the crowds on broadway he could barely keep from shouting, "Look at me! Look at me!" because he had four weeks' salary in his pocket and Sam Aaron, the famous producer, had asked him to write a play and he was filled with a resolve so big and hot and bursting that he wanted to cry . . .*

He had reached Sloane Square. He stopped and waited for the gray and black Bentley which was a half-block away. He seldom gave it a thought, but the Bentley represented something to him, and it was solid evidence of his financial security; not because it was a fine and expensive motor car, but because he had not paid two or three hundred dollars more for a different radiator that would have transformed it into a more glamorous Rolls Royce. He had run through most of the experiences and pleasures of wealth. In the early days there had been the long rows of expensively tailored clothes, the solid gold accessories, the fine burnished leather goods, the spacious and elaborately furnished apartments. Then, there had been the second stage, when he collected expensive paintings, rare art objects, kept horses and a country place. Now he was at another phase. If anyone had asked, he would have said that money was not particularly important, that he preferred to live a life as simple and uncomplicated as possible. This was not wholly true; not true at all, in fact. Many of the possessions and most of the expensive tastes still were there. He simply took them for granted. Once he had been pleased when people exclaimed over his possessions; now it embarrassed him.

The Bentley drew up. He stepped inside, leaned back with a weary sigh, and chose one of the newspapers placed in a neat pile on the seat. "The office, sir?" Harold asked.

"Yes, please," he said.

THREE . . .

Even after years he had not become hardened to stepping into a theatrical reception room and running a gauntlet of importuning faces. For that reason alone his offices in Bond Street were a joy. He stepped directly out of the elevator and unlocked the unmarked door to his private office. A large, elaborately furnished reception room was around a corner and down a corridor.

As soon as he entered he went to his desk and pushed a buzzer. He had scarcely hung up his topcoat and hat when Mrs. Mears came in, stepping and smiling briskly. Mrs. Mears was graying and matronly and she had two grown sons. Years before she had been a repertory actress, but had left the stage when she married. When her husband died, she had taken a secretarial course and gravitated back to the theater. There was scarcely anyone in the theater she didn't know—and know about. He was lucky enough to get her services because the producer for whom she had worked for years had died shortly after he arrived in England.

With no greeting, except her smile, Mrs. Mears said, "Anthony Lancaster is outside again. He's been waiting the better part of an hour. This is the fourth time in the last fortnight."

"Oh," he said. He sat down slowly to think that over. There had been exasperation in Mrs. Mears's voice, but a trace of sympathy, too. He understood that. That was the way Anthony Lancaster affected people who knew him. For forty years he had been one of the most famous actors in the English-speaking theater, and his face was still so well known that he could have tied up traffic in Piccadilly Circus if he wished. But what people who besieged Anthony Lancaster for autographs didn't stop to recall was that he had not been gainfully employed for almost a decade. One reason was that he drank and was undependable. Another reason was that he was nearing seventy and still thought of himself as a leading man. But there was something else even more pathetically wrong with Anthony Lancaster. He had played so many roles, had been a counterfeit for so long that he had lost any genuine identity. Even in private conversation, he spoke lines from his plays. People who didn't know better usually called Anthony a ham. That was essentially correct, of course. But the sad thing was his hamminess had become a kind of crippling paresis.

"Who else is out there?" he asked.

Mrs. Mears looked at her pad. "Mr. Grimes is here; he's the little man from your auditors. All the rest are hopefuls."

"Any of them have appointments?"

"Just one. A Judith Cockburn."

He looked puzzled. Mrs. Mears said, "She's the little baggage you saw in *Three Penny Opera*. She says you told her to get in touch." He nodded. Now he remembered her very well, a serious little girl with wide eyes and an odd twist to her mouth. She had a bit part in the brothel scene in a production in a shabby little club theater. She had stood out so spectacularly that he and Cynthia had gone backstage to congratulate her, and he had promised to recommend her for something if she gave him a call after the play closed.

He reached for the stack of mail on his desk and hefted it with a slight grimace. "What won't keep?"

"It'll all keep for a day or two," she said.

He looked pleased. "The box-office report?"

"Right there on your desk," she said. He found it and studied it briefly and looked up. "What . . ."

She said, "It's down three percent because of the tickets you donated to that charity auction at the Savoy."

He nodded. "Full tonight?"

"Yes."

He opened his wallet and thoughtfully removed two five pound notes and reached in his desk drawer and found an envelope and slipped them in it. "I'll see the auditor first, then the Cockburn girl," he said. "Tell the hopefuls, I regret—to write or telephone for an appointment." He handed her the envelope. "Give this to Anthony and tell him I'm busy."

She took the envelope, but looked hesitant. "Won't he be offended?"

"Yes, I guess he will be—too offended to come back again, I hope." He paused. "It's not that I mind giving him money. It's simply that I'm not doing him a favor by keeping him drunk. He can get television work. I know he's had offers. All he has to do is stay sober for a few hours—and the sooner he's forced to do it, the better."

Mr. Grimes was a slightly stooped, angular man, of medium height in his late fifties. At first glance he looked too deferential, but his handshake was firm and his eyes were level. He said, "Good day, sir." But the *sir* carried more civility than meekness. He was dressed like any middle-class professional man, except that his dark suit was old and shiny and frayed at the cuffs, his low stiff collar had been laundered too many times, and his tie, which was striped with either his regimental or school colors, was limp with age. Even so, Mr. Grimes' thinning hair was combed so neatly, his collar so clean and suit so well brushed that he seemed to have a luster, like old pewter that had been cleaned too often.

He took a chair and placed his bowler and rolled umbrella beside him with precision and opened a worn attaché case and took out some papers. "We've been dealing with your tax situation, sir," he said, "and I think you'll find these in order."

He took the papers from Mr. Grimes and scanned them quickly, flipping the pages until he found a total. "This final figure is what I owe?"

"That is correct, sir," Mr. Grimes said.

"It's quite reasonable."

Mr. Grimes' voice was dry. "It depends on the viewpoint, sir." He made a steeple with his long fingers. "The total amount is, of course, much less than your assessment would be in the United States. But you are aware, I think, that your assessment here is based only on those monies remitted to you in this country. In addition, your allowable deductions have been . . . rather staggering. The figure bears no relation to your real income."

He studied the figure again and looked pleased. "It's about a third less than I pay at home."

Mr. Grimes nodded. "Yes, sir, that's the benefit you derive from disowning your country."

He looked up annoyed, "Disowning my country?"

Mr. Grimes said calmly, "Fiscally speaking, sir. It's an expression we use." He paused. "Rather an . . . unpalatable one, perhaps."

"Damned unpalatable," he said, flatly.

Mr. Grimes was unruffled. "Yes, rather an apt one nonetheless, sir."

"What's so damned apt about it?"

"Well, you are given a choice, sir," Mr. Grimes said. "The decision is yours whether you will pay taxes here or pay them to your own country. I assume you were advised of that?"

His annoyance turned to anger, but he kept his voice flat. "I take it you think this is wrong."

"On the contrary, sir," Mr. Grimes said, "I calculated it myself. I know it is correct."

"You know what I mean," he said. He knew his voice was bullying, but he was too angry to care. "You think it's ethically wrong."

"I am afraid that is not in my jurisdiction, sir," Mr. Grimes said.

"Are you trying to pretend you wouldn't do it?"

"It is a choice I have never had the opportunity of making, sir," Mr. Grimes said, calmly.

His voice had an edge to it. "Are you implying you would not do it if you had the chance?"

Mr. Grimes sat quietly, his eyes still level and direct.

"Well?"

Mr. Grimes said, "Since you put it that way—no, sir, I personally wouldn't do it."

"And why wouldn't you?" he demanded.

Mr. Grimes sat quietly for a moment or two, then said, "I'm afraid, there's no point in explaining, sir." His manner became almost brisk. He retrieved his hat and umbrella and said, "I think you'll find everything in order. If not, don't hesitate to call upon us." He stood up, ignoring the cold, hostile face. "Good day to you, sir."

He watched him go, congealed with anger. He was calm, too calm as he gave the buzzer a jab. *After he talked with his auditors one little bastard would . . .*

Mrs. Mears entered.

"What do you know about that man?" he asked.

She looked surprised. "Mr. Grimes?"

"Yes."

"Why, not a great deal," she said. "He's been with Abercrombie and Harris for ages. He used to do Mr. Johnson's taxes. A nice little man, I think; rather tragic, too. The King gave him an audience during the war. He lost three sons, all airmen, I believe, and his wife was killed during the blitz." She paused. "He's had rather a hard time of it, I imagine."

"Oh," he said. His anger died as quickly as fire quenched with water. And it seemed he could feel, literally feel the ashes hard and heavy in the pit of his stomach. He wearily rubbed his face.

"Do you want to see Miss Cockburn now?" Mrs. Mears asked.

"Five minutes," he said. "Give me five minutes."

He stared moodily into space for a while, and then, without realizing it, stood up and slowly paced his office. No wonder the poor seedy little bastard felt the way he did. After the

· · · 35

sacrifices he had made it must seem pretty sleazy to bilk your country out of a few lousy dollars. And he was right, dead right. He had disowned his country. Even when he was bluffing and bullying he knew it. And it hadn't hurt; it hadn't hurt a bit. It still didn't hurt, really. And why should it? He had disowned everything else that was important. It was easy once you acquired the habit. He had become hardened too . . . a hard man who reaped where he had not sown and gathered where he had not strawed. And for what? What? Suddenly, he realized that he was standing in front of the window. Strange that he had found his way to the window. He had avoided it, tried to pretend it wasn't there, ever since that night when he had stood there drunk and had come within . . . He looked down at the roof of the setback of the building six stories below. The slate shingles were black and white and laid in an intricate geometrical pattern. It looked so close . . . so easy. Just one bound, shut down the mind for just an instant and make one quick thrust, shatter the glass and be free . . . No . . . he shut his eyes and slowly, almost as if he were resisting an actual force, he backed away from the window. It was cheap, not difficult, just too damned cheap.

". . . and where do you think you're goin', buddy?" "Pres-Journal," he said, holding up his press card, scarcely looking at the big cop on the door, keeping his eyes glued to that booth in the back. it was worth the trip, all right, might even make a short at the bottom of page one. man kills self in chili parlor. he walked back slowly, eyes on the booth, smelling the coffee and the chili and the frying hamburgers and the grease and the stale beer, not missing a word of what the sobbing waitress was telling the two plainclothesmen, "No. Cross my heart, I diden know what the durn fool was up to. He hadda coupla beers an' was jus' as calm as you please, an' he called me over an' handed me this here paper napkin with her name an' phone number on it an' said, 'Call her up for me,' and then he done it—he done it—he done it under the table. Boom—jus' like that. It like to have scared me to death." and there he lay, head and one arm on the scarred, ringed and sticky table top, no blood, *no gun no anything, just a bad haircut and a cheap hunched up sports jacket, and a scrawny neck and a hand and one side of an empty face that looked like a poor wax imitation because it wasn't lifelike and was a mottled gray color, and he glanced down and saw that he was standing squarely in a pool of blood which looked as thick and as sticky as syrup and he was filled with revulsion and contempt and he thought, 'Oh, you poor no good fool . . . fool!— It served you right because dying any other way was too good for a weakling like you . . ."*

He found his chair and composedly, ever so composedly, he sat down, feeling the tightness leave his muscles, hiding the distress that hammered away at him inside.

Judith Cockburn entered slowly, much too slowly, and the moment he saw her he was on to her little game. He was surprised; surprised, but mostly irritated because after years he seldom let himself in for such mistakes. Her cream-colored silk blouse was too tight and too many buttons had been left undone. Her black silk pants clung to her slim legs and thighs like a second skin. Her wide eyes were heavily made up with light green mascara, but there was only a touch of lipstick on her full lips and her long auburn hair was draped wantonly over one eye. She seated herself and with a slow casual twist which somehow managed to be suggestive, she shed the bright red jacket draped over her shoulders. He saw that she carefully kept her stomach pulled tight so that her full young breasts strained against her blouse.

He looked at her non-committally, unsmiling. "How have you been, Miss Cockburn?"

She leaned forward with a slightly breathless air. "You'll never know how much I've been looking forward to seeing you again, Mr. Fraser."

He decided to get it over with quickly. "Burton Ashley is casting a new play and he has three small parts which haven't been filled yet," he said. "I think maybe you could manage any one of them. They aren't . . ."

She interrupted with a gasp of delight. "Oh, how wonder-

ful! I'm ever so grateful to you, Mr. Fraser. *Ever* so grateful."
She was leaning forward even more now, hugging her left
shoulder with her right hand, and as he watched unbelievingly,
she let her right hand slide down her arm from shoulder to
wrist with a caressing motion. The gesture was so ridiculously
sensuous, so false and overdone, that for a moment his annoyance almost gave way to amusement.

He wanted to be sure she understood. "None of the roles is
very big, three or four sides, at the most."

"Oh, that doesn't matter, Mr. Fraser," she said. "I'll do anything you think I should do. *Anything.*"

Looking at her eager face, her straining breasts, he realized
it was the literal truth. She would do anything he asked, allow
any indignity, submit to any sportive vice, because she thought
he could help her along to stardom and glory. He had met
hundreds like her in his day. He stood up. "All right, Miss
Cockburn, I'll call Mr. Ashley and tell him you'll be around
tomorrow to read for him."

Before he could do anything to prevent it, before he had
even anticipated it, she was up and behind his desk. She thrust
out both her hands. He took one in a formal handshake. Her
clasp was too tight, her voice too effusive. "Oh, thank you,
your darling man. *Thank* you."

He nodded and disengaged his hand. She had to tilt back
her head to look up at him and there was something so gro-
tesquely shameless in her heavily made up eyes and on her lips,
something so false about her whole supplicating manner that
once again he had the embarrassing feeling that he was watching a poor parody. "I'm thrilled because you've taken an interest in me, Mr. Fraser," she said.

He grunted with annoyance. "Good-bye, Mis . . ."

She moved closer, too close. Her out-thrust breasts nudged
his coat. "You do think I have talent, don't you?" she asked.

Suddenly, he was fed up with the whole tawdry business. It
was really an insult to his intelligence. "For God's sake, how

do I know," he said, coldly. "I don't care. I've offered you a chance at a job—now take it and run along!"

She stepped back as if she had been struck. Her jaw was slack with surprise, and for the first time he saw the little girl's face hiding behind the makeup and the sexy impudence. Then he saw that her fingers were trembling, and in that moment he realized why all along he had sensed something so phony about her behavior. She was just a scared kid putting on an act. He felt weary and apologetic and sad. She was just a kid—a stupidly ambitious kid. So young, so nervous, she had even botched a simple seductress routine. He said quietly, "Sit down, Miss Cockburn."

She took her seat and gave him a quick apprehensive glance and lowered her eyes.

He sat down. "Cigarette?"

She took the cigarette he offered, avoiding his eyes while he lit it for her. She took a great gulping puff and blew the smoke out quickly.

"How old are you, Judy?" he asked.

"Nineteen."

"I'm forty-six," he said.

She looked up and cautiously met his eyes. He smiled at her, and after the slightest hesitation, she gave him a small smile in return.

"Why the Salome bit, Judith?"

She lowered her eyes and studied her cigarette intently. Finally, she opened her mouth wide with a sigh that carried embarrassment, and weariness. "They said it was my big chance," she said. "They said it had never happened before. They said you were . . . interested in me, and if I . . . if I made an impression you could do a lot for me."

He understood. He understood it perfectly. The buzz of excitement in the dirty, shabby dressing rooms when word spread that he and Cynthia were out front . . . the thrill, the joy, the envy, when a name playwright and director came back and singled out one of them and offered to help her. Yes, he could almost write it—the congratulations, the awe, the covetous glances, the endless words of advice.

"Suppose I had succumbed to your charms, Judy—would you have gone through with it?"

There was the barest hesitation. "Yes," she said.

"Why?"

"Because you can help me . . . because you can get me good parts."

"Is it that important?"

"It's the most important thing in the world," she said. Her voice was intense and her eyes were direct. "It's the only thing in the world that's really important."

He sat back slowly. He gazed at the paneled wall opposite, studied the small Renoir sketch Cynthia had given him for his birthday, looked for a long time at the untidy stack of manuscripts in the corner. It was the truth. God's sweet truth. And there was nothing he could do to change it. He was not certain he wanted to change it. He felt sorrow, but also pride . . . compassion, but also envy. He spoke slowly, "I can do something to help your career, Judy. I never think about it much nowadays, but I really do have something precious to give to someone your age. I don't suppose it will seem so valuable to you, because you're young and it will sound like advice. Maybe it'll make me sound pretty square. But it's the only thing I know to be really true that I've learned, after all my years in the theater." He smiled at her, thinking how pitifully young and vulnerable she looked. "I don't know what makes talent, Judy. Neither am I sure I always recognize it until it becomes so obvious I can't miss it. I'm speaking of genuine theatrical talent—not simply young men with long hair who make silly girls squeal, or people who can imitate the sound of a ping-pong game, or who stand on their heads and play a fiddle. Neither am I speaking of motion pictures where it often happens that little girls with unusual faces and hulking young men with broad shoulders are led and trained like muzzled bears until they can go through a two minute sequence. All this probably sounds silly to you; it is silly, but you may as well accept the fact that it is what most people, nearly all people, believe to be talent.

"You and I know better, Judy. You and I know that true theatrical talent is more than a clever trick. It has nothing to do with looks. It is the ability to discard one's self, shed one's real personality and, if necessary, change one's appearance and become someone entirely different, and to do it with such conviction and such sensitivity that every gesture, every expression, every emotion and every nuance, is not only believable, but magical and poetic and thrilling. And it is not done once; it must be done and sustained, once . . . twice a day, for weeks, months, and sometimes, even years. How is it done, Judy? What rare gift is it that permits some people to take a few lines of business and some speeches and create out of them characters who give new limits to our imaginations, cause our eyes to weep, our anger to flash—our very hearts to become instruments on which they can play any tune they wish? It is not only the business. Nor is it only the speeches. For often the directions are followed and the speeches are said and we are not affected at all. But then there comes along someone who has an extraordinary gift. We gather together, and, suddenly, we see in the familiar business something wonderfully intense and purposeful and exciting, and we hear in the worn speeches a depth and a meaning and a beauty we never realized was there. That's talent, Judy. I don't know the whole secret, Judy. But I do know part of it. Every actor who has achieved greatness in the living theater has had marked intelligence. For it takes intelligence to have imagination. Imagination is necessary for understanding, and understanding is necessary for sensitivity. The oddest thing about this is that it has to be said at all. Yet it is a fact that a great many people don't believe that actors have to have intelligence. Maybe it's because actors are artists, and like all artists, often they concentrate on their art to the exclusion of everything else. Maybe it's simply because there are too many dumb fourth- and fifth-rate actors.

"So intelligence is the first requirement of a good actor or actress. And the second requirement sounds so platitudinous that I almost hesitate to say it. It is hard work—unceasing, untiring hard work. I can't even begin to list all the odd qualities and special skills great actors and actresses may have, but I do know they have one thing in common. It is intelligence honed to a single exquisitely sharp edge by hours of hard work in learning their craft. Maybe that is talent, Judy. Maybe it's that simple: brains and dedication."

He smiled at her. "There's no other way; no cheap, quick steps to genuine theatrical fame, despite what anyone tells you. It has nothing to do with any concern for your morals. For many great actresses have been as wicked as Jezebel. But it wasn't wickedness that made them great. I didn't offer to help you to lure you to my bed. I was interested in you because you showed intelligence and ability. No matter what you've heard, most producers and directors are primarily interested in the same thing. No professional will run the risk of letting a whore ruin a costly production, Judy. It's simpler and cheaper just to keep her.

"Oh, I don't pretend that some people haven't reached the top in the theater through guile, and by sleeping around. But they haven't stayed on top unless they also had the necessary talent. For what it really comes down to, Judy, is it's the public you must beguile, not some producer or director. And I honestly don't know any way to do that, except through ability."

He smiled at her and she smiled back. He said gently, "So go home now and tomorrow morning wash your face and put on a nice suit and go around and read for Burt Ashley. You'll get the part—and a great many more, bigger and better."

She stood up and they shook hands. "Thank you very much, Mr. Fraser," she said. She walked across the room but paused with her hand on the doorknob. She turned and looked at him hesitantly. Despite her costume and her makeup, she was now the bright little girl who had attracted him. "You . . . you're a nice man, Mr. Fraser," she blurted, and fled.

He was still looking at the door with a thoughtful expression when Mrs. Mears entered. She smiled slightly. "You are still *virgo intacta*, I presume."

He didn't hear her; his mind was engrossed with something else. He said, "Please call Burt Ashley's office and tell them Miss Cockburn will be around tomorrow to audition. Tell them she's a friend of mine and I recommend her highly."

"Very well," Mrs. Mears said.

She stood waiting until he looked up. "More?" he asked.

She smiled. "Yes, Mr. Samuel Pepys called. He wants to see you this afternoon, if possible. He wants to do something on you and the play."

He smiled. Samuel Pepys was the name of a column in the *Evening Star*. It was literate, amusing and irreverent. He enjoyed it. "What's his real name?" he asked.

"He didn't say," she said, "just said he was Samuel Pepys."

"All right," he said, "tell him that I'll be at the theater at six. We're going to run through that café scene that's gone sour. Right now I'm going to get a drink." He walked toward the closet for his hat and coat.

"I gave the envelope to Mr. Lancaster," she said.

He paused. "Oh?"

"He looked embarrassed for a moment, then he laughed and said that you shouldn't have bothered, that he had forgotten all about lending it to you. He said to tell you he was going to spend a few months with Noel and he'd get in touch when he returned."

Something in her voice made him wait. "Is that all?" he asked.

She hesitated. "Well, not quite all," she said. "He was very jolly about it, as if it were a joke, but he said to tell you that he was a star when you wore nappies and that he would be around to dance on your grave."

He was silent a moment, then he sighed. "I guess he will, at that."

FOUR . . .

His mother came from Alabama. ALLAH-bam-er, she called it in her soft voice, and from the time he could remember anything at all, ALLAH-bam-er was the most exciting, joyous, carefree place he could imagine, infinitely nicer than the Land of Milk and Honey his father preached about, probably even nicer, guiltily he felt, than Heaven where everybody merely lived in mansions and the streets were paved with gold. In ALLAH-bam-er the streams had a buoyance that allowed anybody to swim, little boys rode ponies everywhere, caught fish bigger than they were, ate all the chocolate fudge and strawberry shortcake they wanted, and everything their happy hearts desired was supplied by black people who laughed and sang and said funny things all the time. When he was five his mother took him to ALLAH-bam-er for a visit. So ALLAH-bam-er was the first memorable disappointment of his life.

When he was eleven, he and Jimmy Hendrix were exploring the ruins of the old Renfroe house, when far back in the dark and damp cellar that smelled like the inside of a toadstool they found a green bottle labeled REIMS-CHAMPAGNE-BRUT. He knew all about champagne. It was a delicious nectar so costly that only rich people could afford it, so precious that people in the picture show smashed their glasses when they drank it; it was the imprisoned laughter of the peasant girls of France, it was . . . well, it was simply the best drink ever discovered by man. They took the bottle to the gully behind the ice house, and with flushed, excited faces and bright eyes and fumbling fingers, they managed to get it open. So REIMS-CHAMPAGNE-BRUT was the second memorable disappointment of his life.

He sat at his regular corner table in the Westbury bar, going through the afternoon papers, a half bottle of champagne in a bucket at his elbow. When he took his first taste of the chilled, tart and effervescent wine, he always relived the disappointment of the little boy in the gully. The truth was, he didn't care for champagne much though he drank it almost exclusively. He simply found its taste less objectionable than whiskey; its effect more subtle but just as satisfactory. He also could drink quite a lot of it without getting really drunk, or suffering too much the next morning. He went through the papers quickly, but thoroughly, absentmindedly tossing off the wine almost as quickly as his glass was refilled by a hovering waiter. He paused only once to read with close attention an item in one of the gossip diaries: "Cynthia Barr created a sensation at Le Tabac in the early morning hours when . . ." He read the item carefully, not caring, or even noting, that it was a wholly imaginary and fanciful account of how Cynthia had broken a shoulder strap while dancing a mad Watusi with a well-known peer, but unconsciously assessing it as publicity and determining its origin. Since the name of the play was not mentioned, he knew it had not been planted by Cynthia's press agent, but came from the club.

He put the papers aside and lit a cigarette, and for the first time became aware that the wine had given him a mild and pleasant lift. For the first time all day he had almost shed his persistent and nagging depression. He finished off his glass, looked at his watch, briefly debated whether he had time for another half-bottle. He decided he did. He raised his finger to the waiter.

While he drank his second bottle of wine he studied the people who were now beginning to fill the tables, unerringly picking out the Americans: the men with their light suits with narrow lapels and their neat haircuts and their fresh, almost boyish faces; their wives with their smart suits and astonishingly wide mink stoles, and their pampered, demanding faces. They were so different from the British; the men with their heavier, almost too formal dark suits and their languid manners, and longish haircuts; their wives with their placid and poised faces and their suits which nearly always narrowly missed smartness but were made of materials which were finely woven and durable.

He liked people. He liked to watch them, study them. It was not merely because they were the material with which he made a living. It annoyed and distressed him when often he was described as a satirist. He had seethed recently when Mrs. Mears called his attention to a biographical sketch in a British Theatrical Who's Who, which began: "For two decades Paul Fraser savagely has delineated the ordinary failings of ordinary people."

He had a . . . an affection for people, really. There was a strikingly lovely young English girl at the table near the door. She had shoulder length blonde hair, classic features, the flawless, almost translucent complexion which was a heritage of so many Englishwomen. She was listening to someone with such wide-eyed and wondering adoration that he felt a small twist of envy. He looked at her companion. He was a sharp-faced young man with a sullen expression and a yellowish unhealthy pallor. There also was a large pimple on his neck. *There be three things which are too wonderful for me, yea, four which I know not: The way of an eagle in the air; the way of a serpent upon a rock; the way of a ship in the midst of the sea; and the way of a man with a maid.* He looked away.

Two American soldiers were in the press around the bar. Both were pfcs, and they were such trim, good-looking young men, so painstakingly pressed and polished, so healthy looking with their tanned faces and close cropped hair and shiny cleanliness, that he felt a surge of pride. But how young they were, so terribly and pathetically young ... He had been a soldier, too. He stared moodily at his glass. But like everything else he did, something went wrong. He had been willing to risk his life, even eager to risk it, and after all these years he still felt cheated because he hadn't had a chance. As a young newspaperman, he had stood in line to volunteer for the Army on the Monday morning after Pearl Harbor. It simply never occurred to him that he wouldn't be given a uniform, a gun, and sent off immediately to fight in some foxhole. Lord, how little, how unbelievably little, people knew about the Army in those days.

He had been sent off posthaste, all right—to a motion picture documentary unit on Long Island. Two months later, he was summarily commissioned a second lieutenant, and somebody must have made a mistake because he didn't even have a gun. From then on he fought a constant, badgering campaign to get overseas. Not to kill the enemy; by then that was too farfetched and heroic even to mention. He simply wanted a chance to take films of damage the enemy had inflicted. It was late in 1944, and he was a captain, before, finally, he was sent to England as second in command of a film crew.

He drained his glass and the waiter refilled it with the last of the wine. But he was wounded in the war. Yes, he was wounded gravely. If he thought about it long enough, his scars still pulsated with a faint memory of pain. He rubbed his cheek thoughtfully. She had sun-streaked blonde hair, level gray eyes, and the softest, most expressive mouth he had ever seen in his life. He saw her for the first time across a luncheon table at Sardi's, and from that moment he couldn't bear to have her out of his sight. He could almost write a history of those strange, unreal, feverish wartime days just by remembering Anne . . . the standing in line to telephone . . . the precious weekend leaves . . . the salty, tear-stained kisses . . . the long, aimless happy walks through darkened streets . . . the tiny out of the way places that bootlegged steaks . . . the gagging taste of synthetic Scotch . . . the dear, tender, foolish, promising letters . . .

Always the letters. When he reached England they came every day, sometimes twice a day. After four months they came less frequently, as promising and as tender as ever, but less frequently. Then they stopped. Just like that—they stopped. It was two weeks, two weeks filled with frantic worry and fear, before the brief sympathetic note arrived from her mother . . . *"a blow, but these things happen, and we must make the best of them. I know you want her to be happy, and he's a fine man and they are divinely . . ."*

He emptied his glass. Was it foolish—maudlin, perhaps—for a man of his age to . . . He thought about it. Yes, he supposed it was. It wouldn't play . . . it wouldn't play at all. He looked at the girl with the adoring face. With a woman it was different. He could make an audience weep over a spurned woman. There would even be audible sobs if he caused her to destroy herself because of love. But there was sympathy for a man only if his loved one died. And even then it had to be played with delicacy, or else he was weak. There was something basically funny and ridiculous about a spurned lover. It was easier to play him for laughs. A betrayed husband was a cuckold, yet we did not put horns on a betrayed wife. We gave her sympathy. It was always so. Bathsheba was remembered as a glamorous, fascinating woman, who lived to sit at the hand of her son, the king. But who remembered poor old Uriah? Who cared that he fell at the gate, and as his blood drained in the dust and his eyes glazed with death, he probably gasped out her name?

It was odd, and somehow it was damned wrong and unfair. Perhaps it was true that every time a woman loved, truly loved, she gave everything, demanded nothing. Perhaps there was a reason for giving her extra consideration because her elemental love left her helplessly submissive. But if a man was lucky, very lucky, there came a time when he became helpless, too. Not tender affectionate love, not a superior indulgent love, not even the old throbbing in the glands . . . but gripped by all the demands of a male's elemental aggressive love. That love had such force, it rose to such heights, that it became uncontrollable and senseless in its desire to overpower, possess, submerge. No man was ever the same after experiencing a love like that. Never.

He carefully pushed back his glass. No, after all these years, he was not ashamed to have compassion for that young captain. The real truth was, it still hurt a little when he remembered that poor young man who set his face, and with his eyes blind and burning with tears that refused to flow, walked, walked, walked, through the blacked out streets of London while grief ripped and tore and devoured him inside until he thought he surely would die.

He beckoned to the waiter. "Emil, after I leave, give those two young soldiers at the bar a drink and put it on my bill."

Samuel Pepys was a slightly built, boyishly handsome and obviously bright young man in his late twenties named John Leigh. He had an upper-class accent, a slight stutter which probably was a result of torture suffered in one of the better public schools, and he wore a beautifully cut blue suit and brown suede shoes. He also badly needed a haircut. He was waiting near the box office of the theater, and after he introduced himself, he said, "I ho . . . hope I'm not inconveniencing you, sir."

"No inconvenience at all," he said, feeling pleasantly elated from the wine and liking Leigh at first sight. "I have to sit in on a rehearsal in the theater for a few minutes. Then we'll have a drink and talk."

"Wh . . . why a rehearsal now?" Leigh asked. "I saw the play ages ago and it seemed very finished—marvelously finished, if I may say so."

He nodded. "It was. This is sort of a cleanup operation. You may recall the café scene. There are about twenty bit players onstage at one time and most of them have taken to milking their parts. The scene's running three to five minutes longer than it should."

Leigh's face was bright with interest. "How does one . . . milk a part?" he asked, as they walked across the lobby.

He smiled. "My own expression, Leigh. Padding the part is what it's usually called. The actors are adding little bits and pieces of business, gestures and grimaces. Chewing the scenery a bit too much. When you crowd enough actors together in a scene it usually happens, especially when they're all young-sters." He nodded to the elderly head usher who rushed to hold open one of the glass paneled doors. "How long have they been at it, Peter?"

"Better than three-quarters of an hour, sir," Peter said.

As he paused in the foyer to shed his coat, he heard Larry Dalton's light and penetrating voice saying wearily, "No. No. Not there. Please take it from the entrance." Larry was his as-sistant director. He had a phenomenal eye for detail, a marked gift for interpretation, but, unfortunately, he was just a bit too blatantly homosexual. It made him a trifle too precious, a shade too petulant to command the authority a director should have.

He gave his coat to Peter and nodded to young Leigh to follow him. As he walked across the thick worn carpet, smell-ing the familiar odor of cleaning fluid, brass polish, mildewed flats, dust, grease paint, sweat, new rope, and old drains; he felt a faint stirring, a nostalgic shadow of an icy thrill of antic-ipation and excitement creep up his spine. Once that freezing electric thrill had been sharp, peremptory, whenever he en-tered a theater; indeed, there had been a time when it was almost numbing, a delicious numbness that almost caused him to hold his breath. It had not vanished completely. But it had almost. That was the way things were, he supposed . . . It was the difference between the anticipation felt by a young bride-groom when he heard the light step of his beloved, and the anticipation felt by a middle-aged husband when he heard the firm matronly tread of his wife.

It saddened him because the sharp thrill was no longer there. Yes, it saddened him very much. He was not sure when it had begun to fade, but he knew the exact hour when he first felt it. He was twelve and his mother took him to see a play with real live actors in Indianapolis. It was called *The Passing of* the Third Floor Back, and it was supposed to have a moral a minister's son could appreciate. But he wasn't aware of a moral at all. He sat enraptured, not moving, scarcely daring to breathe. The school plays and the church pageants he had seen had not prepared him for anything so breathtaking, so wonderful . . . so real. He had left the theater in a daze and he was not aware of anything until he and his mother were on the street car going to the railway station and she was shaking his arm and laughing and saying, well, tell her . . . tell her— how did he like it? He shut his eyes and leaned back and said, "Golly, oh, golly," and he was embarrassed because he was afraid tears would be squeezed out of his tightly closed eyes and run down his cheeks.

He motioned young Leigh to a seat in the back row and seated himself on the aisle. The footlights were up full force, flooding the stage with a bright white glare. The members of the cast were in street clothes and boredly standing in their places. They were all bit players, for the principals in the scene had not been called. Larry Dalton was at front stage center straddling a chair backwards. He ran his hands through his long hair with an exasperated, harassed motion, but his voice was still reasonably patient. "Will you please tell me, Ruth," he said, speaking to a tall brunette in a red dress who played one of the waitresses, "what motivates all that hip tossing?"

She was sullenly defiant. "It gets a laugh."

Larry stroked his forehead. "That's the whole bloody point, my dear girl, it isn't supposed to get a laugh." He pointed a forefinger at three young actors slouched at one of the tables. "It gets a laugh because Dick and Robert and Ian there have taken to leering at you. Now please settle down all of you and run through it again. If we wanted a laugh there, we'd bloody well have written in a laugh there."

From his aisle seat, he watched closely. Consciously, and usually unconsciously, as well, he had learned to avoid the corny old cliché that actors were children. But when you got a stageful of actors together and they were bored, or resentful, they often behaved exactly like a classroom of mischievous kids. Sometimes it was best to handle them accordingly . . . sometimes it wasn't. It had taken him years to realize that. Larry still didn't realize it. Thank heaven, he had had a chance to learn it before he started directing. In the early days, he had thought you directed actors by making friends of them, treating them as equals, deferring to them, letting them have their little say, changing lines to suit their whims. He still detested directors who bullied actors, who thought they were animal trainers with a chair in one hand and a whip in the other. But, yes, there were times when it was best to treat actors like bright, intelligent children. For the main thing was not to act indecisive, betray doubts. For actors, like children, responded to authority, needed authority; it made them forget their own insecurities. And . . . to be brutal about it, young actors were scared to death about losing their jobs. He stood up and walked down the aisle slowly. He was almost at the orchestra pit before Larry realized he was there and turned and flashed him a smile, "Why, hullo, Paul."

He acknowledged the greeting with a nod and said quietly, "Foots down." Larry shouted, "Foots down," and after a moment or two, the bright footlights dimmed. He wanted to be sure they all saw him. He stood there calmly, looking at the stage, stood there until they straightened up and lost their boredom, stood there silently until they began nervously to fidget, and some of the younger ones lowered their eyes and looked uneasy. He spoke calmly, quietly, almost pleasantly, "Ladies and gentlemen, you all are professionals. That is why you have been employed. This is a professional theater and we are presenting a professional performance. I don't have to tell you why we all have been put to the bother and the expense of this call this afternoon. This scene has gradually become disproportionately long. Furthermore, it is not being played the way I wrote it or directed it. If any of you has forgotten the original directions, I shall be glad to run through them with you. If any of you feel awkward in your roles, I should like to try and straighten that out. I am at your disposal." He waited. Nobody spoke, nobody moved. After the silence grew heavy, he nodded. "Very well. I am sure that a second call won't be necessary. I shall be watching your performances with interest this evening—and every evening. Thank you all." He nodded to Larry. "Thank you, Larry." He turned and slowly walked back up the aisle. He heard Larry say briskly, "All right, let's go through it once more now. Quickly—and we'll all have time for a pint before curtain."

Young Leigh greeted him with a tentative, impressed smile. "I say, that should stif . . . stiffen them up a bit."

He smiled. "There's a pub in the lane around the corner. Let's go have a drink."

As they were leaving the theater, Leigh asked, "I suppose it does get tiring after a bit—I mean, doing the same thing over and over again."

He nodded. "Yes, it does. I don't object to a little improvising if it doesn't get out of hand. One shouldn't muzzle the ox that treadeth out the corn."

"Quite," Leigh said. After a short silence, he said, "I don't think I'm acquainted with the quotation."

"The Bible," he said. "One of my bad habits . . . quoting the Bible. It annoys my friends sometimes."

"Are you a stu . . . student of the Bible, Mr. Fraser?"

"Hardly that. It's just that I was exposed to it during my formative years. My father was a minister—a preacher; he read aloud a chapter of the Bible every morning and every evening. That's a lot of Scripture to have thrown at you. Some of it sticks."

Leigh remained silent, digesting this. Finally, he said, firmly, "Yes. Quite a bloody awful lot of Scripture, I shou . . . should think."

He smiled. He found himself liking Leigh better all the time. "That's only part of it, Leigh. I also went to a small liberal arts college that was endowed by the church. Most of the male students were studying for the ministry. We all pretty much boned over the same courses until the sheep were separated from the goats in our senior year."

"Wh . . . why did you go there?"

"One reason was that my father went there. But the compelling reason was that I couldn't afford to go anywhere else. Tuition was free because my father was a minister."

"Your father wanted you to become a clergyman, I suppose—fo . . . follow his footsteps, and all that?"

"I suppose he did. We never spoke . . . really spoke of it. He knew I hadn't the call."

"The ca . . . call?"

He smiled. "That's more or less a fundamentalist expression, I suppose—Saul seeing the light and receiving his call on the road to Damascus. What I meant was, my father knew I didn't feel I had a vocation for the church."

. . . the only sound in the world was that loud, rasping, irregular tortured gasping and his mother's low sobs . . . the sound of that awful, choking, suffering breathing that filled the hallway and the house and he felt guilty and ashamed because he kept thinking over and over again, if he must die, please, let him die now . . . let him die quickly and stop torturing himself and us with that awful gasping . . . that terrible rasping wheezing . . . and old Doc Barnes came out of the room, looking worn and beaten and said, "He wants to see you, Paul." and he walked in slowly and the room was resounding with that awful noise and he was lying on his back in the big old familiar bed, his chest heaving, his head thrown back and he was waxen and somehow unreal and ugly because his face was so tight and skull-like and he was not wearing his false teeth and his mouth was an ugly pulsating slit and he leaned over the bed, feeling almost distaste until he saw his fine eyes, sunken, but burningly alert and he was filled with a hurting flood of pity and love and he thought, yes, this is my father, my beloved father . . . my laughing, strong daddy who used to toss me around in his strong arms and ride me on his shoulders, and he said, "Dad . . . it's Paul, Dad . . ." and that ugly mouth twisted in an attempt to smile and you could tell he was trying to stop his wheezing and slowly . . . painfully, he gasped, "son . . . missed . . . you . . . son . . ." and he tried to smile and said, "Dad, . . . all right, Dad . . . and the eyes dimmed someway and he said, "Proud . . . son . . . proud . . . you . . . always love . . ." and he said, "I love you, too, Dad," but he didn't hear and the wheezing grew louder and louder and then stopped and he said clearly, "Love God, son . . . love . . . God" and he let his breath out in a small sigh and his eyes were empty and he was not inside that waxen face any more . . . and he said, "Dad . . . Dad . . ." and a choking painful agony filled his chest and a ragged voice inside him cried, "Daddy, . . . Daddy! . . ."

FIVE . . .

It was a typical side-street pub. A bit too drafty, a bit too unswept and undusted, and a bit too deliberately quaint. He led the way to a table in the private bar. "I'm having champagne," he said. "Will you join me or had you rather have something else?"

"No, pooh sounds marvelous," Leigh said. Pooh was slang for champagne in London's young upper-class circles.

He ordered from the barmaid and smiled at Leigh. "Well, what is Samuel Pepys' interest in me?"

"The first thing I should like to ask is . . . well, rather embarrassing," Leigh said, not looking embarrassed at all.

He knew what was coming. "I should like to ask if you and Cynthia Barr are married?" Leigh asked.

He had been right. It was a question he had been asked dozens—no hundreds, of times during the last five years. Some columnists had reported that they had been married in Mexico, in Europe, and once Hedda Hopper had even reported a false report that a marriage record had been unearthed in Guatemala. But nobody except he and Cynthia knew for certain, and in some unspoken way, they had reached an agreement to keep it that way. In fact, they had never had a discussion about the matter, but from the first they had evaded the question when it was asked.

He looked at Leigh with a straight face. "Why don't you ask Miss Barr?"

Leigh said, "You kn . . . know very well she won't tell, either."

The barmaid placed glasses and a bare bottle of champagne in the center of the table. He filled their glasses and tossed his off as quickly as the gaseous effervescence would permit, looking at Leigh above the rim of his glass.

Leigh smiled. "Well, there was no harm in asking, was there?"

"No harm at all," he said, refilling his glass.

Leigh took a sip of champagne. "If I may say one more thing, if I were married to Miss Barr, I jolly well would tell everybody about it."

He smiled. "I'll tell her you said that. She will be pleased."

"How do you think the British theater compares with the American theater?" Leigh asked.

He put his glass down slowly. "We could stay here all night discussing that one, Leigh. But I can give you a quick answer. A pretty obvious one, I'm afraid. Judged strictly as productions, American shows are infinitely better than yours. Our musicals are so much better that no comparison is really possible. As for straight plays, they have to be better than yours even to survive. As you know, on Broadway a play has to be either close to a smashing success or it's a failure. That's certainly not a good thing. It robs our theater of a lot of vitality. But I don't suppose it will destroy us. It never has; every year there's a lot of mourning about the poor state of the theater. But, somehow, it keeps on flourishing."

"Which country has the better actors?" Leigh asked.

He shrugged. "Good actors are good actors—like good plumbers are good plumbers. Your ordinary run-of-the-mill actors are better than ours, I think."

"Why do you think that is?"

He refilled their glasses. "Training, mostly. Not only because actors here have more opportunity to appear in plays and learn their craft, but because they are more apt to get classical training."

"I take it you don't think very highly of modern training methods."

"Oh, Lord . . . on the contrary I'm in favor of any kind of training that makes actors think. And that includes all the old methods as well as those supposed to be new. I'm not opposed to any method that helps an actor get inside a part or shuck off his inhibitions. If he can do it by jumping on a table and acting like a slot machine or a percolater, then fine. There is too damn much attention paid to developing the individual personalities of young actors. Shaw paid old Irving the absolute ultimate in compliments when he described him as faceless. For a good actor must be faceless to play a variety of parts, and I think classical training is more apt to teach him to subjugate his own personality to a role. I like classical training because it stresses the fundamentals. You'd be amazed to know how many actors there are who simply can't walk around a stage well."

Leigh laughed.

"No, I'm serious," he said. "There are a lot of actors, even distinguished actors, who are so stiff and graceless that delivering them lines is like speaking to a stone wall. A really accomplished actor is so light on his feet, that you feel if you went —poof, you would blow him away. Instead of spending so much time teaching kids to imitate overstuffed chairs, I wish more teachers would show them how to develop some grace."

They had finished the bottle. He felt warm and relaxed, almost happy. "I suppose we should have another bottle."

"What do you think is the greatest fault of the theater today?" Leigh asked.

He smiled. "That's an easy one, Leigh. We get the wrong kind of audiences. We do everything we can to alienate ordinary people. Leave the slobs to TV and Hollywood, we say— Give us the sophisticated, the brainy, the fashionable. Well, the result is most of the time the legitimate theater caters to the jaded, the show-offs, the mindless jerks, who are ready to praise anything that is supposed to be smart. It saddens me to belabor the obvious, Leigh, but it just happens to be the simple truth that the greatest dramatists of history have written for the general public."

Leigh looked slightly stricken. "B . . . but surely you th . . . think the avant-garde theater has a place?"

He grinned at Leigh. "My heresy is even worse than that, Leigh. I'm not even sure I know what avant-garde theater means. What is it? Some pathetic, brooding little fairy spewing out his moral anarchy? Some unstable, frustrated, bitter young punk letting loose with his anger and venom? Is it some unwashed pot-smoker putting down a lot of hallucinatory gibberish which audiences don't understand, and he can't explain? Or is it some smart, cool cat taking advantage of the fact that there are always a lot of fools who are impressed by something too murky to be understood? I could go on and on, Leigh—but what's the use?"

He shrugged. "Actually, after almost twenty years, I've learned to accept all this with a modicum of peevishness, Leigh. What really does upset me is that every year, more and more, the theater seems to be forgetting its basic purpose. It's not altogether the fault of playwriters, either. Too many productions are being turned over to precious young men who should be decorating bordellos. Not only is the theater becoming too arty for art's sake—it's becoming damned silly. We use too many sets that destroy illusion instead of enhancing it —too many things that scream—Look! forget the play, and see how clever we are. The big thing at the moment is to try to make audiences gasp with disbelief when the curtain goes up and they see the sets. The honest truth is, Leigh, good players with a good play don't need fancy sets. They don't need anything much, except enough room to move around in."

The wine arrived and he refilled their glasses. Leigh took a swallow and said, "I say, this is a pleasant interview. Do you have a suitable quotation for the occasion?"

He raised his glass and said, "I will fetch wine, and we will fill ourselves with strong drink; and tomorrow shall be as this day, and much more abundant. Isaiah."

Leigh looked at him with admiration. "You are rather astounding." He finished off his glass with a flourish. "I'm not sure I agree with you about everything, though. One of the reasons I like American musicals is the clever way they manipulate things about."

He refilled their glasses. "I don't mean musicals. Musicals aren't my line. I mean straight plays. Illusion is the only staple we have to offer in the theater; if we package it too prettily, we end up selling the wrappings and not the product." He studied Leigh a moment and grinned. "You came to the wrong man for a lecture on what my Cynthia calls the arty-farty thea-tah, Leigh. I can't speak trippingly about expressionism and constructivism and the role of the *regisseur*. But I can tell you a lot of other things. I can tell you what it's like to sit in a crummy hotel room in New Haven and write a second act for the fiftieth time. I can tell you what it's like to rehearse all night and walk out of a theater so dog tired you can't see, a couple of gallons of coffee sloshing in your belly and your mouth charred from smoking too much. I can tell you what it's like to stand in the back of a theater and hear audiences laugh when they're not supposed to laugh, and not laugh when they're supposed to.

Leigh smiled. "But it has been worth it, hasn't it? I mean—"

He shook his head slowly. "I don't know, Leigh. I truly don't. I love the theater . . . I've spent nearly my whole life in the theater, and I truly don't know whether it has been worth it or not." He paused, then brightened. "You know, Leigh, when I first started in this business, the man who helped me more than anybody, the man who was my dearest friend, was a producer named Sam Aaron. I used to think that Sam was a man of no pretense. Now I know better. Sam avoided pretense so much that he was really guilty of pretense. He was born on New York's Lower East Side, and even after he became rich and famous he still looked and acted as if he should be sitting on a front stoop in some tenement district. He spoke a sort of rough New Yorkese and from the things he said, he seemed to have no imagination at all. But he really had the most profound knowledge of the history of the theater, the surest

60 . . .

ability to spot what was right or wrong with a play of any man in his generation. Sam was a wise man—too wise to be a phony. He knew there were no situations that were new. They only seemed new because people came along who had an ability to present them differently.

"Sam had two favorite expressions he used when he read a play. One was, "Keep duh horses outta it," and the other was "Get ridda duh nuttin's." The crack about the horses came about because when he was a young man Sam produced a play in which he had an actor come riding onstage on a horse. The theater was small and the horse was big and instead of being impressed, the audience was panicked with laughter. By keeping 'duh horses outta it,' Sam meant never do anything in a play which required the audience to stretch its imagination to a point where things became ridiculous. 'Duh nuttin's' Sam talked about were lines or business in a play which didn't advance the action or give some necessary insight into the characters.

"I've never known two better guides to writing and directing plays. Maybe that's my fault." He looked thoughtful a moment, then smiled. Don't get the impression that I'm saying that all plays should be produced with some sort of grim Bolshoi realism. Imagination and fantasy are the breath and life of the theater. It's all right to build a castle out of children's alphabet blocks, but for Heaven's sake, don't make it Elsinore Castle."

The wine was beginning to have its way with him. There was a slight stiffness in his facial muscles, a warmness across the back of his neck. He knew he was drinking too much, and, somewhat absently, he remembered that he hadn't eaten all day. But he didn't feel hungry, and he did feel relaxed and calm. He took another large swallow of wine and burped thoughtfully. He looked at Leigh and decided he liked him very much. Yes, he was a nice fellow.

Leigh also was looking at him solemnly, his cheeks had a bright flush. He said, "I agree with you, Mr. Fraser. I . . ."

He said, "Paul. Call me Paul."

"Very well," Leigh said. "I agree with you, Paul. There is a proper place for everything in the theater."

"Not only the theater, Leigh," he said, gravely. "For everything there is a season, and a time to every purpose under the heaven: A time to be born, and a time to die; a time to plant and a time to pluck up that which is planted. Ecclesiastes."

"Hear. Hear," Leigh said.

"Not hear, hear, Leigh," he said. "It's amen, amen."

"Yes, quite," Leigh said. He thought it over. "Amen, amen," he said.

"Excellent, Leigh," he said. "A very sensitive reading."

It was amazing how quickly the wine had attacked him. They had had only one—or was it two, bottles? One minute he had felt only a slight pleasant glow, but now there was a soft and delicate fuzziness about everything. It was as if they had lowered the overhead lights and put a big filtered spot . . . amber, no, amber and blue—on Leigh and him. He felt wonderful. Wonderful, indeed, and he had to be sure the feeling didn't fade. He refilled their glasses and noticed that the bottle was three-quarters empty. "I think we should have more refreshments, Leigh," he said. He raised his arm and with great dignity signaled the barmaid.

"Amen, amen," Leigh said. He raised his glass in a toast and tossed off his wine with one swallow. He sat expectantly until his lips erupted with a soft burble. He smiled, a pleased, proud smile, and held out his glass to be refilled. They drank in silence for a while before he said, "There is one question remaining. I should like to hear about your work in films. Tell me about Hollywood."

"Hollywood," he said thoughtfully. "What can I say about Hollywood? It can't be nice, Leigh, because it is unfashionable to speak well of Hollywood, and I do not wish to be thought unartistic." He reflected. "I will say this about Hollywood. There are some people in Hollywood who have talents that are sublime, and if you are a wicked and envious man such as I am, it causes you to gnash your teeth. For these few people create sagas and symphonies out of strips of camphor and cellulose nitrate that are so wonderful that you wonder how anyone can be so gifted. And there are other people in Hollywood making films who are too vulgar to be allowed to do anything except make brassieres for Guernsey cows. It is not Christian to punish all for the sins of a few—or even for the sins of many —and probably Hollywood suffers more than it should. We do not say books are bad because there are many bad books. Nor do we say newspapers are bad because there are many bad newspapers. So it is not as simple as saying Hollywood is good or bad. And that is all I care to say about Hollywood and Art for the nonce. I hope I have enlightened you, Leigh?"

"Amen, amen," Leigh said.

The barmaid arrived with a new bottle. He carefully upended the old bottle and filled their glasses and handed the empty bottle to her with a grave nod. "The wine is excellent here," he said. "Give my compliments to the vintners."

"Amen, amen," Leigh said.

They sat in silence, working their way through the new bottle, raising their glasses in a dignified salute each time he refilled them. When the bottle was half empty, Leigh leaned forward and studied him carefully. "I hope you don't mind my mentioning it, Paul, but you are rather a tall chap, you know."

He nodded. "I am tall for my age, but when I was younger I was even taller for my age. When I was seventeen I was amazingly tall for my age, because I was as tall as I am now and I suffered great embarrassment. I was so tall that when I went to dances girls had to cling to me about the hips and I always seemed to be kneeing them in intimate parts of their anatomies. Wouldn't that have embarrassed you, Leigh?"

Leigh was looking at him with great sympathy. "Frightfully," he said. "Yes, frightfully."

"I was also very frustrated, Leigh—terribly frustrated. For I suffered an urge to kiss a girl properly, and somehow the mechanics of it were just too involved. I had to bend down so far to kiss a girl that I always lost my nerve before I succeeded. Wouldn't that have frustrated you, Leigh?"

"Indeed it would have," Leigh said. "Yes, indeed, it would have."

"But finally I found a solution to my problem, Leigh. By pure luck I found a solution. I met a girl who was six feet one in her stocking feet and she was a blonde and strapping as some Munich Brunhilde. A big, strapping girl, and she was rather pretty in a big strapping way. You'd never in a million years guess what her name was, Leigh."

Leigh was spellbound. He hiccuped twice, and shook his head.

"Her name was Karen Klaatz," he said, "and she was a butcher's daughter. Her name was Karen Klaatz and she was six feet one in her stocking feet."

Leigh shook his head with wonder. "Fancy that," he said. "A butcher's daughter."

"Yes, her name was Karen Klaatz," he said. He filled their glasses and held up the bottle and shook it disappointedly. It was empty. He looked at his watch and then looked at Leigh.

Leigh was still mulling over what he had said. " 'Strawd'-nary," he said. "A butch . . ." he hiccuped, ". . . er's daughter. Fancy that." He raised his glass and emptied it with two swallows.

He grinned at Leigh and Leigh grinned back. "You have a talent for drinking, Leigh," he said. "As you grow grayer you should become a champion."

Leigh said, " 'S my fondest hope. My fondest hope."

"I have to go to the theater now, Leigh, and after the performance Miss Barr and I are supping with some friends. I would be honored if you would join us. Honored, indeed."

"I would accept with pleasure," Leigh said, "but I had some vague hopes of sporting my oak this evening."

He considered that. "How does one sport his oak, Leigh?"

"Sorry," Leigh said, "I forgot you are a foreigner and do not speak our language." He covered his mouth and hiccuped several times. "Sporting one's oak means courting a young lady."

"And what is its origin, Leigh?"

"It entered the language because of a custom we followed at Cambridge," Leigh said. "We had heavy oak doors to our rooms, and on those rare occasions we were permitted to have young lady visitors and did not wish to be disturbed we closed them. This was known as sporting one's oak." He reached for the champagne bottle.

"It is finished, Leigh," he said. "We will find more. Wine is a mocker, strong drink is raging: and whosoever is deceived thereby is not wise. Proverbs."

"Amen, amen," Leigh said.

He looked at Leigh fondly. "Leigh, couldn't you bring your young lady to sup with us?"

Leigh looked thoughtful, then beamed at such brilliance. "A capital idea," he said. "Jolly good—really jolly good." He paused. "But first I must fetch her."

"Where is she, Leigh?"

"Far down in the docklands," Leigh said, and hiccuped. "Far away in the docklands at the Mersey Street Settlement House."

He pondered that carefully. "Leigh," he said severely, "are you playing rakehell with the lower classes?"

Leigh vigorously shook his head. "No such thing. 'Pon my honor as an English gentleman, no. She is marvelously solvent —Huddlesfield mills, and all. She is there as an angel of mercy. She is an angel of mercy and she succors the poor."

"Very well, Leigh," he said. "We will fetch her. I happen to have a motor car I use for just such purposes. I have a motor car with a faithful old retainer, who drives it day and night." He reflected. "Yes, he drives it day and night and refers to me affectionately as that sleepless son-of-a-bitch." He raised his sleeve and squinted at his watch. "If we leave now, Leigh, we can just about make intermission at the theater. We will see Miss Barr, and then we will fetch your Huddlesfield angel."

Leigh was trying to coax a few more drops of champagne from the empty bottle. "A capital idea," he said, "—really a capital idea."

He called the barmaid and paid his bill, and when he started to rise, the floor seemed to lurch under his feet. He sat down again slowly. He was drunk; not too drunk, very pleasantly, very happily, drunk. He tried it again, rising slowly and placing his hand on the table for support. He swayed slightly but the floor was stationary, and he discovered he could walk with no trouble if he planted his feet firmly. Leigh was making his way to the door with the careful cautious gait of a barefoot man walking on sharp stones.

Outside the pub, they halted, swaying slightly, taking deep breaths of the heavy, slightly foggy night air. "I don't want to be unduly inquisitive, Leigh," he said. "But do you have to write a column tonight?"

"No, it will keep," Leigh said. "It will keep until morning." He paused thoughtfully. "If I can remember what it was you said."

"You will think of something, Leigh," he said. They advanced cautiously to the center of the cobbled lane and started in the direction of the theater. "Yes, you will think of something," he said. "I know because I used to be a newspaperman myself. I hate to phrase it so tritely, but it is gospel."

"I am not surprised to hear that," Leigh said. He thought it over. "No, I am not surprised at all. I hope you will forgive my saying it, but in my quiet, unobtrusive way I have rather a genius for people. I sensed there was a journalist lurking behind your golden and opulent exterior."

He was immensely pleased. "You are a genius, Leigh. In your quiet, dignified English way, undoubtedly you are. Yes, I first became a newspaperman when I was fourteen years of age."

"I say, that was rather young, wasn't it?"

"No, in point of fact it wasn't, Leigh. If I had been more truthful, I probably could have become a newspaperman when I was twelve years of age. It is a sad story. Would you care to hear it?"

"I would, very much," Leigh said.

"Well, when I was twelve I was a newspaper boy, Leigh. I delivered newspapers on a bicycle, and every afternoon when I went to the back door of the newspaper to pick up my papers I was overcome with a peculiar feeling. I can't explain it. It was a very small newspaper, and I would stand in the doorway, watching the flatbed press run, and looking right through to the front office where the editor sat correcting proofs and reading copy. His name was Hall and he was a big man. I couldn't understand it, but I was overcome with a feeling that I belonged there somehow. It fascinated me and it filled me with some kind of desire I had never experienced before. Well, one summer day, the urge grew so strong that, almost before I realized it, I was walking through the dirty press room and I went right inside the office and walked up to Mr. Hall. As I said, he was a big man and he had shaggy eyebrows and shaggy hair. He looked a bit like an English sheepdog, in fact. He looked at me through his eyebrows and said, 'What is it, Sammy?' That was one of his peculiarities; he called all little boys Sammy. I said, 'You got any jobs around here, Editor?' He looked me over and asked, 'Why do you want to work here, Sammy?' I didn't have a reason I could express, so I said the first thing that came to mind. I said, 'I want to make some money.' He had a big blue pencil in his hand. He raised it and pointed to the door and said, 'Get! If you want to make money go deliver your papers.' Now, I ask you, Leigh, wasn't that sad?"

"Very sad," Leigh said. "It sounds almost Dickensian somehow."

"It crushed me, Leigh, crushed me. But I was persistent, and I thought I was clever. Two weeks before school ended the next summer I quit my paper route, and on the very afternoon school let out I summoned up all my courage and walked in the front door of the newspaper office and went up to Mr. Hall. He looked at me through his eyebrows just as he had the first time, and he had a blue pencil in his hand. I said, 'Can you use a boy around here, Editor?' To my amazement, he remembered me. He said, 'Still trying to make some money, Sammy?' I said, 'Oh, no sir, I don't care about money. I just want something to do.' He raised his pencil and pointed toward the door. He said, 'Get! If you want something to do, go fishing.' Wasn't that heartless, Leigh?"

"It moves me," Leigh said. "It moves me greatly."

"Well, the next summer I almost decided not to go near the newspaper office, but I knew I never would forgive myself if I didn't. I wanted to work there more than anything else in the world. I put on my best blue suit and slicked down my hair and went to see Mr. Hall. Nothing had changed. He lowered his head and looked at me through his eyebrows, and he even had a blue pencil in his hand. I didn't have as much aplomb as I had before, I was scared to death, in fact. I said, 'I'm looking for a job for the summer, Editor.' He sat back and said, 'Still trying to make some money, Sammy?' I said, 'No, sir, that's not it.' 'Just want something to do in your spare time, Sammy? Why do you always pick on me?' I said, 'I . . . I just don't know. I like the way it smells around here.' He raised his pencil and my heart sank, but he threw it on the desk and he roared with laughter. He said, 'That's a fine answer, Sammy. Come to work tomorrow morning.' "

" 'Strawd'nary," Leigh said.

"It was the biggest day of my life," he said. He paused. "No," he said slowly "—no, I don't guess it was . . ."

. . . he was breathless because he had run all the way home, but he stopped in the hallway beside the big mahogany hatrack with the marble top and waited until he caught his breath and then he walked into the dining room where they were having supper and he said, "Hello," and then quickly, much more quickly than he had planned, he said, "I've got a little piece in the paper today, a piece I wrote all by myself," and his mother said, "Paul, why, Paul, you mean you've written a story after being there only three days?" and his dad said, "Well, what do you know about that!" and he put the paper on the table and his dad reached for it and asked, "Where, son, where

68 . . .

is it?" and he said, "It's on that page—I just happened to be reading that page," and casually, very casually, so he wouldn't seem too excited, he pointed it out and said, "There—there it is, right there at the bottom of that column, and his mother said, "How wonderful, oh, how exciting, read it out loud, dear," and his dad cleared his throat and read, "Dr. Barnes and John Anderson caught a nice string of crappie and perch out at Wheeler Lake yesterday. Fishing was also reported good below the dam at the lake," and his mother said, "Isn't that wonderful? Let's cut it out and save it, Paul," and his dad lowered the paper and said, "It's fine, son—clear and right to the point. Nobody could say that clearer and better." and he said, "Aw, it's not much, just a little . . . squib." but with them looking at him like that, he knew that never again would he ever write anything that made him feel so proud . . .

SIX . . .

They entered the stage door of the theater with great
dignity, the stiff conspiratorial dignity drunks frequently have when they find themselves among people who are sober. He looked at his watch and saw that the
second curtain intermission was about half over. He motioned
to Leigh to follow him and walked down the corridor toward
Cynthia's dressing room, nodding stiffly to stagehands and
members of the cast he passed on the way. The door marked
with a large gold gilt star was half open, and he paused and
listened a moment. He nodded gravely to Leigh and they
eased into the room. Cynthia was seated at her dressing table,
holding court for a half dozen or so members of the audience
who had come backstage. She was seated with her head held
high, holding her right arm out stiffly, and she was saying,
". . . is the worst thing you can do. So I would sit very calmly
and quietly, trying not to be frightened because adrenalin ex-
cites dogs, you know. If anyone else became excited and started
to get up or came toward me, I would say in a normal conver-
sational tone, 'No, stay where you are, stay where you are,
everybody, and just pretend that nothing unusual is happening.' I would just ignore him, absolutely ignore him, and I'll
bet anything that he would go away. Even wild animals won't
bother people who lie still and pretend to be unconscious, you
know." She lowered her arm.

There was an appreciative murmur from the visitors. She
flashed them a smile, and, suddenly, saw him standing just
inside the door. "Oh, hello, lover," she said. "I was just telling
them about that awful dog."

He nodded soberly. "With such a performance, his mouth would drop open in admiration," he said. Everyone laughed. She studied him through lowered eyelids with a mocking, knowing smile. He and Leigh stood near the door until a buzzer sounded and the visitors made a hurried departure. After she had shaken hands with the last of them, she closed the door and grinned and threw her arms around his waist.

"Two in a row, lover? What's the celebration?"

He nodded formally toward Leigh, who was looking owlish. "I should like to present Mr. Pepys, a drinking companion in whom I am well pleased."

"Hello, darling," she said, giving Leigh her hand. She surveyed them both and laughed. "Your name isn't really Peeps," she said to Leigh. "Nobody is named Peeps."

Leigh bowed low. "It's m . . . m . . . my nom de plume, fa . . . fa . . . fair lady," he said, suddenly recovering his stutter.

He looked at Leigh with companionly pride. "It's the name he drinks by," he said.

She studied Leigh with amused speculation. Then she grinned. "You're not Samuel Pepys? That darling Samuel Pepys, who wrote all those nice things about me?"

Leigh bowed again. "The same one, ma . . . madame."

"Then you are a darling," she said, patting him on the cheek. "Much too nice to be associating with this . . . this Elmer Gantry."

"Mr. Pepys, who claims his real name is Leigh, is joining us for supper," he said. "We are on our way now to fetch his young lady."

"How nice," she said. "Where are we going, lover?"

He thought about that slowly, carefully. "To be truthful, I haven't yet made arrangements," he said. "I have been busy —busy on matters of great importance. Is that not true, Leigh?"

"Amen, amen," Leigh said.

The call-boy came up the corridor intoning the signal for curtain. She smiled and went to her dressing table and hurriedly smoothed her makeup with a tissue. "Why don't we go directly to the Moroccan place, lover? Nate and Dolly are meeting us here. I've asked Charlie to stop anybody else who starts back. No more goddamned levees tonight." She turned from the mirror and paused and was about to kiss him, but remembered her makeup, and thumped him sharply on the chest instead. "Good-bye, darlings, see you later," she said, and left.

He looked at Leigh thoughtfully. "What do you say to the Moroccan place?"

Leigh said, "I am a great admirer of some Moroccan things. I like Morroccan leather goods very much."

He nodded. "Very well. We shall stop at the crush bar downstairs and pick up a couple of bottles and go and find your young lady." He paused. "On second thought—one bottle. For we must remember the admonition: Hast thou found honey? Eat so much as is sufficient for thee, lest thou be filled therewith, and vomit it. Proverbs.

Leigh nodded. "Amen, amen."

When he bought the Bentley, he had been offered the choice of a built-in bar, makeup table or writing desk. He had chosen the writing desk; now he deplored his lack of foresight. As the car turned the first corner, the champagne bucket would have toppled from the desk onto the floor if Leigh had not rescued it and placed it between his legs.

He apologized. "It was purely a case of nice-nellyism, Leigh. I thought a bar would be a bit gauche. I should have realized it was a necessity."

Leigh finished his glass of champagne, and carefully poured himself another. "Bars in motor cars are gauche," he said, loyally. "You were quite right. For a rich barbarian from across the sea, you have a sense of style. It's m'fondest wish to emulate you."

That pleased him. "Oh, you will do better, Leigh. Far better. I am a man of only small talent."

"I do have one 'strawd'nary talent," Leigh said. He tossed

off his champagne and patted his chest delicately. "Mustn't get the come-ups," he explained. He burped, and nodded approvingly. "I do not often boast about it, but I am perhaps the world's greatest authority on Jonathan Swift."

"Do tell," he said, delightedly. "When I was a child in my father's house I was very fond of *Gulliver's Travels*. It once was even my favorite book. Edify me about old Jonathan."

"Very well," said Leigh. He took a deep breath. "Jonathan Swift, as the whole world knows, was born at Number Seven Hoey's Court, Dublin, on November thirtieth, in the year sixteen six-seven, only a few months after the death of his father . . ."

As Leigh talked, he slumped back against the seat and closed his eyes. He felt good for a change, maybe a bit too drunk, but good all the same. His raillery with Leigh had been just what he needed. Why couldn't he stay cheerful and full of bounce like this all the time? He opened his eyes and looked out the window. They were deep in the docklands section now, threading a narrow street behind huge warehouses. It looked interesting. Maybe he should come down here and poke around . . . *Oh, for God's sake, stop kidding yourself, boy. You're full of wine now, but you can't stay drunk all the time. What about the morning? What about all those long and dreary mornings?* Enough of that . . . He turned to Leigh.

" . . . was singularly devoid of passion," Leigh was saying. "Of friendship, even of tender regard, Jonathan was fully capable. But Vanessa's ardent and unreasoning passion was beyond his . . ."

"Enough, Leigh," he said. "That will do nicely for now. Suppose we have a drink?"

Leigh said sorrowfully, "It is finished. It must have spilled. 'Pon my word, I had scarcely a drop."

He laughed and Leigh joined in. They were still laughing when the car pulled up before a large corner building which was obviously the settlement house. Diagonally across the street, on another corner, was a large, well-lighted pub. He nudged Leigh and pointed. "While you fetch your lady I will go yonder and order wine. We will fortify ourselves before going back to civilization."

"Capital, capital," Leigh muttered. He was having trouble getting up. While Harold opened one door and reached in to assist Leigh, he managed to get the other door open and, somewhat unsteadily, make his way across the street to the pub. The private bar was spacious, old-fashioned and completely deserted. He found a table and a plump genial little man, who was obviously the publican himself, came over immediately.

"Do you have any champagne?" he asked.

"Any kind you name, guv," the man said proudly.

He ordered his favorite Krug and three glasses. The man returned almost immediately and with a flourish thumped the unopened bottle in the center of the table. "Here we are, guv—right out of the fridge."

He had scarcely managed to get the bottle open before Leigh appeared, blinking owlishly, accompanied not by one woman, but two. The pert, fashionable mod, little blonde clinging to his arm was his girl friend, Wendy Balfour. The other woman, quietly chic, brunette, perhaps in her mid-30's, he introduced as Madame Valois. Leigh stammered, "I have ta . . . taken the liberty of offering Ma . . . Madame Valois transportation."

He smiled at Madame Valois. "Good show, Leigh," he said. "You are a credit to the care I lavished on your upbringing." While the publican brought another glass and he poured the wine all around, he had a chance to study Madame Valois. She sat quietly, appearing to be viewing them all with amused detachment. She was an attractive woman. Unusually attractive; hair so black that it had blue highlights; enormous, expressive eyes. "Are you also an angel of mercy, Madame Valois?" he asked. She raised her eyebrows, puzzled, and looked toward Wendy Balfour for help.

"Madame Valois is a sponsor of Mersey House, Mr. Fraser," Wendy said.

It followed. He had dressed enough women to know that her deceptively simple gray suit was not a manufacturer's item. Her pearls were genuine and matched. Yet there was something vaguely off-center about her, too; no high shine to her grooming. Women were often like that when they dressed for themselves, not a man.

"And what does a sponsor do?" he asked.

Madame Valois looked at him without changing her expression of speculative amusement. "Very little, I'm afraid. It has been almost a year since I have been down here." Then Leigh launched into a droll and fanciful account of their troubles with the champagne bucket in the car, and he added his comments, and he did not have a chance to talk with Madame Valois further. He did notice that she continued to observe their hilarity, rather than share in it; she also refused a second glass of wine, though she sipped her first one slowly, apparently savoring it.

When they returned to the car, Leigh and Wendy insisted on taking the jump seats, and immediately put their heads together and began a low conversation in their upper-class accents which sounded like a subdued gargle. Madame Valois had paused before she entered the car to give Harold her address, and as he sat with her on the back seat, he couldn't think of anything to say. He had a feeling that she had been put off by his drunkenness, and he was sorry about that. Finally, he said, "We are joining some friends and going to Le Casbah for supper, Madame Valois. We'd be happy if you could join us."

"Thank you," she said, "but I'm afraid it is impossible."

"The invitation includes your husband, too, of course," he said.

"It is very nice of you," she said "but my husband is not with me."

Ordinarily, he would have let the matter drop. But he was intrigued with this attractive, oddly withdrawn woman. He looked at her and smiled. "Then there's really no reason why you can't join us for a bite to eat."

That should have at least brought a polite smile. But in the dim light from the street lights they were passing, he could see that her face was calm, composed. "To be quite honest, Mr. Fraser," she said, "I don't care for cabarets."

He thought about that. "You know, to be quite honest, neither do I," he said.

Her face did not change expression. "Then why do you go?"

He mulled that over. Then he grinned. "I really don't know. Don't we all do things we don't particularly care about doing?"

"Not all of us, Mr. Fraser."

"Oh, come now," he said. "Don't you ever do anything you really don't care to do?"

"Certainly," she said. "But they are necessary things."

He laughed. "I try to avoid the necessary things."

"Then you are being very foolish," she said, calmly. "A man of your talents should know better."

He felt pleased, and asked shamelessly, "What do you know about my talents?"

She looked at him composedly. "Oh, I have seen some of your plays, Mr. Fraser." She paused. "I found them very amusing."

At least that was something. He felt vaguely gratified. He also knew enough about feminine blandishments to know that this woman wasn't trying to be coy or using the old needle technique. She simply spoke as if . . . well, as if she had been injected with truth serum. It was intriguing—and disturbing. Maybe she simply didn't have a sense of humor? He wished he was sober enough to figure her out.

Her apartment house in Belgravia had a circular driveway that went to the front entrance. After she made her good nights, there was no reason for him to get out of the car; but he did, anyway, standing half in and half out of the open car door. She offered her hand, and as he took it, he said, "I hope we can meet again sometime, Madame Valois. May I give you a call?" She seemed to hesitate, and he grinned and said, "I don't drink all the time, you know." She smiled slightly and said, "No, I should not think so." Then she said, "I am sorry, but I shall be leaving London within a day or two." She said good night again, and entered the door.

When he rejoined Leigh and Wendy in the car, he said, "I liked that woman."

"She's very attractive," Wendy said.

"Who is her husband?" he asked.

"I haven't the foggiest," Wendy said.

He asked, "But she is French, I take it?"

Wendy nodded. "I assume so, but she must have spent a lot of time in the East. I heard her speaking both Hindustani and Urdu today."

"P'haps she's a Madrasi," Leigh said helpfully. He began to sing,

"I love a Madrasi,
A beautiful, fair Madrasi . . ."

It must have been almost midnight when they arrived at the Moroccan place. He was drunk, really drunk now, and he had only a dim, jumbled recollection of the last few hours. He and Leigh and Wendy had sat drinking in the bar at the theater until the final curtain, and then they had gone on to Cynthia's dressing room and polished off a few more bottles with her and Nate and Dorothy Bernstein. He was very fond of the Bernsteins; Nate was head of the West Coast office of the agency that represented him and Cynthia, and Dorothy had once been fairly successful in pictures, playing kittenish blondes. Dorothy was still kittenish, for that matter; most of their laughter in the dressing room had been over her exchanges with Leigh when she thought his name was really Mr. Peeps.

Yes, it was a good party; he liked them all. No matter how drunk he was, he could still think. And he felt sad because he had lost his elation. As soon as Ali, the fawning little maitre d' he loathed, had ushered them to the big corner table Cynthia liked, he had ordered a couple of magnums of wine. But as soon as he had a drink, he knew it was no use. It was too late; he was over the hill now. So, maybe he couldn't walk so well, maybe his coordination wasn't so good. Ah, but he could still think. He knew he was just plain drunk; and he was tired and drained out and fed up. This stupid place was part of the trouble. He looked down with distaste at the big black table with its garish brass inlay, sullenly eyed the crimson satin upholstery which was too soft and thick and too heavily tasseled. But he had to admit the lighting was clever. He reflected on it professionally. Somebody knew how to achieve just the proper suggestion of decadence; somebody had worked hard to get the exact shade of flat reddish light that washed all color from the human face and replaced it with a kind of luminous violet shadowing. He looked across the table at Wendy Balfour, who, as usual, had her head close to Leigh's. Her pert little face looked like a death's head. He studied Cynthia, who was talking animatedly to Nate . . . telling him about the dog, no doubt. Her eyes were blue cavities. Two violet shadows erased her cheek bones and made her face look sharp and avaricious; she had no mouth at all because the red light obliterated her lipstick. What in hell was wrong with everybody, anyway? Women wanted to look beautiful, and once beautiful women chose places lit by the flattering soft glow of candles—

He realized Cynthia had put her hand on his. She was looking at him in her level, amused way; she was always amused when he was drunk. "What did you do today, lover?" she asked.

They were all looking at him. He wanted to sound expansive and gay. *What had he done?* He thought about it carefully, but he couldn't remember a thing. He tried to grin, and to gain time he asked, "Would you care to hear about my day?" He realized his voice was blurred.

"Yes, tell us, lover," Cynthia said.

He looked at all their smiling faces; they looked like badly made up characters in Marat/Sade. He remembered something. He said solemnly, "I saw a beautiful adoring girl—a

beautiful girl looking at a man with adoration in her eyes."
Everybody laughed, and Cynthia asked, "Were you the man,
lover?" He shook his head sadly, "No, I wasn't the man. I
wasn't so lucky."

It was all coming back now. He started to speak again, but
just then there was a burst of wailing music and a tinkling
of bells. A belly dancer had come onto the floor. He looked
at her disinterestedly. She was a pouty, dark little girl, wearing
a skimpy net bra and a gold metallic girdle which fitted just
below her hip bones. A red rhinestone was pasted in her navel.
He watched a few moments while she placed her hands across
her forehead, palms outward, half closed her eyes, and with a
small secretive smile began to undulate her hips. He sighed
and looked down at the table. He wished they had let him
finish. He was about to tell them how he had insulted a silly
old actor, and had tried to help a silly young one. He might
even have told them how he had disowned his country—become a Benedict Arnold, fiscally speaking, of course . . .

"Just look at that little bitch," he heard Cynthia say. He
looked back at the floor. The little dancer had her knees bent,
her pelvis thrust forward, and was gyrating her hips slowly.
Occasionally, without a break in her slow grinding, she rotated
her breasts, then her protruding little belly with a suggestive
spasm. What in hell was amusing about that? Why did Cynthia like to come here? He thought about it. But why pick on
Cynthia? Why did he come here . . . Suddenly, he thought
of Madame Valois. She said he was foolish . . . nicely—but she
said it all the same. And he was. Very well, he would leave.
He was drunk, but he could still think. He was tired and fed
up and he would simply leave. Nate and Dorothy would understand. He could explain to Leigh tomorrow. Slowly, deliberately, he stood up. Only Cynthia looked at him. He gave her
a reassuring wink. She would think he was going to the men's
room. Smiling at his cleverness, he carefully, stiffly walked toward the foyer, looking neither right nor left. He kept walking
until he passed through the front door and felt the cool night

air on his face. He was drunk, all right. "I'll call your car, Mr. Fraser." The doorman was a shadowy blur. He shook his head. "Leave car f'guests," he said thickly. "Get me a cab."

That must have been what happened. He could never remember the trip home; whether one of the servants let him in, or he used his key. The next thing he knew, he had shucked off his clothes, and was standing at the washbasin in his bathroom, automatically following the ritual he always followed when he had been drinking heavily. He carefully brushed his teeth. Next, he dropped two seltzer tablets in a glass of water and slowly drank the fizzing mixture down. He followed this with three milk of magnesia tablets. Then he opened his mirrored medicine cabinet and reached for a bottle of sleeping tablets, preparing to take two. But when he shut the mirrored door, he looked directly into his face. He stood there looking blankly at the blank eyes, slightly red-rimmed. The face he saw was sallow, utterly weary—finished and old. He looked from that defeated face to the bottle he held, three-quarters filled with capsules. There was nothing dramatic or agonizing about it. He made his decision without having to even think about it; he was cool, and it was final. But, first, he had to take some precautions.

It was automatic, almost as if he had planned it carefully. Steadily, not staggering the least bit, he walked into Cynthia's bathroom. He rummaged around looking for a lipstick. When he couldn't find one, he opened a jar of cold cream. Using his forefinger, pausing now and again to dig out more cream, he wrote on her mirror: "Let Me Sleep." He stood back a moment and sized up his handwork. It would do. He was rather proud of it, in fact.

He returned to his own bathroom and carefully washed and dried his hands. He was really functioning with impressive dignity, he decided. He carefully drew a glass of water and poured his palm full of the red capsules. He swallowed them effortlessly—again, and still once again. There . . . the bottle was empty. Pleased with his own craftiness, he opened his laundry hamper and dropped the bottle inside. He was preparing to snap off the light, when he noticed a single red capsule had fallen in the basin. He carefully retrieved it, popped it in his mouth, and swallowed it without water.

It was all so easy. So simple. He had always known it would come to this. And he was absolutely right. He felt pleased . . . and vastly relieved as he turned back the covers and got into his bed. That was all he remembered—almost all. It may never have happened, but before he dropped into that deep darkness, he had a vague recollection that he felt a sense of panic because he had forgotten to say his prayers. That was odd, because he had not prayed for years. Maybe he imagined it, or maybe the drug dredged up a childhood memory. Because it seemed he said:

> *Little Jesus, mild and meek,*
> *Protect me while I sleep . . .*

SEVEN . . .

When he was a young newspaperman, working on a New York newspaper, he once had been plagued by a stomach ache that persisted for days. He stoically ignored it until one predawn morning he came awake in his room in a small hotel on 39th Street and found the minor pain had become a hot and urgent agony. He did not have to be told what was wrong; he knew as surely as if the word *appendicitis* had been branded on his throbbing belly. Gritting his teeth against the pain, he rose and dressed, found a taxi, and turned himself in at a large and ugly old hospital, just off Third Avenue. As soon as it was established that he was employed and reasonably solvent, it was surprising how quickly things began to happen. Almost before he knew it, he had been enemaed, shaved and daubed red to the breastbone, and was being wheeled into an operating room. A large man, swathed in white, except for glinting metal rim spectacles, clutched his arm firmly, poised a needle, and said genially: "You're going to find this pleasant, son. Count to ten slowly."

Surprisingly, he had found it pleasant; he had scarcely begun counting when he was enveloped in a sudden, velvety oblivion that was fathomless and absolute. It also was a revelation. Somehow he had always thought that going under anaesthesia would be like falling into a deep and reluctant sleep. Perhaps it was naïve of him, but he had never dreamed that anything could cause him simply to cease to exist. He had always believed that deep inside his secret self, that something which psychiatry had popularized as the unconscious, that awareness his father had taught him to regard as his immortal soul, would always remain inviolable. As he pondered on it later, he had never been able to decide whether he should feel comforted or disturbed to discover that it simply was not so. If a drug injected into his arm could obliterate him so completely, couldn't death do the same? Yes, the thought disturbed him, but it was consoling to know that if he did plunge into that plumbless chasm of nothingness, forever and finally, he would be past caring or regretting.

But the oblivion he experienced now was neither enduring nor pleasant. He was never able to sort out all his impressions or even put them in sequence. He did vaguely remember that once he heard the murmur of voices and felt a wrenching discomfort that was almost pain. Another time, he felt that his bladder was bursting. It seemed he heard a running stream in the distance, and for some reason, he was trying desperately to reach it so he could relieve himself; but something held him back. Then, he heard a woman's voice, half-exasperatedly, half-resignedly, saying, "Oh, all right. Go ahead." And he was standing in the stream, blissfully making water, making water, while the roaring current pounded against his legs and spray and mist flew past him. On several occasions, it seemed he was being dragged along. He definitely recalled being turned over repeatedly. Once when this happened, he opened his eyes and was surprised to see Willie Hunt-Groves standing above him. That was odd. Somebody must be sick if old Willie was here.

It must have been later that he felt himself being jostled roughly and he opened his eyes again. Willie's face, with its silly bushy moustache, was just a few inches away from his own. He started to ask Willie irritably what the hell was going on, when he realized one of his arms was draped around Willie's neck; he turned his head and saw that his other arm was around the neck of a plain-faced woman wearing a nurse's cap. Why, he was sick. He was sick and Willie and a nurse were trying to make him walk. He tried to say something and couldn't. *I've had a stroke*, he thought. *I've had a stroke and I can't talk and I can't walk.* Then he realized that his throat and chest were terribly sore, dull, aching soreness. No, it was pneumonia. Of course, it was pneumonia. He knew all about pneumonia. His father had been unconscious for days and almost died of pneumonia when he was a boy. He tried to help Willie and the nurse by moving his feet. His throat and chest hurt quite a lot, and he was thirsty. Nothing would taste quite as good as a glass of cold milk. He exerted himself desperately in an effort to say "Milk," and he was surprised when finally the word he croaked out was, "Brandy." Willie turned his head and his big block teeth showed in a grin. "Hah!" he said loudly. "Not likely, old man. Not bloody likely."

Then Willie had him in a chair and was making him drink something hot that tasted awful and seared his sore throat and burned all the way down to his stomach. He wanted to be cooperative because he knew Willie was only trying to help, but, finally, he lost his temper when Willie and another older doctor began to work him over. It was like a bad third-degree sequence in a 1935 Republic picture. They kept asking his name and where he lived and how old he was; shaking his shoulder roughly and telling him to wake up, and shoving fingers in front of his face and asking him to count them. Part of his anger at first was with himself because, no matter how hard he tried, he simply couldn't find the right words to answer them. He did eventually, though, and he also bawled them out, until they let him fall asleep again.

The next time he awakened, he was himself again. It was night and the only light in the room came from a goose-neck lamp on his bedside table. A nurse was standing in front of the dresser mirror, primping at her hair. He watched her a moment, and started to say hello, but then he decided he might as well play it broad. "Where am I?" he asked.

She turned in surprise, and when she saw his smile, she smiled back. "This is the London Clinic."

"How long have I been here?" he asked.

She said, "I'll get your doctor," and left the room.

A minute later, he heard the rapid tapping of heels, and Cynthia burst through the door and he was smothered in her kiss, her cool furs, and the fragrance of her perfume. "You big bastard," she said. "You had me playing East Lynne all over the place."

He grinned at her. "I feel fine." He saw Willie Hunt-Groves standing at the foot of the bed, his florid face beaming. He was about to ask what it was all about, when Willie said, "So you decided to take a few pills, did you, old man?"

Instantly, it all came back. He felt an immense sense of relief; not because he still was alive, he didn't give that a thought until later; but because the mystery was solved. "So that's it," he said almost elatedly. "My God, I'd forgotten all about it."

"How many pills did you take?" Willie asked.

He reflected on it, remembering everything he did while standing at the washbasin. "I'm not sure," he said. "It was about three-quarters of a bottle."

"Hah! Thought so," Willie said, looking pleased with himself. "Enough to take care of three—four blokes your size. You almost bought it, y'know, old man. Damned tricky there a while." He laughed. "Thought you'd softened up the old brain for good."

Cynthia called him a horse's ass, and kissed him. Suddenly, he realized how sore his throat was, a soreness that seemed to extend to his stomach. He told Willie about it.

Willie gave his happy snort. "Shouldn't wonder," he said cheerily. "Had the Arabian pipeline stuck down there a while —bringing things up and taking them down. Two-way traffic. S'pose you've got a bloody awful touch of gastritis, too. Be surprised if you don't." He beamed at him. "Like olive oil?"

"I think so," he said.

"He adores it," Cynthia said.

"Going to order you up a big flagon," Willie said. "Want you to guzzle down a whiskey glassful every hour. Best thing there is to soothe the old belly. Should help the gullet, too."

Somehow it seemed terribly funny. Just the sort of remedy Willie would suggest. Then, while Willie guffawed and Cynthia studied him with her amused, rapt look, he told them what he remembered about awakening, how he thought he had a stroke or pneumonia. Finally, after a lot of laughter and conversation, Willie told Cynthia she had better be leaving, and she gathered up her furs and kissed him good-bye. Willie left with her, but reappeared a few minutes later with a hypodermic and jovially gave him a shot in the rump.

He looked at Willie, all his elation now gone. "Tell me what happened, Willie."

Willie still looked pleased with himself. "Cynthia found you. Came home about four, but couldn't sleep. Finally, went in to check on you. Didn't like the way you were breathing. Shouldn't wonder. She bloody near roused London." He chortled. "Had everybody cracking about and tumbling out of bed, except the Prime Minister. Got you here posthaste."

"What time this morning.

"Yesterday morning, old man," Willie said. "About sixish." He looked at his watch. "Bit more than thirty-six hours ago." For the first time, he lost his cheerful air, and looked weary. "Bit of a scramble there for a while. Thought we'd lost you. Pumped you out, and washed you out, and still couldn't tell." He grinned again. "Gave you enough stuff to keep you near the point of bloody convulsions all day yesterday, but still couldn't get you awake completely. Finally, had to let you sleep some of it off."

"Thanks, Willie," he said.

"Hah!" said Willie. "Way I earn my living."

He had a sudden, uncomfortable thought. "Did the papers get wind of it, Willie?"

Willie looked almost contrite. " 'Fraid they did, old boy. Ambulance drivers, and all. Bit of a splash yesterday. Reported you got too many pills and were hauled in." He beamed again. "Nothing to worry about. Told them myself last night it was just bad reaction to normal dosage. Few of them waylaid Cynthia this morning. She laughed it off, told 'em it was too much bubbly." Willie stood grinning at him for a while, then said a bit too casually, "Don't s'pose you'll make another try, old man?"

He shook his head. "No, Willie."

"Good-o. Didn't think you would." Willie retrieved his black bag from the dresser, and said offhandedly, "S'posed to send a head doctor round to have a chat. Bloody textbook procedure. Might be a good idea at that. Don't s'pose y'mind seeing him?"

"Yes, I do, Willie," he said. "I don't want to see a psychiatrist, or anybody else."

Willie hesitated a moment, but then he beamed. "Hah! All right, old man."

It was not until sometime during the night that he finally began to reflect on what he had done. They had propped him up high in bed to ease the now gnawing discomfort in his esophagus and belly. After his nurse had aroused him and given him a shot glass of Willie's olive oil, he lay there wide awake, staring into the stilly darkness. He supposed he should feel some regret, maybe even fright. But he simply couldn't. Neither was he particularly thankful. He only felt empty; not happy that he had been saved, nor unhappy because he had not died. The only thing he really felt was annoyance because of the inconvenience: the unnecessary pain, the stupid publicity, the embarrassment over making a silly, ineffectual ass of himself.

But the more he pondered on it, the more he realized how dangerous, how utterly sad . . . yes, even how frightening, his attitude was. Here he was, a man forty-six years old, probably two-thirds of his life lived, and he was lying in a hospital bed, an attempted suicide, saved only by the grace of God and bluff old Willie Hunt-Groves. That made him a failure, all right. He had said it many times before, only now it was not mere self-abnegation, but a solid fact; he could not change it with the old palliative about his money and success. And it would still be true no matter how drunk he got. No, drinking would not help. It was dangerous; he had almost thrown himself out a window when he was drunk, he had broken down and cried before Cynthia, and, finally, he had . . . He thought about the events leading up to the time he swallowed the pills, recalling all the details. It had been a typical day, wasteful, aimless, stupid.

What went wrong? Once his days had been joyful, challenging. Maybe he should go back to Indiana for— No, that was silly, futile. One of the symptoms of his discontent was the habit he had developed of dredging up memories of happier times. He didn't actually have any roots that could be restored by going back to the scenes of his childhood. He had discovered that on the couple of occasions he had gone home before his mother died. He couldn't find any real identification with that strange town, where buses roared, where trolleys once clanged, where familiar old houses had either been modernized or fallen into decay, where old streets had been widened and paved, and where new stores and supermarkets covered the vacant lots where he ran carefree and played ball as a kid. It saddened him, really. So did the tight-faced, hearty and graying men, and the plump, simpering matrons, who had been his friends and loves when he was young. And they bored him, so caught up in their piddling little affairs; so smugly proud because the mid-century affluence allowed them to drive garish cars, belong to the country club, and drink bonded liquor, fondly believing they were living like the rich because they had tawdry imitations of all the things only the envied rich could afford when they were young. Anyway, were they really so different from the people he knew now? Wasn't it one of the Van Dorens who said he had never met anyone new after leaving his small midwestern town? It was a true observation; when you ventured out to see the elephant, you had to expect a certain amount of disillusionment. People were people. Once, when he had been invited to spend the night at the

White House, he had come out of his room in the morning
and had been amused to see the President striding down the
corridor, picking his nose. Yes, presidents picked their noses,
and glamorous actresses had pimples on their behinds, and
dexedrined old trout on the best-dressed lists had hot and
cold flashes. Sometimes they had more money and they paid
less attention to conventions, but the people he and Cynthia knocked around with—the people the press smart aleckly
lumped together as The Jet Set—weren't really much different
from the people he grew up with. No, the trouble was not with
the people he knew, but with himself.

What about his work? He thought about it, and for the first
time in years, he was completely honest with himself. He
knew he must have some bump of talent; everybody said so.
But he had never really given it free rein. He had used his
talent in being a scoffer; not writing true comedy with its deep
insight and pathos, but merely in poking fun at people; following the same successful formula all the time, not cutting
too deep, just deep enough to expose their silliness and petti-
ness. His early plays already were so dated that they were seldom performed except by small-town amateur groups. It was
unlikely any of his plays would be performed even ten years
after his death. He was really nothing but a money-spinner.
Oh, he loved the theater, all right, but he hadn't contributed
to it. He was always taking—not giving.

He had to change his life. There was no other answer. He
had to shake it up and even alter it completely if he was to
survive. Maybe after he did that, he also could give his life
some purpose. He lay there in the darkness thinking about it,
and he began to make plans. It didn't take as long as it seemed,
but it was difficult—wrenchingly difficult. It never occurred
to him that he was suffering through the predicament any man
faces when he aspires to a better, more meaningful life. He
knew it, and felt it, but he would have scoffed if anyone had
told him that the threshold to a higher, more worthwhile
existence always is straight and narrow. To take even the first

step across it, he had to part with a number of things which he knew to be disappointing and valueless, but which, nevertheless, he had grown accustomed to carrying; the trappings had really become part of his ego and for that reason alone they were difficult to discard. But he lay and pondered, and he fought and he ruthlessly discarded. He came to Cynthia last, reluctantly, guiltily. He adored Cynthia, but Cynthia was part of his trouble, or, at least, symbolic of his trouble. She represented the kind of life he had grown to detest. Maybe she could also change? But did it matter? He had to either marry Cynthia or leave her, and he knew the answer to that. But still, the more he thought about it, the more he cringed at the thought of hurting Cynthia; he simply didn't know how he was going to tell Cynthia. He only knew that with Cynthia he had to be honest and straightforward.

He was thinking about Cynthia when, finally, he fell asleep. He thought about her when he awakened and, abstractedly, while he good-naturedly bullied his day nurse until she allowed him to go to the bathroom and have a shower instead of giving him a bed bath. Cynthia was lurking in his thoughts all during the time Willie was there guffawing, poking around, and assuring him that he was almost in the pink, really in the pink. He thought about Cynthia almost constantly, until eventually she arrived in a breathless rush and he felt her blasting kiss. And, then, it proved to be surprisingly easy.

Cynthia said brightly, "Lover, I've decided to leave the show."

He studied her a moment, thinking how vibrantly lovely she looked. "Why, Cynthia?"

"Oh, I've been getting bored with it for ages, lover. Now that you need a rest I thought maybe we could run down to that sweet little place in Portofino. Maybe even go on to Majorca and . . ." She stopped when she saw his face.

"No, Cynthia," he said. He wanted to give her a smile, but he didn't feel like it. "I'm sorry."

"But why, lover? You know that bitch Sybil is dying to take over the part." She grinned. "I hate myself for saying it, but she'd be good, too."

"It's not that, Cynthia. It's just—" he tried to keep his voice casual—"well, it's just that I want to go away alone for a while. I want a chance to be alone."

For a moment, a long moment, he saw the surprised, naked look of shock and despair in her eyes. He had hurt her; he hadn't wanted to—but he had hurt her very much. But Cynthia knew how to defend herself. She lowered her eyes briefly. Then she was gazing at him with her familiar look of mocking amusement. "Is this bam-bam, thank you, ma'am, lover?"

He was tempted to smile and deny it, but he forced himself to be partly honest. "I don't know, Cynthia. Maybe it is."

Smiling, taking her time, she opened her bag and found her cigarette case. She lighted one of her tiny cigarettes and blew out the smoke. Grinning, almost teasingly, she asked, "Find somebody else, lover?"

"You know better than that, Cynthia," he said.

"Where will you go?" She still looked amused.

"I don't know," he said. "I guess I'll go back to New York first, then maybe I'll go out to Indiana for a while." He looked at her seriously. "You're very dear to me, Cynthia, and you always will be. You know that. But I've simply got to go away alone and think things out."

She laughed. "Nobody can go home again, lover. Don't you know that?" She eyed him speculatively, mockingly. "You're not exactly a barefoot boy with cheeks of tan any longer, you know."

He smiled. "I know."

Suddenly, she stood up quickly, almost abruptly, and snubbed out her cigarette in his bedside ash tray. "All right, lover," she said, airily. "If that's the way it is—that's the way it is." She adjusted her furs, and stood looking down at him with a bright smile. "Get thee off to a goddamned monastery, or whatever it is. I'll keep a light in the window, if you ever decide to come back. 'By. See you before you go." For the first time since they had been together she left without kissing him. She simply gave him a small wave and left the room quickly, too quickly.

He felt awful after she had left, miserable and depressed. He knew why she had left so quickly. He knew how much he had hurt her. He had hurt himself . . . yes, it hurt very much. But he knew he was right; it was not much consolation, but he was right.

That night, after his nurse had cleared away his dinner tray, and he sat propped up reading the evening newspapers, Arlie Beimann came into the room. He was both surprised and annoyed. Arlie, a small, rotund man, with a slight Austrian accent and dark, searching eyes that were magnified by heavy black eyeglasses, was Cynthia's analyst, and he did not like him. He did not care for psychiatrists in general, in fact; perhaps they sometimes helped the genuinely mentally sick, but he considered analysts who catered to the rich and well-to-do as phonies. He had another reason for resenting Arlie; from things Cynthia had said, he knew Arlie probably knew all about their sex life.

Arlie stood at the foot of the bed, smiling. "How are you feeling, Paul?"

"All right," he said, shortly.

Without being asked, Arlie calmly seated himself in the chair across from the bed and took out a blackened and battered briar pipe, which he never seemed to light, but fondled between his hands.

He looked at Arlie, disliking him, and when Arlie did not speak but only looked at him smiling, rubbing his pipe, he said, "You know your big trouble, Arlie? You're a lousy casting job. You look exactly like a Viennese psychiatrist."

Arlie smiled placidly. "All psychiatrists look like psychiatrists, Paul. No matter what appearance they have. Would you like to know why?"

"No," he said. "What do you want, Arlie?"

"This is a professional visit, Paul," Arlie said.

"Well, you can trot along. I don't need you."

Arlie puckered his lips wryly. "When you use that tone, I'm convinced you don't, Paul." He studied his pipe a moment. "My patient is Cynthia. Not you."

He lay looking at him, not saying anything.

"Cynthia has a problem that I can't help her resolve until I know how it came about."

He still said nothing.

Arlie rolled his pipe in his hands, and looked at him with his large, searching eyes. "Cynthia tells me you have decided to break off your relationship. Do you mind telling me why?"

"Yes, I do, Arlie," he said. "It's none of your business." He paused. "But I'll do it anyway. I won't go into all the reasons, but I'll give you one good one: I don't love Cynthia."

"Are you sure, Paul?" Arlie asked.

That nettled him. "What kind of damned silly question is that?" he asked.

Arlie looked at him calmly. "I meant it to be a reasonable one, Paul." He stroked his pipe. "Partners in a relationship do often get angry about something, build up resentments . . ."

"It's nothing like that," he interrupted, trying not to lose his temper entirely. "I'm very fond of Cynthia, probably fonder than I've ever been. She should know that." Finally when Arlie continued to look at him, he said, "I'm fed up with the kind of life Cynthia and I lead. It's useless and stupid. I want a change."

Arlie looked at him placidly. "What makes you think Cynthia is any happier with the life you have together, Paul?"

That definitely angered him. "Cynthia is a big girl," he said coldly. "She knows how to take care of herself." When Arlie smiled slightly but did not answer, he demanded irritably, "Well, what the hell's so funny."

"Nothing is funny, Paul," Arlie said. He looked down thoughtfully and rubbed his pipe between his palms. "Cynthia is a strong personality. But she also is a woman, and maso-chism is biologically intrinsic in the female, so . . ."

"Don't give me any Freudian double-talk, Arlie," he said angrily.

Arlie looked up and smiled slightly. "All right, Paul." He paused. "But it wasn't Freudian, you know." He said seriously, "Would it really surprise you to know that Cynthia also is un-happy with the life you lead together? Didn't you really know that she has always hoped that you would marry her? Haven't you always known, Paul, that she would go anywhere, lead any kind of life you want?"

He lay silently, thinking about it, feeling his anger evapo-rate. Yes, he knew it was true. Cynthia would do anything he asked. He realized he had always known it.

Arlie asked quietly, "What is it really, Paul?"

He shook his head, feeling glum and depressed. "I don't know." He looked at Arlie and tried a quip. "Why don't you tell me? You're the expert."

Arlie smiled. "I'm not so gifted, Paul. Only rarely can I tell a patient what is wrong. All I can do is offer some clues so we can try and discover the problem together."

That made sense. For the first time, he found himself not resenting Arlie quite so much. He could see why his calm sen-sible manner, his obvious intelligence, might help many peo-ple, Cynthia even. He said wearily, "I don't know what it is. I wish I did. The old salt has just lost its savor. I'm tired, fed up, disgusted with myself and simply don't give a damn what happens tomorrow." He looked at Arlie. "But whatever it is, I don't need a psychiatrist to tell me I hated my father or loved my mother too much, or piled up hostilities as a kid. I didn't. Anyway, it only started a couple of years ago."

When Arlie continued to look at him, he added, slightly defiantly, "And it isn't the climacteric, Arlie."

Arlie toyed with his pipe and smiled, pleasantly and non-committally. After a short silence, he asked, "But it is some-thing, Paul?"

He said tartly, "Certainly it's something."

"Then let us examine our clues," Arlie said, placidly. "The only reason people turn to suicide is that they feel they have problems which are insoluble. You say you have no obvious problems such as health, finances, or unrequited romantic love, so we must go elsewhere to find the cause of your trouble. We don't have to proceed completely without direction because we know melancholia and despair always are the result of a loss, the renunciation of a goal or some love object, which in your case, we have already established is not romantic. And the goal you have renounced doesn't appear to be sexual." He smiled. "Now, if you were my patient, Paul, there are three areas I should like to examine carefully. First, you are a successful creative person, a writer, and you are automatically doomed to suffer some despair because, whether you admit it to yourself or not, you wish to achieve perfection. That is impossible and always leads to frustration. Second, you are a Twentieth Century man, and merely because of that you go to the rack daily and are tortured, often by things which you consciously ignore. Maybe you simply work too hard and do not relax in a beneficial way. Third, there are things other than the climacteric, which could cause distress to a man of your age. In our middle years, we often sit back and take stock of our inventory. We almost always are despondent over what we find. All of us have to go through a process of learning to accept the man we are, and not despair over the man we hoped to be."

He thought that over. Explained that way, without psychiatric mumbo-jumbo, it made sense. Finally, he looked at Arlie with a small, rueful smile. "I seem to have more liabilities than assets. I guess there's not much hope for me."

Arlie laughed softly. "Oh, it's not that bad, Paul. There's no complete and permanent cure, perhaps, but there are certain balms that can be applied to ease the pain and strain and make them bearable. We'll talk about them sometime if you wish." He placed his pipe in his pocket. "If there is a permanent cure it's known only to a few yogis crouched in secret caves in the Himalayas." He paused a moment. "In your case, Paul, perhaps there would be still another thing to consider. Don't I recall that your father was a clergyman?"

"That's right," he said, a bit defensively. "What the hell does that have to do with it?"

Arlie smiled. "It could matter a great deal. In the long run our conduct depends on our intimate convictions. Our character is developed according to our faith—or lack of it. It's one religious truth from which no one can escape. I am, for example, a Jew; not a very good Jew, but a Jew nonetheless. Have you read Tolstoy's A Confession?"

He nodded. "When I was young. But I'm not a mystic looking for salvation, Arlie. I may suffer a lot of the same complaints, but it's damned sure not because of the same reasons."

Arlie shrugged, smiling his same placid smile. He stood up and came to the edge of the bed. "Paul, I want to ask a favor of you," he said quietly. "Don't make your break with Cynthia final just now. Give yourself a chance to think about it. If you won't accept psychiatric help, at least get out of this beastly climate for a month—two months. Go somewhere and lie back and rest and look up at a blue sky. Then make up your mind. Will you do me that favor, Paul?"

He looked at Arlie, momentarily not disliking him at all, and nodded, "Yes, Arlie—yes, I'll do that."

By late afternoon, the telegrams, the flowers, the ridiculously fancy baskets of fruit had begun to arrive. They did not please him. On the contrary, he looked at them dourly; most of them had come from members of the cast, theatrical acquaintances, or social hangers-on he and Cynthia had attracted —all people who were beholden, or wanted to be beholden, to him. There were some exceptions. He was genuinely pleased when the nurse brought in a bouquet of mixed flowers from the household staff; amused when a bunch of bedraggled African violets arrived with a short note from Leigh: "Bad show

—but understandable. I couldn't count when I arrived home, either." Finally, the flowers became so numerous, their scent so depressingly funereal, that he had his nurse move most of them out into the hall.

He had a bad evening. He missed Cynthia, and he hoped she might come by or at least telephone him before leaving for the theater. When she did neither, he was tempted to call her in her dressing room. Eventually he decided against it. He slept poorly, awakening often, and though he tried to blame the slight, lingering soreness in his throat and stomach, he knew that was not the real reason. He was altogether so glum and depressed the next morning that Willie eyed him speculatively. "Move about more, old man," he said. "Do you good. Want you to go up to the solarium. Might even be lucky and see the sun. Hah." About ten o'clock, restless, and bored with a bad thriller he was trying to read, he decided to follow Willie's advice. In the hall outside his room, he stopped before a vase of carnations that had arrived, and chose a red one as a buttonhole for his woolen robe. The solarium was bleak and deserted; the sun wan and emitting no discernible heat. He found a comfortable chair and picked up an old copy of the New Statesman. After a while, he put it aside, and for lack of something else to do took the carnation from his lapel and began to examine it. Afterwards, he realized Madame Valois must have stood there for some time before he looked up and saw her. He was so surprised that he remained seated for several moments, looking and smiling at her. Her own smile was slight, scarcely lighting her somber eyes. "You may not remember me, Mr. Fraser," she said. "I am Martine Valois and . . ."

"Of course, I remember you, Madame Valois," he said, finding his feet. He laughed. "I wasn't that far gone." It gave him a mild jolt to realize how delighted he was to see her. Her smart little suit was a soft apricot this time; the twinkling white and green stones in her French enamel brooch obviously genuine. And she was just as strikingly attractive as he remembered. In fact, only once or twice before in his life had he seen such a complexion; it had almost an iridescence, a warm, delicate rose tint found in certain sea shells. Another thing that struck him was the fullness of her figure. He had lived for years among women who worked and suffered to achieve a spare slimness. Her figure was not plump, nor soft; she was full bloomed, a strikingly womanly woman. She was extraordinarily good looking, all right. And she had an extraordinary way of speaking. "I have thought about you often since we met, Mr. Fraser," she said.

He realized she was not being flirtatious, not paying him a compliment; she was merely stating a fact. It was disconcerting. "I've thought of you, too," he lied. He wondered about her nationality. She had no accent, but there was a slight formality about her speech which made it obvious that English was not her first language.

She did not acknowledge his remark. Her face was serious, her dark eyes direct. "I realized the other night how unhappy you were. I cannot fully explain why. But I was not surprised when I read what happened in the newspapers. I have been asking myself if I could have done anything to prevent it."

He smiled. "How could you? I didn't know it myself."

"Why did you try to destroy yourself?" she asked.

The question took him completely by surprise. No one had asked it before, not even Willie or Arlie. He wondered if he shouldn't resent it. What was she, anyway? A spiritualist medium? A kooky dame hung up on religion? Just an earnest do-gooder? He looked at her level, calm eyes and knew none of these things made much sense. Instead of resentment, what he really felt was embarrassment. He felt himself flush, and this embarrassed him all the more. He laughed. "I was just plain drunk, madame," he said.

Her eyes were still fixed on his face. "That is not the true cause," she said.

"Perhaps not," he said. He looked at her enormous dark eyes. He shrugged. All right, if she wanted a serious discussion, they would have one. "I don't know," he said, smiling slightly. "I simply don't know how to answer you. I'm solvent, my health is good, but I suppose living has become a burden. And when I got plastered, it seemed like a good idea to do something about it. The wrong thing, I guess. At least, I bungled it."

"You feel lost," she said, "—lost, but also as if you are searching for something you will never find."

Again he was surprised, but also felt a twinge of annoyance. "That's a fair diagnosis," he said. "It's pretty near perfect, in fact." He sat looking at her a while. "But why do you have this interest in me, Madame Valois? Is it professional?"

For the first time she smiled a small smile. "Why should I not take the time to help someone who needs help? Would I pass you by if you were injured? Am I supposed to ignore you because I do not know you well? Would you not help me, Mr. Fraser?"

"Yes . . . yes, I would," he said.

"No, I have no profession," she said. "I often wish I did. I sensed your unhappiness because I once experienced it myself—and I have known others who have."

He grinned. "Did you bungle, too?"

Her face was serious. "No, I might have tried to destroy myself, but before I reached that point, I realized my difficulty."

"And what was that?"

"Mr. Fraser, perhaps you feel lost and you are distraught because you have begun to question the reason for your existence. You are asking yourself the old question: Who am I?"

He laughed. "It's nothing as juvenile as that, I assure you."

Her expression had not changed. "Why is it juvenile? Were Tao and Buddha juvenile? Was Jesus Christ? St. Augustine?"

"I didn't mean to be flippant," he said. "I just don't think that's my problem." He smiled. "I know I don't belong in such exalted company."

"No," she said. "Nor do I. Do you really not understand? Or are you pretending? Why should you alone not ask yourself such an important question? Self-realization does not lead all of us to the same goal. But it does teach us to accept ourselves for what we are, not what we wish, or profess, to be."

He smiled. It was a paraphrase of what Arlie had said. "How do you go about seeking self-realization?" he asked.

"It depends, Mr. Fraser. Some find it easier than others. We are all imperfect creatures, but many of us resist self-surrender more than others. As Newman said, we are all rebels and the first thing we must begin to do is lay down our arms." She smiled. "With our fierce vanity we declare our souls our own, and that is a lie because, in fact, they are not."

He thought that over, and smiled. "Whose are they?"

She said quietly, "When you decide that, Mr. Fraser, you have taken the first step."

"And how do I go about that? Join the church?"

"Sometime, perhaps," she said. "Whatever else one does, it always helps to remember that most human activities one considers so important, so vitally necessary are in reality not worth the time and energy expended. Most of us already know this if we stop and think about it, but we spend all our time in trying to conform within our own petty worlds. If you will remember that, I will have helped you." Abruptly, before he realized her intention, she stood up and held out her hand.

He stood up slowly, surprised. "But I'll be seeing you again?"

"I am leaving London this evening," she said.

"But where are you going?"

"I am going to India on an evening flight," she said.

"India!" he said, surprised. "My God, why?"

For the first time, she laughed. "And why not, Mr. Fraser? It is delightful there this time of year." She looked up at the bleak sky. "The sky is not like this. It is a beautiful blue and one can look at it for hours without seeing a cloud."

Another coincidence. He smiled, "You're not a yogi, are you?"

She shook her head, no longer smiling. "No, Mr. Fraser,

nothing as exalted, as you expressed it. I am only a woman."

"Maybe I should go to India," he said.

"Perhaps you should," she said, disengaging her hand from his. "In India, men who have reached your age and estate often give all their wordly possessions away. They take up a begging bowl and go out to seek the answer to who they are." She motioned to the carnation which had fallen from his lap to the floor. "They sit and gaze at a single flower, just as you were gazing at that one, for hours and they do not feel it is a waste of time."

She was gone before he realized he had not asked where she was going in India, or when she would return. How stupid of him. He sat alone in the solarium for most of the afternoon.

That night, after Willie had finished with his poking, he said, "When I get out of here, Willie, I'm going looking for some sun for a month or two."

"Hah. Jolly good," Willie said. "Envy you."

He hesitated a moment. "How would India do?" If there had been the slightest surprise, the barest quibble, he was prepared to agree how ridiculous the idea was. But he had forgotten how casual the British were about India.

"Damned good idea, old man," Willie said. "Very pleasant out there this time of year. Help get you out of yourself, too."

PART
2

EIGHT . . .

He could not honestly muster up an anticipatory thrill as he journeyed to India. He was far too seasoned a traveler for that. Without being fully aware of it, the truth was years before he had become a member of that affluent and unfortunate band of international migrants who, like giant tortoises, carry their environment around with them. Except for a few obvious differences like language and currency, which were minor annoyances to be endured, it always seemed to him that the people he met and the places he visited in Rome and Paris were about like those in Madrid and New York. Moscow had proved to be as drably dull as Warsaw and Budapest; Cairo and Istanbul had the same atmosphere of oily decadence as Beirut and Tangier.

Once, at his insistence, he and Cynthia had traveled on the famed Orient Express from Milan to Paris, and they had been congealed with boredom and annoyed with the food and service; Tahiti was a honky-tonk with cocoanut palms, and though he had been forewarned the legendary *wahines* had bad teeth, he couldn't decide whether he was amused or disappointed to discover that their worst feature was their big, ugly splayed feet.

. . . Still, there was something different about going to India. Was it merely that he looked forward so much to seeing Madame Valois again? He pondered on that several times during his flight out. Yes, he did want to see her again—he wanted it very much. But there was something else, too; something he couldn't quite ferret out. He had no way of knowing that, like all people who visit India for the first time, he really had a vague presentiment that he was likely to encounter any number of unpleasant things: drought, famine, flood, pestilence, and, perhaps, even cobras in his bathtub. It simply never occurred to him in his mental preparations also to include Indians. And that was a mistake. For, within a few minutes after his plane landed at Bombay, he had decided India's humanity would be his greatest problem. His troubles began when he had to face a battery of splendidly turbaned, but empty-faced immigration officials, who grunted unintelligibly and made him fill out involved and lengthy forms printed on incredibly cheap paper that clogged his fountain pen and caused everything he wrote to become indecipherable blots. Already stiff with annoyance, he then had to locate his own luggage and carry it to the customs counter. More blank-faced, liquid-eyed Indians made him open all of his bags and searched through every inch of each of them with a kind of labored, puzzled thoroughness. They even rummaged through his toilet cases, and from time to time, they questioned him suspiciously in a sing-song English which made them all sound like drunken Welshmen. He decided that whatever other crimes the English had committed in India, teaching the Indians their language was one of the worst.

He emerged into the lobby of the airport seething with irritation. Immediately, he was engulfed in the greatest confusion he had ever seen in his life. After he had been in India a while, he came to realize that, by Indian standards, the crowds at the airport had been orderly and well behaved. But in those first few minutes, when his temper and nerves already were frayed, it seemed he was being attacked by a swarm of slovenly, dirty, yelling, gesticulating, emaciated Indians. Finally, somehow, a scrawny taxi driver, wearing a lopsided orange turban and soiled baggy pantaloons, had him in tow. Shouting, waving his arms, long shirttail flapping, he drove away the hawkers and solicitors, restored order among the wiry little porters carrying his luggage. He and his baggage were loaded into a battered, ramshackle old taxi.

All the way to his hotel he sat staring out the window of the taxi in a sort of amazed, disbelieving stupor. He was not overly fastidious, nor easily shocked, but he felt uneasy and affronted. He had never seen such filth and poverty in his life. This India had absolutely no relation to the India he had read about or seen portrayed on the stage or in motion pictures. In every direction he saw squalor and misery, swarms of flies, ragged, underfed people. At every intersection there was a tangled, noisy mass of bullock carts, dilapidated automobiles, and swarms of heedless, half naked pedestrians.

His driver scarcely slackened his speed, driving headlong into the jams, shouting, honking his horn furiously, nudging people and animals out of the way with his fenders. Before the peeling, dirt smeared walls alongside the road, he noticed that Indians were hunkered down on their heels. He wondered if they were praying, and, suddenly, he realized that they were relieving themselves. He was sincerely offended, not because of prudishness, but because it seemed so incredibly stupid and unhygienic. Even dogs could be broken to grounds.

He was immensely relieved when he arrived at his hotel. It looked as he had expected India to be. The lobby had marble floors and thick Indian rugs and turbaned bearers padding about. There was a profusion of exotic plants, and even a massive old-fashioned grillwork elevator.

A courteous, smiling young Indian in a crisp white suit, who spoke perfect English, greeted him at the reception desk. After he was registered, he was taken up in the slow, old elevator and ushered into a roomy and pleasantly cool suite, with high ceilings and quaint but comfortable furnishings which were a mixture of Victorian and Indian. A barefoot bearer went around, opening shutters and turning on lights, and then gave him a low salaam and went outside and sat on the floor beside the door.

He took a long shower, and still in his terry cloth robe went outside and stood on his broad balcony, looking down at the swarming crowds in the street below. He had to face it: He detested India, and he had made a mistake in coming. He sighed when he thought that right now he could be sitting at a table in his favorite little café on the quayside at Portofino —or looking down from a balcony of the old Negresco in Nice. He did not really dislike those poor, miserable people on the street below. On the contrary, he realized he felt a deep compassion for them. That was part of the trouble, really. It distressed him, almost sickened him, because there was simply not a thing he could do for them. But he had to be honest— neither did he want to go down and mingle with them. He was not some old maid from Duluth who believed that there was something exotic about people who spoke a foreign language or dressed differently. These poor bastards were just God's forsaken. Maybe there were some sights here worth seeing. Just maybe. But he knew he wasn't really interested. Something in him had always rebelled at visiting places which were tourist attractions. He had never visited Napoleon's tomb, nor Stratford-on-Avon—not even the Statue of Liberty. He sighed. Well, he would have to make the best of a bad mistake —stick it out for a decent period, and then go home. He looked glumly down at the crowded streets and felt annoyed with himself, and with India, and also, suddenly, very lonely. He decided to write Cynthia a note.

He found paper in the old-fashioned desk and wrote quickly, trying to be amusing; not mentioning his glum disappointment, except for a few wry comments about his troubles in customs. After he had written a short letter, he read it over, and then added a postscript: "I deserved that boot." As he sealed and addressed the letter, he smiled, as he recalled Cynthia's farewell. She had been gay, almost too brittlely gay, right up until the last. After his baggage had been carried out, she stood near the door grinning, flourishing one of her tiny cigarettes in a long holder. He stooped and received the hot blast of her kiss and looked at her for a moment fondly and said, "Good-bye, Cynthia. Thanks." She smiled at him mockingly and said, "Good-bye, lover. Have fun." He turned, and as he walked through the door, he was kicked; not a playful kick, but a hard, strong boot right in the behind. He turned in surprise, and Cynthia stood there with her face contorted like a child's, tears streaming down her cheeks. She sobbed, "You'd better come back, you big mother," and slammed the door.

He had three visitors that same afternoon. All were young Indian newspapermen, and all were surprisingly alike in some respects. They were skinny and had the same dusky, slightly bluish color and their black hair was long and oiled. They also all wore cheap, badly fitted suits which were too short in the sleeves, and they spoke the sing-song English which he found so difficult to understand.

There was a marked difference in their manners. The first young man smiled too much, hung eagerly on everything he said, was too profuse in his thanks even when offered a cigarette, and, altogether, he was so ingratiating that he found himself disliking him, even though he felt sorry for him. In a fawning, apologetic way, he asked a variety of questions, painstakingly copying down his opinions on the theater and art, how he felt about Vietnam, atom bomb tests, and his views on racial problems in the United States.

The second young man arrived as the first was leaving. He covered almost the same ground, but he was lofty, almost patronizing, scarcely smiling at his pleasantries, refusing to accept a drink or a cigarette, and when he had finished asking his questions, he closed his notebook with weary disdain, offered a limp hand, and left.

The third newspaperman arrived an hour later, and he was openly hostile. There was not much variation in his questions, but after every reply he looked up belligerently and disbelievingly. Every so often, he would repeat the same question. "Boot why iss it yoou haf coom ta India?" Each time he would patiently explain that he was on holiday and was merely looking around. Finally, after he had answered the question for the third or fourth time, the young Indian asked angrily, "Then whhy iss eet yoou are teeking oop my time?" He smiled at the young man's angry face. He knew that old ploy, as a young newsman he had sometimes used it himself to needle or deflate a visiting dignitary. "I'm not," he said. "I didn't ask you to come. Good-bye."

The young Indian slammed his notebook shut and stalked to the door. He turned with a scowl. "Meester Fraser, yoou haf bean less thann honeest wif me."

He was annoyed, but after he thought about it, he felt sorry for the young Indian. Sorry for all of them, for that matter. It was long afterwards before he realized that, by a lucky coincidence, he had learned within a few hours about what to expect when he met middle-class Indians. With a few treasured exceptions, they would all turn out to be either too servile, defensively patronizing, or anxious to pick a fight. Only upper-class Indians and poor peasants seemed to be willing to accept him as a friend or an equal. Whether it was because the middle-class Indians, with their deplorable accents and cheap Western clothes, were suffering from a feeling of inferiority, he never could decide. It simply was something he learned to accept, just as he learned to accept the fact that when an Indian was asked to do something he would give all the reasons why it couldn't be done, before finally doing it.

He had been subjected to the press too many times to be much surprised when, as he breakfasted on his balcony the next morning, he read what the young Indians had written about him. They had misquoted him, wrenched things he had said out of context, but in the main their stories were somewhat flattering, strikingly alike in the ground they covered, and all falsely reported that he was in India to study the Indian theater.

One result of the newspaper stories was that he received a flood of invitations, and he accepted a few of them. Most of the British he met were of the Foreign Office type, calm and steady, but on the dull side. The Americans were provincial and a bit too bombastically idealistic when discussing the various foreign aid ventures that had brought them to India. On the whole they were nice people, often wearing, sometimes slightly pathetic, but kind and hospitable, and it was nobody's fault that he had nothing in common with them. After a few days he had forgotten their names and probably would not have recognized the faces of most of them.

He was surprised at the number of foreigners he met. Within a couple of days, he realized that his chances of meeting Madame Valois by accident were extremely remote. Nobody he met knew her, and though he thought about calling the French Consulate and making inquiries, he never did.

The truth was that, within a few hours after he arrived, he knew he was only marking time until a decent interval had passed and he could return to London. But he did not brood about it, because the trip was serving its purpose, though, perhaps, not in the way he would have liked. Maybe it was something he had worked out in the hospital, or maybe it was simply the change of scenery, but temporarily at least, he had lost his sense of crushing melancholia. He no longer found himself dredging up memories of happier days, which he now realized —and probably realized at the time—had been one chief symptom of his despair in London. Certainly, he was better off for drinking so little. Under Bombay's peculiar prohibition laws, he could not buy liquor unless he signed a formal declaration that it was necessary for his well being. To brand himself an alcoholic seemed a humiliating price to pay for a drink, so he did without, except when invited to drink the liquor and wine of people who were less prideful. He had not had so much rest or been so lazy in years.

He spent the major portion of every day on his balcony, reclining in a deck chair. He had bought a stack of books about India in the bookstall in the lobby, and he plowed through them lazily, pleased with those that described the filth and ignorance as it really was, caustically amused by those that dealt with Indian mysticism and spirituality. Late every afternoon, he would shower and dress and go for a short stroll, picking side streets and staying away from the congested thorough-fares. He already had explored the business district of Bombay, and except for a few sights, such as huge Brahmin bulls lying on the sidewalk arrogantly chewing their cuds while people walked around them, and betel stands, where Indians bought betel nut dabbed with lime and cocoanut and wrapped in a betel leaf, he found nothing of interest. He found much to depress him: the whining beggars, the filth, the solemn crowds. He felt sorry for them, but he also felt that Indians were the most unattractive, glum and solemn people he had ever en-countered. He felt a slight sense of shock each time he remem-bered that Bombay was the most modern and cosmopolitan of all Indian cities.

One afternoon while he was walking through a smelly resi-dential section where the sidewalks were splattered with red stains from spat betel juice, he felt a sharp tap on his shoulder. He turned and found a filthy, almost naked Indian thrusting what appeared to be a large black root almost in his face. It took him several seconds to realize that the man had no nose and what seemed to be a gnarled root was actually his hand, twisted and rotted by leprosy. His reaction was purely auto-matic. He backed away slowly and he actually felt hackles rise, along his spine and on the back of his neck. He looked at the Indian with fear, fascination and pity, and reached in his pocket and found what money he had and threw it at his feet. It was an experience he never forgot.

He had a second memorable experience two nights later when he attended a garden party given by a young man at-tached to the American Consulate. He had found a seat at one of the small tables scattered around and was nursing his drink and watching the crowd gathered under the Japanese lanterns when a distinguished looking Indian in his late fifties came over and introduced himself. His name was Lal and he was a Justice in one of the Bombay courts. As they sat chatting it developed that the Justice had been educated at Harrow and Oxford. He would have been an interesting man anywhere, for he was witty and erudite, as well as being impressive looking, but in India, he seemed a rarity.

After they had talked a while, he asked the Justice a question that had been puzzling him. "How do you account for the fact that so much nonsense is written about Indian mysticism?"

The Justice smiled. "Nonsense is written about every subject, Mr. Fraser. Why should that one be exempted?"

He smiled. "That's true. But something runs deeper here. It seems almost a conspiracy among Indians. Everyone seems determined to perpetuate the myth. Except for a few Western journalists, nobody makes any effort to expose its origin."

"What is its origin, Mr. Fraser?"

"Why, ignorance," he said. "Superstition always flowers where there is ignorance. In the West Indies there is voodoo. It was transplanted to the southern part of the United States where Negroes called it conjeer. I can give other examples. But what puzzles me is why most Indians seem to take pride in the superstition. Why don't educated people, such as yourself, expose it for what it is?"

The Justice sat musing. "How long have you been in India, Mr. Fraser?"

"Only a week," he said. "But does that really matter?"

"I only wanted to know where to start," the Justice said. He smiled. "I will start at the beginning. It is true that we are a singularly ignorant and backward people. There are four hundred and eighty-odd million of us, and only about ten percent of us really can be considered literate. So superstition does flower. It flowers wildly. But superstition is abstract, something believed but not provable. Let us agree that things believed but unproved are all bogus. But what about things that have been proved? This old land has some genuine mysteries also, Mr. Fraser."

He smiled slightly and shook his head in disbelief.

The Justice smiled. "I should like to show you something, Mr. Fraser. It's my one parlor trick and I've been waiting for an opportunity." He took a piece of waxed string out of his waistcoat pocket, pulled it taut, and then rolled it into a ball and popped it into his mouth. He worked his jaw slowly, and after a few seconds the end of the string began to emerge from his right nostril. The Justice reached up and with a deft, casual movement withdrew the whole string. He smiled. "That astonishes you?"

"It does indeed," he said.

Still smiling the Justice replaced the string in his waistcoat pocket. "It astonishes most Westerners. Actually, it's a back to front variation of an elementary yoga exercise. Its purpose is to cleanse the nasal passages. Anyone can learn it with a little applied effort. I practice a few yoga exercises every morning for physical fitness. I've been using that one ever since my university days to impress unbelievers."

He smiled. "It's a startling trick. But it is a trick."

The Justice nodded. "Yes, and a simple one, but until you saw it, you would not have believed it possible. That is my point. At any village festival you will find wandering fakirs doing tricks which will hold you spellbound. For the price of twenty cigarettes they will apparently make their hearts stop. They can make their pulse accelerate in one arm and stop in the other. They can pull their eyes from their sockets and walk around with them dangling on their cheeks. They can bring up their intestines and wash them before your eyes. They can stick sharp skewers through their bodies and not bleed. All of these astounding tricks have been learned to draw annas from the crowd. These fakirs do things that are supposed to be impossible. True yogis never exhibit their powers for the curious. But think of what powers they must have. The things they can do defy all explanation."

"Such as?"

"I have a colleague," said the Justice, "whose mother's brother was a renowned yogi. When my colleague was a child this uncle sometimes spent short periods in his home. Since he was a child, he was the only one allowed to enter his uncle's room, and then only once a day to take him food. He has told me that several times when he entered he found his uncle stretched at full length and floating in the center of the room. He was too young at the time to grasp its significance."

He showed his disbelief with a slight smile.

The Justice smiled. "Your credulity astounds me. Some yogis attain marvelous control of body temperature. They walk about naked in the Himalayas in freezing weather without discomfort. There are some who can dry out blankets dipped in icy water as quickly as they are wrapped around them. There are some who reputedly can fly through the air at express speed, some who can assume the form of animals, some who can live without food, some who can live without breathing for several years. Even some who live forever."

"Seriously," he said, "do you believe any of this?"

"I believe a little of everything except what barristers tell me in my court," the Justice said, lightly. He paused a moment and grew serious. "Yes, I do believe that there are men in India who have powers so marvelous that normal people can't fully grasp them. It's more than simply not understanding them—these powers come from a source beyond our comprehension. There are men who go off into the Himalayas and have themselves walled up in tiny cells which have small apertures through which food can be pushed, but no light enters and they sit there in the darkness for years, concentrating on attaining certain powers. Body control is only one method of reaching oneness with God. There are others who choose different methods."

"But why should India be the repository for all these secrets?"

The Justice shrugged. "The knowledge is here. It's been here for centuries. In addition, India is a country where a man can renounce all possessions, throw away every stitch of clothing he wears, if he wishes. He can wander forth to seek God naked without being hauled off to a police court or an almshouse. He can sit in one spot and die if he doesn't block traffic, for that matter."

"Do any foreigners ever attain these powers? I mean really attain them, not come here to write a cheap book or start a cult?"

"Not often. From time to time one comes along. There's a European named Bhaiji, who has appeared in the last few years. He is considered a true Holy Man."

"I'd like to talk with a Holy Man," he said.

The Justice said, "It isn't easy, Mr. Fraser. And they won't divulge their secrets anyway—it would destroy the very reason they suffered so long to attain them." He smiled. "If I may give you advice, Mr. Fraser, free your mind while you are in my country. Go and see India. Don't search consciously. Simply open your eyes and your mind and your heart, and if old Mother India has a message for you, you will receive it in time."

NINE . . .

It was odd how quickly it happened. He had lazed on his balcony for a week, contemptuously ignoring the city below him. Three days later he was seated beside Sixteen in the front seat of the roomy old Buick, approaching Agra, and there had been scarcely a waking minute, or second, in which he had not seen something interesting or astonishing.

After three days he realized also how naïve he must have sounded when he returned from the garden party and picked up the telephone in his room. "I should like to order a large car with a driver to be sent around at ten in the morning," he said.

"Certainly, Mr. Fraser," a polite voice said. "How long will you require it?"

"I'm not sure, but not too long," he said. "I only want to do a bit of sightseeing. Perhaps run up to the Taj Mahal."

There was a pause at the other end of the line. The polite voice said, "That's . . . quite a distance, you know, Mr. Fraser."

"It doesn't matter," he said.

Even after spending only one day on India's narrow, meandering and poorly macadamized highways, and seeing the primitive facilities for both tourists and their automobiles, he smiled when he recalled the conversation. Everything considered, it was as if a foreigner in a New York hotel had picked up the telephone and casually ordered a car to be sent around so he could run out and see Boulder Dam.

But the car had come anyway, and with it had come Sixteen, tall and stately and immaculate, but also, like all Sikhs, looking fierce and warlike because of his black beard and hawk nose and dark eyes. For the first few hours, he had sat in the back seat, but then he moved up front with Sixteen. He was surprised to discover that his eyes were mild and soft and somehow stricken looking, like those of a *Christus* in an Italian Renaissance painting. Sixteen had served in the Army for twelve years under British officers and his English was understandable but limited. He had the grave punctilious manners of a professional soldier.

After he had talked for a while, he said, "I don't believe I know your name?"

"Singh, sir."

"But I thought all Sikhs were named Singh," he said. "What's your first name?"

"First name Ranjit, sir."

"Is that what your friends in the Army called you—Ranjit?"

A slow grin spread over his bearded features. "No, sir. Friends called me Sixteen."

"Why Sixteen?"

"There fifteen other Ranjit Singhs in Regiment, sir."

He smiled. "All right, I'll call you Sixteen, too." He could not remember anyone who had caught his affection so quickly as tall, bearded Sixteen, who in only three days had proved to be loyal, perceptive, and efficient. He smiled as Sixteen glowered and braked the car as a little girl trotted across the road behind a cow, catching manure as it fell.

He had grown accustomed to such sights. During the first few hours after they left Bombay he stared unbelievingly when he saw women and children squatting around piles of cow manure and patting out cakes which they plastered on the walls of their mud huts to dry. Great stacks of these manure cakes were stacked outside most huts, as they were the basic fuel of India. Cow manure had other uses, too. Once while they had stopped to refuel the car at a large mud hut which served as a filling station, he had watched fascinated while the fat wife of the proprietor smeared the hard packed mud floor of the hut with a mixture of cow manure and water.

During that first day when they sped along the dusty or badly paved roads through the bleak landscape, it seemed to him that most of the population of India was either dabbling solemnly in cow manure or splashing in the scum-coated bathing tanks at the edge of each village. On the second morning, while passing through a small village, he had seen a middle-aged woman stoop and catch a massive Brahmin bull's urine in her cupped hands and sip it. Sixteen had smiled. "Very old-fashioned woman, sir. She hope maybe to have a baby."

He had grown immune to the way Indian drivers passed each other on the narrow roads. They sent their vehicles dashing toward one another like angry charging animals, not giving an inch until the last moment, when they swerved and passed with inches to spare. There was always something to hold his interest. Sometimes it was a village festival and the roads would be jammed with bullock carts and tongas, loaded with singing peasant women in gaudy, bright colored finery, their arms and ankles loaded with heavy silver bracelets, which represented the family savings. Sometimes it would be a single slender and graceful Indian girl, water jar atop her head, who modestly drew a corner of her sari over her face as they passed. In every village, naked little children always crouched at the side of the road, and as they approached some of them invariably would dash across the road at the last instant, in the senseless way of chickens.

Frequently they saw gaily decorated palanquins, curtains drawn tightly, being carried along by *dhoti*-clad bearers. Each time Sixteen would slow the car and smile and explain, "Bride going to house of her husband, sir."

Sadhus and Holy Men of all ages and descriptions were a common sight. They thronged the roads, sat outside small village shrines or temples, and usually appeared with their begging bowls when they stopped. Once he saw eight Sadhus, their bodies smeared with cow manure ash and their long hair and beards matted with cow manure, walking along single file, completely naked. Lingams were as common as lampposts in the Western world, and while undeniably they were a phallic symbol, sometimes with chiseled detail, they were no more objectionable than road markers.

He saw nothing to make him change his mind about India's ignorance and superstition. But somehow it had become more interesting and less annoying. In three short days he had even built up some immunity to the horrible, grinding poverty. On the edge of one village, Sixteen motioned with his head toward a dirty figure weakly crawling on all fours toward the shelter of a bridge. "Sick man, sir," he said. "Crawling under bridge to die."

It wasn't until he lay in bed that night in a modern hotel in Indore that he grasped the enormity of the casual remark. He and Sixteen had watched a fellow man crawl under a bridge to die, and they had done nothing about it, had not really even discussed it. But he realized that even if they had stopped for that man, what about the next? And the next? He tried to put it out of mind.

He really had no great interest in seeing the Taj Mahal. All the replicas and pictures he had seen of it had led him to believe it would be ornate and tasteless, something like the masterpieces confectioners made out of cardboard and spun sugar. It had been merely a reference point, an excuse to get him out of Bombay. But after they reached Agra and registered at their comfortable but old-fashioned hotel, he went out to see it, and he was overwhelmingly glad that he did. It was the first time in his life that he could remember anything being even more wonderful than publicity had represented it to be.

He went back again to see it by moonlight. And, then, feeling a little embarrassed, he slipped out of bed in the early morning darkness. He drove out by himself, and he was standing alone in the garden when the huge red Indian sun rose slowly to the horizon, poised there a while, and with a sudden dash, swept higher and higher, bathing the lovely dome and the slender minarets with a light which, almost more quickly than the eye could follow, caused them to reflect pink, gold, and, finally, dazzling white. He knew it was an experience he would not forget as long as he lived, and he felt lucky, unbelievably lucky, to have discovered at his age something whose beauty could impress him so much.

One of the things that amazed him was that in some districts where poverty was the most apparent, where people seemed closest to actual starvation, game was the most plentiful. Peacocks wandered across the road like barnyard chickens. Doves were so thick that in almost any day three or four dashed themselves to death against the windshield of the car. Small fleet black buck browsed in the fields like cattle. He found it unbelievable that in the midst of this plenty, villagers should be so emaciated, their children pinch-faced from malnutrition. He asked Sixteen about it.

"They all vegetarians, sir," he said. "Very strict Hindus."

"But they would eat game rather than starve to death, Sixteen," he said.

Sixteen shook his head. "No sir. A few maybe, but most of them very strict Hindus."

He smiled. "They would eat each other rather than starve."

A week later, while touring the Jaipur district, he discovered how wrong he was. They were on a narrow dirt side road returning to Jaipur when they topped a small rise and he saw a man, a woman, and a small child lying beside the road. Nearby was a poorly constructed lean-to made from weeds and dead branches. He had seen hundreds of such dwellings, but there was something so unusual about the way the figures ignored the car that he asked Sixteen to stop.

When he stepped from the car, the man and the woman raised their heads feebly. The man began to whine in sing-song Hindustani. The child, a naked boy of four or five, lay unmoving, sprawled across his mother's breast. The man and woman were half naked and they all were filthy, and so horribly emaciated that every bone was visible. The woman's breasts were shriveled and dry like empty sacks.

He had never seen a genuine case of starvation in his life, but he recognized it immediately. "These people are starving, Sixteen," he said.

Sixteen had alighted from the car and was looking at the man impassively. "Yes, sir," he said. "Man says they had no food for long time. He asking us for something to eat."

Sixteen's calm disinterest and the horror of the situation infuriated him. "Well, let's do something about it," he said, coldly. He was about to reach for the child, when he remembered there were some remains of a box lunch packed by the hotel in the car. He went to the car and rummaged around and found two small hard-boiled eggs.

He returned with them and Sixteen shook his head. "They not eat eggs, sir. They vegetarian."

"They'll eat them," he said.

He offered one of the eggs to the whining man. He shook his head weakly.

"Vegetarian, sir," Sixteen repeated.

Angered by the stupidity of it and by his own helplessness, he cracked one of the eggs on the heel of his shoe, peeled and broke it and raised the child's head and started to feed him some of the yellow. The woman rolled her eyes backward until only the whites showed and shrieked and clutched the child to her breast. Weak as he was, the man forced himself to a sitting position and his whine had become a protest.

He straightened up, and with an angry helpless gesture, threw the egg as far as he could. He looked at Sixteen.

"Village not far, sir. It better we go there and get some food and come back."

As they drove away, he sat silently, amazed, angered, and shocked. Finally, he said, "Eggs aren't meat, Sixteen. Why won't they eat eggs?"

Sixteen shook his head. "Strict Hindus think they meat, sir. Strict Hindus not even eat cake and bread with eggs in it."

The village was a huddle of mud huts. He sat in the car while Sixteen disappeared into the narrow dirty main thoroughfare. Within a few minutes he returned with a shaven-headed, toothless man in a dirty *dhoti.*

"This man *patwari,* head man of village, sir. He know people. He say he go get them in his cart and take care of them until they get well. He wants some money, sir."

"How much money should I give him?" he asked.

"Twenty rupees enough, sir."

He gave the man twenty rupees. As they drove away, he asked, "Can we trust him, Sixteen? Will he really take care of them?"

"Yes, sir," Sixteen said. "He good man. He knew about people. He saw them this morning when he passed by. He take care of them until money runs out."

He did not much care for New Delhi. Like all capitals it strove for grandeur, but somehow its magnificent buildings seemed as empty and characterless as a new hat in a store. Besides, like most people who are apolitical, he had a contempt for most politicians and New Delhi had the wildest assortment he had ever seen. Long-haired, bearded patriarchs, wearing robes and sandals, were almost as plentiful as solemn bespectacled young parliamentarians wearing black coats and striped trousers. They were symbolic of the indecision he had encountered in most Indians: whether to be proud of the old ways and traditions or accept progress and move into the twentieth century.

Nearby Old Delhi at least had the virtue of having made up its mind. As far as possible, it clung stubbornly to the old ways. He found Chandni Chowk, its main thoroughfare, one of the most appalling, and yet fascinating, streets he had ever seen. Sleek new automobiles, large trucks, bicyclists, antiquated trolleys, and crowds which worked in a swarming unwholesome, glistening mass, like maggots on a carcass, jostled and pushed up and down it day and night. Only huge and scarred old Brahmin bulls were given any deference on the crowded street. They wandered where they liked, browsing on vegetables in the open markets, placidly emptying bowels or bladders on the sidewalks, creating little oases of calm wherever they decided to lie down and chew their cuds.

On one corner in Chandni Chowk he saw a dozen or more lepers, most of whom had their legs and arms eaten away completely, sitting in boxes on wheels which were pushed around by other lepers not so badly afflicted. In shops he visited on the same street he saw a faultless 18-carat diamond, an emerald and ruby necklace which was priced at a hundred thousand dollars, literally basketfuls of smaller diamonds, rubies, sapphires, pearls, and aquamarines, as well as Moghul paintings and Hindu sculpture which any museum would have coveted.

His air-conditioned hotel was luxurious, the food was not bad, and New Delhi was the first city he had discovered in India which had after-dark amusement. The New Delhi papers carried stories of his arrival, and, as in Bombay, he received a spate of invitations. He accepted one or more almost every night, but he usually was more bored than entertained. The one refreshing thing about New Delhi was he had an opportunity to meet many of the American newspaper and magazine correspondents assigned to India. He was pleased to discover most of them felt as he did about India's vaunted spirituality, and he was pleased to learn that many of them were writing books exposing it for what it was. He stayed in New Delhi a week, but, for all he learned, it was a week wasted.

He had debated whether he should wind up his visit with a trip to Calcutta or to Benares. Some people had advised him to see Calcutta because it was the worst city in India. Others had insisted he should see Benares because it was the oldest and considered the holiest. He had no real interest in either. He left the decision to Sixteen. "What will it be, Sixteen—good or bad?"

Sixteen smiled. "Always pick good, sir."

All during that second day after they had left New Delhi

and were approaching Benares, he was glad Sixteen had made the decision. For nowhere else in India had he seen such peace and contentment and plenty. The soil was rich, black and crumbly, like good chocolate. Water was knee-deep in the paddy fields, and cane grew as high as a man's head. The cattle and bullocks were sleek and well fed. Fat little babies tumbled about the doors of mud huts, and old men squatted in the shade of towering banyan trees, puffing their *hookahs*.

Both sides of the road were thronged with pilgrims going to or returning from Benares. Some of them were Holy Men wearing robes or clad only in loin cloths with vermillion caste marks on their foreheads. Now and then he saw a gaunt and wild-eyed Sadhu, usually smeared with cow dung ash, sometimes carrying a trident. But most of them were ordinary Indians, and sometimes there were whole family groups. As they approached the city the crowds grew heavier, and Sixteen had to weave the car in between bullock carts and tongas and carts filled with Indians of all classes and castes, dressed in holiday finery. There was something different about the crowds somehow, and it was some time before he realized it was because so many of the people were smiling. There was a gaiety and an excitement overhanging the whole procession which he had never seen in Indians before.

"This must be the best part of India, Sixteen," he said.

Sixteen smiled. "Some of it very bad, too, sir. You wait."

As they entered the outskirts of the city, then began to creep through a labyrinth of narrow and crooked streets, he discovered what Sixteen meant. For no stench he had encountered in India was even remotely as putrid as the one which filled the car; it defied all description. It was heavy, seemed to cling like musk, and somehow it seemed malignantly evil. Sixteen put his handkerchief over his nose and mouth, and he did the same. Sixteen grimaced, "Very old city, sir. People live here long time."

He held his handkerchief to his face and looked at the bazaars, swarming with flies, bustling with haggling crowds.

Mangy dogs sniffed at refuse heaps. Ash-and-dung-besmeared Sadhus were everywhere. Fat and oily Brahmans in cinnamon-colored robes with caste marks on their foreheads waddled along majestically. Dirty and horribly deformed beggars crouched at every intersection, whining piteously. He heard the sound of conch horns, temple bells, the chant of prayers. In one narrow street they squeezed slowly past a tonga. It was occupied by a Muslim woman, covered with a dingy white *burga* with a lattice work of threads over her eyes. As they passed, less than a yard away, he saw one sandaled foot peeking out from under the robe. It was small and soft and the color of beaten gold and there were jeweled rings on two of her curled toes. The next sight he saw was a black and wrinkled old crone with wild eyes and matted hair picking something out of a drain.

He sat and thought about the remarkable contrasts in India, and he thought about them again when the car began to emerge from the crowded and crooked bazaar district and they began traveling a broad and well-paved street. His hotel was cool-looking and spacious and sat behind a high mud wall which was dazzling with a fresh coat of whitewash. It had a broad and shady verandah, and as he stepped from the car, he noticed there even were broom marks on the hard-packed, immaculate driveway.

The burning ghats stretched along the Ganges had a strange fascination for him. On his first visit, on the afternoon he arrived, he had been somewhat repelled, not so much by the process of disposing of bodies, which seemed cheap and hygienic, but because of the seemingly indifferent and calloused way in which it was done. On each of the following three mornings when he left the hotel for an exploratory foray into the stinking city, he told himself he would not return to the ghats, but he always did. Usually he started on some portion of the congested thirty-six mile circuit around the city called the Panch Kesi. It was the magnet for pilgrims to Benares, for if they made the complete circuit, visiting all the temples and shrines on the way, they automatically were forgiven all their sins. If they happened to die on the Panch Kesi, and many aged or ailing pilgrims came to Benares for that express purpose, they automatically were united with Brahma, the Mighty, and did not have to be reborn again.

Most of the sights he saw seemed repulsive or stupid. Mendicant fakirs who stretched their hard and skinny bodies on beds of spikes, or who buried their heads in sand piles were merely silly. Those who held their limbs at different angles until the muscles atrophied and the ligaments froze were insane. He had been in the theater too long to be impressed by street magicians who could grow mango plants from seeds or produce on a dirty handkerchief any scent which was requested. Snake charmers annoyed him. He would have liked to visit some of the temples, but since he was a foreigner, with no caste at all, he was not sure he was permitted to transgress.

He did find the burning ghats truly unique. They stretched for several miles along the sluggish, mellowish Ganges, row after row of small stone or brick platforms. The rich and the famous, as everywhere, were launched on their last journey with great ceremony. Great crowds of male relatives, friends, and professional mourners, beating gongs and drums and chanting lamentations, followed the body, which was bound to a stretcher and covered with fine shawls of silk or cashmere. The body was carried down the stone steps, worn by centuries of use, and dipped in the Ganges. It was then placed on a ghat and covered with great piles of sandalwood and camphor. Innumerable vessels of *ghee*, or clarified butter, were poured on. A hot coal was placed in the mouth and on the chest. The eldest son circled the pyre seven times before he ignited it. As the flames and billowing smoke rose, there was a mighty shout, a Brahman said incantations, and the paid mourners beat their breasts and chanted. There were no women present, and he wondered if that was why genuine tears and hysterical grief were so strangely absent.

The poor got short shrift. The body was covered with cheap muslin, and sometimes there were only four bored stretcher bearers. There was scarcely enough wood to cover the body, and sometimes it was not completely consumed. Several times he saw charred but recognizable hands and feet and skulls on the ghats.

After the embers cooled, the ashes of the rich were sprinkled with grains of rice and parched corn and spices and left to lie for three days before, ceremoniously, they were consigned to the river. The remains of the poor were dumped in as soon as possible.

Crowds of men, women and children submerged themselves in the river where the ashes were thrown, praying, bathing, splashing about, and frequently drinking or gargling the water.

He found it horrible in some ways, but in others it was peculiarly moving. For it showed a calm, almost too matter-of-fact acceptance of the inevitability of death. And before they were burned the rich were stripped of their expensive shawls and the poor of their skimpy coverings. Naked they came into the world, and naked they departed. Rich or poor, they all were consigned to the sluggish waters of the Ganges.

As he stood on the stone steps of the ghats one afternoon, he began to study the swarms of pilgrims and family groups who surrounded him. Nearby a poorly dressed mother nursed a child. A little boy was squatting solemnly, emptying his bowel. A wrinkled old woman lay sleeping peacefully. A skinny young peasant in a dirty dhoti leaned back on his elbows and held his feet aloft while an older man tried to remove something from his heel. A naked little boy was carefully washing his face in a stagnant pool of water. A bent and wrinkled old man bared his gums in a smile and began jabbing and gesturing excitedly to his worn, stooped wife, as he caught what was obviously his first glimpse of the sacred river. A young girl, eyes modestly downcast, sat eating a chapati. A beggar with useless, dragging legs propelled himself toward the river with his elbows. A village mother, dressed in garish country finery, laughed as her toddling naked son dashed after a sparrow.

For a moment it was almost as if a curtain had been drawn and he saw beneath the flies, the filth, the stench. For the first time he felt an identification with all of India's seething, urinating, smelly, ragged, starving, and ignorant masses. And just as men always feel humble and small when confronted with the immensity of creation, he felt dwarfed; for he was just another man, just another soul. Sooner or later they all would be intermingled in the same mighty stream; and in the final accounting, he would not be judged because of his tailors, his education, his skills, his money, or his hygiene, but on his soul alone. He stood there for a long time.

Sixteen was waiting, and he sat silently during the ride back to the hotel. He alighted at the front steps and walked up to the verandah. Then he saw her. She was seated at the far end of the verandah with a tea tray before her, and she was wearing a pale rose linen dress only slightly darker than her lovely complexion. There were 480 million people in India, but on the large quiet verandah, there were only the two of them. He stood watching her a moment, and she was seated there as calmly as if she had been awaiting his arrival.

TEN . . .

He was halfway across the verandah before she glanced up and saw him. She did not seem surprised; but sat quietly, watching him gravely with her large dark eyes until he reached the table. He suppressed his elation and spoke with mock casualness, "Why, hello, Madame Valois. Imagine seeing you here."

Her smile was slight, but her eyes were bright with amusement. "Good afternoon, Mr. Fraser. Would you care for some tea?"

He sat down slowly. He felt a sense of shock to realize how glad he was to see her. For several seconds he simply stared at her. She looked exactly the way he remembered; the same enormous eyes, the unbelievably glowing complexion. She was a beautiful woman. Suddenly, he grinned. "I must say, you don't seem very surprised to see me."

"I am not, actually," she said. "I have been following your progress in the *Times of India*." She sat composedly, eyes somber now, apparently not the least disconcerted by his close and admiring appraisal. Then, unexpectedly, she flashed him another small smile. "Besides, I knew you were here. As I drove into the hotel this morning, you were driving out."

"But . . . what—why didn't you stop me?" he demanded.

"You were traveling much too rapidly," she said. Her slight smile had disappeared as quickly as it appeared. She picked up her tea cup and looked at it thoughtfully, before taking a sip. He noticed that there was a tiny feathering of gray in her hair near the temples that he had not detected before. Her cologne was light and elusive. In a few minutes, he had discovered something else. She was one of those unusual people whose eyes were their most expressive feature; her large eyes were perhaps more eloquent, more revealing than her face or lips could ever have been. But though they could change in a twinkling, reflecting her moods, there was something unfathomable about them also—something darkly tragic. He wondered what it was.

"I'd almost given up all hope of finding you," he said. "You don't realize what a remarkable coincidence this is."

"Perhaps not as remarkable as you think," she said.

He grinned. It was the kind of enigmatic statement he would have expected from her. "You mean you saw it all in your crystal ball?"

Her smile was slight. "No, Mr. Fraser, I meant that most people who visit India come to Benares. When they come to Benares they usually stay at this hotel. For eight years I have been having tea on this verandah every afternoon. I have grown accustomed to seeing people I have met before."

"You live here?" he asked, surprised.

"Yes."

"But you weren't having tea here yesterday afternoon—or the afternoon before."

"No, I have been away for three days, visiting my husband."

Without thinking, he dropped his eyes to look at her left hand. She was not wearing a marriage band. Only when he looked up again and met her calm gaze did he realize how obvious his glance had been. He felt a twinge of embarrassment, and was trying to think of a quip to cover it when, fortunately, a bearer approached.

"Do you wish tea?" she asked.

He nodded and was about to give his order, but she spoke to the bearer in Hindustani and he padded away.

"Is your husband near here?" he asked.

"Yes, quite near," she said. She sat silently, sipping her tea, offering no explanation or elaboration, completely impassive.

He was both amused and intrigued. What an unusual woman she was—so completely direct yet so mysterious. But that was nonsense. Nobody was really mysterious. Maybe she was just humorless. Or maybe she was just acutely shy under her wonderfully poised exterior.

He waited until the bearer brought his tea, poured him a cup, and then went away, before he spoke. "You realize, don't you, that you are responsible for my being in India?" He already knew her well enough not to expect her to respond with feminine coyness. But he did expect some kind of protestation, pleased or flustered—perhaps, even a trifle coquettish. Instead, she looked at him calmly. "Are you sorry you came?"

He decided to match her honesty. "I don't know. I've seen some interesting sights, but perhaps I am sorry."

"What have you seen?" she asked.

She sat quietly while he gave her a brief account of his travels. Her dark eyes brightened with amusement at his wry comments, grew thoughtful when he made some bitter comments on places and people. He finished by telling her of his visits to the burning ghats. They sat silently for a while, and he said, "So you see, I'm not sure whether it's been enjoyable or an ordeal. I'm not even certain whether I like the place or detest it. Odd, isn't it?"

"I don't find it odd," she said, "because I often feel the same way."

"But I thought you were . . ."

She shook her head slowly. "Because I have been coming here for so long, you assumed I enjoy it? No." Her eyes were brooding. "I do not believe a Westerner with normal sensibilities ever becomes completely adjusted, completely at ease, here. It is too much like living in the midst of a slum. No matter how well ordered or how comfortable one's life is, it still is impossible to escape the poverty and dirt and misery. Indians are immune to it because they grew up with it. They are amused or resentful when they see how affronted we are. If they are resentful, they usually accuse us of materialism and say we are only interested in comforts which are unimportant. What they do not realize is that to become immune to the misery and suffering of others is in itself cruel and unnatural. There is no virtue in pain or misery or starvation—perhaps there is in the way they are borne—but, essentially, they are evil and wrong."

"You're right, of course," he said. "But even in the short time I have been here I have discovered that building some immunity is necessary."

"But one should not make a virtue of the necessity," she said.

He smiled. "Who's to say? Maybe it is a virtue. At least the Indians seem to have a lot going for them. Didn't most of the great mystics and ascetics seem to find poverty ennobling . . . Buddha giving up a palace, Jesus renouncing the world?"

The shadow that always seemed to be present clouded her eyes. "That is an incorrect interpretation," she said. "Such men did not renounce the world merely because they found poverty ennobling. Nor was it simply because they refused to have more than the poorest of their fellow men. Their motives were far more complicated. They had reasons that were extraordinarily special, reasons that ordinary people do not have and are not supposed to have."

He made his voice bantering. "Don't tell me you don't think India's poverty gives her some special claim on spirituality? Isn't there some rare and wonderful knowledge buried under all the muck and confusion?"

She looked at him for a long time. "Yes, there is," she said.

He was disappointed in her. "Oh, come on now," he said. "Do you truly think that India has some unique spiritual force, some special mystical enlightenment to offer?"

"I know it has," she said quietly. She placed her tea cup on the table and, almost abruptly, stood up. "It has been pleasant seeing you again, Mr. Fraser," she said.

He got to his feet slowly, both surprised and annoyed. "But

you can't run off like this," he protested. He smiled. "I've come halfway around the world to see you."

Her face was expressionless, but he saw that dark, almost tragic shadow in her eyes. For a moment she seemed about to speak, but she stood quietly, simply looking at him.

"Perhaps we could have dinner together," he said.

She hesitated, and he thought she was going to refuse. Finally she said, "Yes. I am free for dinner." She paused. "Suppose you come to my apartment."

He grinned. "That's fine. Thank you."

She had started away when he said, "Just a moment. I . . ."

She turned. He smiled and said, "What time?"

She gave him one of her slight smiles. "Of course . . . about eight. Any of the bearers can tell you how to reach my apartment."

Off and on during most of the afternoon, and especially while dressing for dinner, he thought about her. He had a gift for cataloging people, but so far she had eluded him completely. All he really knew about her was that she seemed to be French and was obviously well-to-do. His years in the theater had given him an eye for clothes, and he knew the simple linen frock she had been wearing that afternoon, like the suits and furs she had worn in London, were couturier items. She was a bit older than he had thought, probably in her late thirties, but he couldn't be sure. She was that rare type of beautiful woman who probably looked older than her actual years when she reached maturity and would remain more or less ageless until she actually reached her dotage.

He found her compellingly attractive—yes, more attractive than any other woman he had met in years. More attractive than any woman since Anne. And he was not certain what the attraction really was. He was used to meeting beautiful women, but she had . . . well, there was that air of mystery about her, something almost tragically mysterious. He smiled wryly as he tied his tie. How sophomoric could he be? Her mystery, her tragic air would disappear after he saw her a few times, more's the pity. He grunted. She probably was miserably unhappy, bored stiff with her marriage. Her husband undoubtedly would pop up in a few days, probably a dapper, suave little Frenchman. Maybe an importer or art dealer, who was out now scrounging for bad Indian sculpture or temple paintings that he would sell at inflated prices. He paused. Yet . . . there was something . . . yes, something extraordinarily wonderful.

He was not surprised to find she occupied an entire wing on the top floor of the hotel. He had discovered most foreigners who lived in Indian hotels had such commodious accommodations. When he arrived a few minutes after eight, a tall dignified Indian, who wore a white jacket and dark trousers, and who looked more like a butler than a bearer, opened the door for him. He ushered him into a huge drawingroom. "Please be seated, sir," he said. "I'll tell madame you are here." He looked around the room, pleased and surprised. Most of the furniture was black teak, almost contemporary in design, but somehow it retained an Asian flavor. There were a number of Moghul pieces scattered around, including an immense chest banded with silver and covered with faded red and gilt hunting scenes. An off-white Indian carpet covered the floor. There was a profusion of Indian and Western paintings, bric-a-brac and green plants. One entire wall was covered with books. A tall teak table with a large brass top stood in another corner, covered with bottles of liquor and liqueur. A record player was hidden in the book shelves somewhere and he smiled when he realized it was softly playing the score from My Fair Lady. It was an elegant room, a beautiful room, with just enough clutter to make it look lived in and comfortable. It opened directly into a dining room and he caught a glimpse of a black teak table, more paintings and silver and crystal.

He sat down on a large teak sofa which was upholstered in rough textured handwoven white Indian silk. A low fire burned in the fireplace, and above the mantel, which was strewn with bronze Hindu figurines, there was a large portrait of her painted when she was in her teens. At first glance it seemed that she had not changed much, except that she now had the fullness of maturity. But then he saw that the young girl's small smile was brighter and cheerier and her dark eyes were not so tragic. The artist had done a remarkable job in capturing her glowing complexion.

He was admiring the painting when she said, "Good evening, Mr. Fraser." She wore a long, flowing, heavy black silk hostess gown which was cut severely but opened in front and had a suggestion of *décolletage*. She wore red embroidered Kashmir slippers, and her hair was pulled back into a single thick braid, Indian style. As he stood up to greet her, he thought again what an unusually beautiful woman she was. The gown showed off the ripeness of her figure, and he was amused because, unconsciously, the director in him decided it was the figure of a Neapolitan movie actress. He wondered what she would say if he told her so.

The thought died as soon as he looked at her face, for while she had her usual small smile of greeting, her eyes were as dark and somber as when they had parted.

"I admire your room very much," he said.

She looked around slowly, as if appraising it herself. "It is an improvement over the usual Indian hotel accommodations, I suppose," she said. "I lived in so many hotels for so many years, I finally felt I could not bear them any longer." She looked at him. "May I offer you a drink?"

"Yes, thank you—whiskey and water, if it's available."

The bearer had entered the room. She turned and said something in Hindustani. She seated herself in a chair near the sofa.

"Did you live in India even before you came to Benares?" he asked.

"Yes, I spent my first winter here in 1946," she said.

"Then you were here when the British still were in control," he said.

She nodded.

"Were they really as bad as the Indians claim?" he asked.

She shook her head. "No, most Indians still parrot the propaganda that was used during their fight for independence. The British did commit blunders and crimes here, but I believe most of them were blunders and crimes of the times."

The bearer served her a sherry and gave him his drink.

"What do you mean?" he asked.

She regarded her glass thoughtfully. "Well, you would be amazed to discover how many Indian grievances date back to Victorian times. They still judge all British actions by mid-twentieth-century standards. They simply overlook the fact that the worst excesses of the British took place when the British also were handling their own lower classes roughly. But I believe there will come a time when sensible Indians will admit that the best thing that ever happened to them was the period of British rule."

"Did you ever see Gandhi?" he asked.

"Yes, many times."

"Was he a saint?"

"Certainly not," she said. "He was a very shrewd and clever politician, who also happened to be an unusually good and idealistic man. He taught India many useful things. He was a great man. He had to be to unite the Indian masses against the British as he did. For centuries they had not cared who ruled them. They felt that a change in government really didn't concern them, but was merely the good or bad fortune of their masters."

"Indians still are remarkably fatalistic, aren't they?"

"Yes. It is inevitable because of the Hindu interpretation of transmigration. That is also one reason why they have such an indifference to the misery of others. Over the centuries fatalism has become ingrained. If a poor Hindu's only water buffalo dies, he beats his breast and blames it on the sins of a former existence. If a pious Hindu merchant develops cancer, he sighs and meekly accepts it as his fate. Perhaps it is all just as well. There are so many educated and Westernized Indians in cities that most foreigners forget that ninety percent of all Indians live in villages and still follow the old ways. They believe in Hindu codes which give detailed accounts of sins and the effect they will have in rebirth. They meekly accept life as it is and expect their neighbors to do the same."

The bearer announced dinner. When he walked in and saw the table set with gleaming silver and softly lighted by candles, he smiled and said, "This is great—a treat."

She said, "I am afraid you will get only hotel food, but it does seem less tiresome when it is eaten outside the dining room."

After they had been served soup, he said, "Transmigration has always intrigued me. It's a lot more interesting than the Christian Heaven."

She did not say anything.

"You don't agree?" he asked.

She remained silent for a long time. "I do not think about it that way," she said.

He smiled. "But living a lot of different lives is more appealing than sitting in a mansion in Heaven?"

She did not smile and her eyes were serious.

He was puzzled and amused. "Have I offended you by my blasphemy?"

"No, I am not offended. It is only that I do not believe that Heaven—not a fanciful Heaven, but a reunion with God—and reincarnation are incompatible."

"You mean it's possible to have a melding of Hinduism and Christianity? Not a bad idea."

"I did not use labels," she said quietly. "I do not believe God is unreachable to men who seek Him in any manner, because we are alive to Him, living in Him, and I do not think any of us is given a separate and neutral life. I do think God has bestowed some truths which are available only to a few living men."

"I am not sure that all theologians agree with you," he said. "At least, not the evangelistic ones I studied."

She shrugged. "I am no longer impressed by theologians," she said. "The uses of theology are too obvious. In all religions, theology only obscures the truth or tries to give it a bias. A disparagement of theology always follows clear appreciation of truth. It has been so each time a great prophet has appeared —Christ, Buddha, Mohammed. To theologians truth is only another name for the current belief."

"That's not always true," he said.

She started to say something, but looked down at her plate instead. After a while she looked up and her mood had changed. "If you are interested in transmigration, you might be interested in an odd experience I had once. It was on my third trip to India. I was staying in Darjeeling and making side trips to nearby villages. One morning I was walking along a mountain path to get a better view of Mount Everest, when I passed a small mud hut. A gray bearded old Sikh was seated in the doorway and he spoke to me in a heavy American accent. I have never been so surprised. His name was as American as his voice—Frank Jones. He was from Detroit, Michigan and had lived there until he was sixty. He was eighty-two when I met him, but he was wonderfully preserved and active and alert. He had wandered all over India, and ten years before he had built the mud hut and settled down there to die within sight of the Himalayas.

"I had a long talk with him that day, and I went back to see him a number of times. I used to take him small gifts and presents of food. He told me the most amazing story. He said that when he was a child and first learned to speak, he had what seemed to be a peculiar disability. He persisted in giving strange names to things, and sometimes when he spoke to people everything he said was an odd gibberish. In time he outgrew it, but he always remembered some of the names he had given objects because it seemed that they should be called that.

"He grew up and became a soldier in the First World War,

and he married twice and had a variety of jobs. He was never very successful. He drove a laundry van and worked in a motor car plant, and did various things of that sort. He said that he had always had a deep interest in India and anything that came from India, but he was not a bookish man and he was too poor to travel, so he never did anything about this interest. Then one day when he was forty-five years old he was reading a magazine when he came upon the word *kara*. He repeated the word several times, and, instinctively, he placed his hand on his right wrist where Sikhs wear their *karas*. He remembered that when he was a child he had called any bracelet a *kara*. He visited a library and found several books on the Sikhs. He ran across other words and expressions in *Gurmukhi*, which is the basic language of the Sikhs, and he discovered many of them were the same words he had spoken as a boy. He said that if he repeated any *Gurmukhi* word several times he was aware of its meaning.

"The discovery changed his whole life. For years he read everything he could find about the Sikhs and their customs. When he was sixty his wife died, and he took his small savings and bought a passage to India. He wandered about the Punjab on foot, a pack on his back, hoping to find some landmark or some sign which would tell him where he had lived and who he had been. He had a bad time of it. He was ill several times and his money ran out and he had to work for the villagers or depend on their hospitality. Four years after he landed in India, he walked into a small village one day and he knew he was home."

"How did he know?" he asked.

"I asked him that, and he simply looked helpless and said, 'How do I know the sun will rise tomorrow?' He was not able to discover who he had been, but he knew he belonged. He settled in the village and took the religious vows of a Sikh and eventually married a Sikh widow who had a small holding of land. When she died, he set out again, hoping that he might find something else familiar that might tell him who he had been. He never did find anything, but mountains had a strange fascination for him. He returned to his village periodically over a period of years, but finally sold his land and began to wander the mountain ranges. He had given up the search when I met him, but he seemed quite content."

"He was a fortunate man, wasn't he?" he said.

She pondered. "No, I do not think he was. It must be dreadful to know part of the truth and never be able to discover all of it."

"How do you know it was the truth?" he asked. "I think he was lucky simply because he found some peculiar quirk in his mentality which gave purpose to an otherwise unsuccessful life."

"Yes," she said, thoughtfully. "Yes, he was lucky in that respect. Everyone should have a purpose in life." She looked at him. "What is yours, Mr. Fraser?"

He thought about it. "I don't know. I seem to be in between purposes at the moment."

"That is a natural result of the process of living, is it not?"

"Must it be always?" he asked. "It makes it seem a particularly unhappy process."

"It often does seem so," she said. "But we should continually redefine happiness also. Otherwise it would lose all meaning."

"Have you always been lucky enough to do that?" he asked.

"No, I have not always been so fortunate, but when I return to France and see my friends, I do sometimes feel that I am more fortunate than they are. For I have some friends whose idea of happiness has not changed since we were young girls and thought true happiness was stuffing ourselves with chocolate eclairs. Only now the eclairs are gowns and jewels and motor cars."

"But don't you envy people like that a little bit also?"

"No. How could I? For they are not truly happy. The things I have learned in my life have not always pleased me, nor have the ways I learned them always been arbitrary. But still I am glad I have learned to distinguish between counterfeit and genuine happiness. Even if I have not always been fortunate enough to attain it."

"And what is true happiness?"

"It is a personal matter, not only with me, but with every one."

She served coffee before the fire, sitting on the floor beside a low table in front of the white sofa. She looked more relaxed than he had ever seen her, and he sat captivated by the way the light from the fire reflected on her incredible skin. It seemed to have a soft rosy glow under the surface. When she placed her cup on the table, on an impulse, he reached forward and placed his fingers on the back of her hand. She sat perfectly still, not moving, not looking at him. When he removed his fingers, she withdrew her hand. Her face was imperturbable and in the shadows her large eyes were black and unreadable. He said, "That was rude, I suppose, but I wanted to see if your skin was as glowing as it looked. You have the most beautiful skin I have ever seen." She inclined her head in a slight nod. He said, "I know you have heard that so many times that it must bore you."

She looked at him silently, then gave him her small smile. "No, I like to hear it. I now am old enough not to be vain about the skin God gave me, but it is pleasant to hear." She paused reflectively. "My father used to say that my complexion was a curse put on him because he was a painter. He said that he could never get it right."

"Did he try often?"

"Not really," she said. "He was much too busy with other things." She looked up at the portrait above the mantel. "He did that when I was sixteen. I thought he would never finish it. Everytime he studied it, he would bring out his brushes."

"It's excellent," he said. "I was admiring it earlier."

She looked at the portrait, nodding slightly.

"Were you close to your father?" he asked.

"We were very close," she said. "My mother died when I was six, so there were just the two of us. He cared for me until I was old enough to care for him. He was a wonderful man."

"He was French?"

"No, Greek. He was born in Athens. My mother was French. My father came to Paris as a young man to study painting, but he was always sadly out of joint with his times. He was a classicist and he thought any experimentation at all was sacrilege. He even accused Turner of fakery. He eventually became a restorer. He was an extraordinarily gifted man, and when I was a girl I used to think that if we had been born in a different century he would have been immortal. Now I am not so sure, for I realize he probably was lacking in the originality that makes a great artist. I thought about my father often when they were trying that poor man in Holland for counterfeiting Vermeers. He apparently had the same sort of talent as my father. Papa could have copied Rembrandt or Vermeers or even Raphael and most experts would have been deceived. That was his gift."

"Did you live in Paris?"

"That was always our home, but after my mother died my father and I were vagabonds. When I was quite young we spent most of our time in England, where Papa had commissions, restoring church paintings mostly." She dropped her eyes.

"You seem to have regretted the experience," he said.

"Yes, I did," she said. "Whenever I visit England now, particularly London, I always find it difficult to believe I disliked England so much as a child. Perhaps it is I who have changed, but I believe England has changed more. Papa and I always seemed to be living in some tiny, grimy little village, where the women were suety and wore flapping, shapeless dresses, and the men clumped about in big heavy boots and grunted to each other in monosyllables. They thought my father was funny, were frightened of him really, because he was a foreigner and had an accent and wore a beret.

"At the other extreme, there was the village vicar and his

friends. They thought that since Papa was a painter, he had to be cultured, and he went through torture because they were always giving teas for him and making him talk about things he knew absolutely nothing about."

She paused with a small pensive smile. "Poor man—and poor little daughter who was trapped with him. The arts are culture, but I have never been able to understand why most people believe artists are cultured, or even are interested in culture. Musicians seem to be the only exception. Most painters I knew as a young girl, and those I have known since, were more interested in discussing women or where the *bouillabaisse* was good or how to grind colors than they were in discussing the arts."

He smiled. "And writers generally end up by discussing money."

After a short silence, he asked, "How long did you remain in England?"

"Until I was thirteen," she said.

"And then?"

"I attended a convent school in Passy until I was sixteen. The war had come and it was during the German occupation. I scrounged the markets for enough food to feed us, and I attended classes at the Sorbonne until I was eighteen."

"And after that?"

"I was married," she said. She turned to the table and asked, "Would you care for more coffee?" The abruptness of the gesture and her tone made it clear that she did not wish to be questioned further. It was so obvious that neither could pretend it was not deliberate.

He looked at her musingly. "No, thanks, I don't care for more coffee," he said.

There was a heavy silence before she asked, "Where will you visit tomorrow?"

"I have no definite plans," he said. "There doesn't seem to be much left. I would like to visit a temple, but I'm hesitant about going inside."

"But there are many temples you can visit," she said.

"Do you know one?"

"Yes, several."

"Would you go with me to one?" he asked.

She nodded. "Yes—yes, of course."

"But there are many temples you can visit," she said.
"Do you know one?"
"Yes, several."

ELEVEN . . .

The worn stone steps of the temple were crowded with
a swarm of beggars and fakirs. Some were stretched
out sleeping in the hot, bright sunshine. Others held
out their hands and whined beseechingly. One fat sullen man
in a long dirty white robe wore a heavy iron device hooked
through his lips to enforce a vow of silence. Another almost
naked figure had dozens of shriveled lemons hooked to his
skinny black body. As they threaded their way up the steps,
he advanced grinning, removing and replacing one of the
hooks in his chest. Martine looked at him levelly. "*Jao. Jaldi
kare,*" she said. The man scowled and backed away.

He was impressed. "I know *jao* means go," he said, "but what
did you add?"

"*Jaldi kare*—it means fast and very fast," she said. "Men
who deck themselves out like that are not fakirs, only disgust-
ing performers."

A fat, shaven-headed old temple attendant in a faded cinnamon robe sat half-dozing near a row of shoes and sandals
near the temple door. She spoke to him in Hindustani and he
produced felt covers which he slipped over their shoes.

For some reason, he had expected the interior of any temple
to be dark and gloomy and heavy with the odor of incense. Instead this one was bright and airy and the marble floors were
so clean that they glistened. Three bearded and robed ascetics
were seated on small carpets in the middle of the temple in
earnest discussion. A small group of men and women were
seated on the floor before a large shrine which had a gold and

crimson pyramid cover and which contained a massive brass idol. Other people wandered about as casually as visitors to an art gallery, pausing before brightly colored idols which stood in niches which covered the walls from floor to ceiling. A young Indian girl, barefoot and wearing a pure white sari, entered with a garland. She went to the large shrine and plucked the flowers from the garland one by one and tossed them at the base of the idol. There was a burst of laughter from a group of young Indians who were walking in a pavilion which ran around all four sides of the temple.

"This temple is dedicated to Vishnu," Martine said. "He is one of the Gods of the Hindu Triad, and the most popular. He is represented by the large figure in the main shrine. Of course, like most Indian gods he has dozens of forms and probably a thousand names. Hindus believe he has had nine incarnations so far. One more will come at the end of the world. Oddly enough, they believe he was Buddha in his last earthly life, although Buddhism is the only major religion which is considered so heretical it cannot be blended into Hinduism. Hindus believe that Vishnu came back as Buddha deliberately to try to woo men away from Hinduism and test their faith."

He looked at all the idols around the walls. "How can they possibly keep track of them all?"

"They can't," she said. "No more than most Christians can remember all the saints. Some scholar once said that Hinduism is a religion which has neglected to throw out its dirty water. God has been piled on god and myth on myth until it's such a vast thing that nobody can grasp all aspects of it. Actually, the Hindus have no theology—only mythology and philosophy. Despite all this, they are, strictly speaking, monotheists."

"How can they be with so many gods?"

"They believe there is a supreme god, but since ordinary mortals with their limited intellects cannot possibly visualize him, it is all right to create images of his various aspects which they can understand. For that matter, they can worship stones, serpents, monkeys, or even dunghills because God is everything and everywhere."

They walked slowly along one wall. "To simplify things for himself, each Hindu has three principal deities," she said. "The first is the god of his village or town, the second the deity of his family, and the third is a personal god which he can select for himself. Once I met a Hindu who, by a rare coincidence, had resolved all his gods into one. He was quite proud of it. Of course, all pious Hindus are expected to worship other gods, too."

She paused before an alcove which contained a figure of a jet black woman with a bright red tongue, ten arms and a garland of skulls around her neck. "As you probably know, this is Kali, in whose name so many crimes have been committed." She looked at the figure thoughtfully. "Mostly literary crimes, I suspect. There are many reports about human sacrifices in rituals for Kali, but like the reports about children being blinded or mutilated so they will make better beggars, it is difficult to find any proof. Some of the reports could be true. In a country of this size with so many ignorant people, I suppose anything could be true, but the idea of human sacrifices is as shocking to good Hindus as it is to Westerners. The same thing is true of most sensational temple ceremonies one reads about from time to time. There is a sect in India which holds a communal sex orgy in its worship of a goddess named Shakta, but it is as small and as obscure as Western sects which hold black mass. There also are some temples in remote, backward communities which still have priestesses who are prostitutes. This is the basis for many of the lurid stories one reads."

They stopped before another alcove which contained a figure with the body of a squat and chubby man and the head of an elephant. Her dark eyes brightened. "This is my favorite god, Ganesha," she said. "He also is one of the favorite gods of most Hindus. See how they have showered him with flower petals? Ganesha is the god of prudence and sagacity and Hindus pray to him to remove obstacles whenever they undertake anything—build a house, start a journey, have a child. He was the eldest son of Shiva and Parvati, a couple of principal deities. Parvati fashioned Ganesha out of oil and ointments and various impurities of her body and made him a doorkeeper to stop her husband who liked to surprise her while she was in her bath. Shiva came along and Ganesha tried to stop him from entering the bath, and Shiva cut off his head. Parvati was so heartbroken that Shiva sent out servants to bring him the head of the first living creature they met. It happened to be an elephant. So Shiva clapped the head on Ganesha's body —and there he is."

He was watching her as she spoke. She was wearing a sleeveless lime green silk dress. With her eyes bright and her voice animated, he decided he had never seen her look so lovely. She looked up and caught his gaze, and slowly, very slowly, the light faded from her eyes and they grew dark and melancholy. She looked back at Ganesha. "Shiva, incidentally, is the god of Benares," she said. "That is a clue to his antiquity, for no one knows how old Benares really is. It already was an ancient city when Buddha came here six centuries before Christ was born. Some scholars believe Shiva worship is the oldest faith of man. There is definite evidence that he was worshipped in the Indus valley as far back as five thousand years ago. He usually is portrayed as a typical Hindu Holy Man with long hair and a begging bowl in one hand and a skull in the other. If you look about you will notice that most pilgrims to Benares wear Shiva's mark. It is three horizontal lines drawn across the forehead with cow dung ash."

"You obviously have gone into Hinduism deeply," he said.

"I have not retained as much as I should," she said, "but I have studied it . . . for many years now."

"You aren't a Hindu, are you?"

"That is impossible," she said. "A Hindu can be almost anything he pleases. He can worship any gods, or no gods at all, and remain a Hindu. But a person who is not born a Hindu cannot become one, even if he says all the prayers and follows the rituals."

"What is your religion?" he asked.

"I believe in God. I call Him God, and I pray to Him as God."

"You are simply a Deist?"

"No, because that implies I believe in God but do not accept revelation of His existence, and I do."

"Why aren't you a Christian? Since you attended a convent school, I assume you were born one."

"There are many reasons, but to begin with I cannot accept the Apostle's Creed."

"You don't believe in the divinity of Christ?"

"No, that is not quite correct, either. I believe that Christ was in communion with God. I also believe that His teachings and His actions were divinely inspired. What I cannot accept is the view that men must acknowledge Him if they are to be redeemed. I do not even believe that His purpose was to establish a new religion. Nor do I believe He intended men to worship Him. I believe His purpose was to teach men to dispense with dogma and pettifogging theology that obscured their knowledge of God and obstructed their relations with God. Instead men with their imperfect knowledge decided that the Jewish doctrine of the Unity of God could only be completed with the Christian doctrine of the Trinity. The Great Teacher was forgotten in the Lord."

"But didn't Christ Himself say, 'I am the way and the truth and the life: no one cometh unto the Father save through Me'?"

"Yes, I do not question that He may have said that. Perhaps even in those exact words. But I believe He was reassuring Thomas and the other disciples that the lessons He had taught, the knowledge He had imparted was divinely received; it was the way of truth and life, and if they did not forget what He alone had taught them, they would follow Him to God. He also said, 'Whither I go, ye know the way.' He did not say He was the guide, nor did He ever say He was the example. He merely said He had taught the way."

"But don't you believe that the men who originally interpreted Christ's teachings were themselves divinely inspired? St. Paul, in particular. Surely, he couldn't have set out and conquered Macedonia, Greece, and Rome unless he had been given divine guidance."

"Yes, I think such men were infused with a divine spark. But it came from the enlightenment Christ had received. They had not experienced the same direct enlightenment. Even the disciples were often confused and prone to error. All men— even Paul, who was working at second hand—were subject to the errors of men. It was men who allowed the pure and simple doctrine of Christ to become diluted and distorted by Graeco-Roman myths and ceremonies. Such ancient myths as the Immaculate Conception, the worship of the mother and her dying and rising husband or son under the names of Cybele-Isis and Attis-Osiris—to name the most obvious examples. I do not mean the early church was guilty of deliberate distortion. As it converted it also absorbed, because men brought to the church their superstitions and legends. And even those who joined the church free and unencumbered still could not fully grasp the pure meaning of Christ's words. They could not, for nothing personal—personal belief, personal feeling— is ever absolutely understood by others. It must be lived."

"But what you're forgetting," he said, "is that Christianity actually is not the teachings of one man with a blending of Graeco-Roman myths and culture. Even aside from the Atonement, Christ's life was the culmination of centuries of striving. It was much more than the birth of a great man. It brought a pure distillation of knowledge. Christians have always acknowledged what went before. I remember I was taught the very name Jesus Christ is symbolic of the fact that He fused truth that already existed with truth which He imparted. For *Jesus* is the third person singular of a Semitic verb, and *Christ* is the passive participle of a Greek verb. This proves other cultures meet in Christianity. It's not so strange, it was the crowning achievement of many centuries of groping. Anyway, I can't accept all the assertions that Christianity embodies pagan myths. It hasn't anything to do with the fact that I am a Christian, though a poor one, I'm afraid. It's because I've learned many of the assertions are so far fetched. I've often read, for instance, that the use of wine in the Communion service is a relic of the religious awe of intoxication, supposedly springing from the fact that Persian kings appeared in the temple drunk during festivals in honor of Mithras. To me, that simply doesn't make sense. And it has nothing to do with what I may or may not believe about the Eucharist. It simply seems much more obvious that wine is used in the Communion service because it was served at meals and, therefore, became a part of the ceremony at the Jewish Passover."

He smiled at her. "But, anyway, I don't think these things are of much importance to ordinary Christians. It's probably better to leave them to theologians to argue over."

"Then what are Christians supposed to believe in?" she asked. "How do you define religion?"

He pondered that a moment. "A longing of the spirit, I suppose. As the Psalmist put it, 'My soul thirsteth for God.' I believe most men are born with that thirst. If they retain it, I don't honestly think there is a more direct way for them to quench it than through Christianity. For Christianity starts and ends with one tremendous notion: that if we comprehend the sayings and follow the actions of a single man Who was the Son of God, we are saved through His grace and led to His Father. It's a fairly simple notion, really, when you think about it. Not only is every man permitted freedom of action; it is even held forth as a divine promise." He smiled. "Provided, of course, that freedom of action is based on truth—and the knowledge of truth depends on learning from the Son of God."

She shook her head. "That is not simple at all. It implies that Christianity is the only true light and those who do not carry it are wandering in the outer darkness. I can never accept that. The important thing is to believe in God. I believe Christ felt the same way. Whether He is accepted as divine or not, Christ was not a destroyer. He did not kill anything that was not already dead. There are more Hindus, more Jews, more Buddhists, more Moslems today than ever before. Altogether they outnumber Christians and they always have. I do not think people who follow these religions fail to perceive the true light, nor do I believe that the thousands upon thousands of generations of men who lived before Christ's comparatively recent birth floundered hopelessly in the dark." He was about to protest when she halted before a niche. It contained a small and rather badly made plaster figure of Gandhi. "Most Westerners are amused or appalled when they see Gandhi in the Hindu pantheon," she said. "I do not think Gandhi was a saint, but it does not offend me. The Roman church continually is beatifying new saints, and in some Jewish synagogues the name of Einstein already is graven on scrolls along with the names of Moses and Abraham. Religion is only permanent rightness and the love of God. If it satisfies religious ritual to exalt righteous men, I do not understand why anyone should object."

He smiled slightly. "But you do believe that ritual essentially is meaningless? You feel every man has a right to pursue his own separate bent, as you do?"

She looked at him. "I have not said that at all. I have said that rituals, prayer books, codes, and all the trappings of individual religions are not necessary. They may be good or they may be bad. But they do produce a herd psychology. I also said that I thought many useless things were added and some precious things were lost when the Christian fathers were interpreting the gospel of Christ. But I am not following a purely personal bent. For I believe in God. God remains the same; God is unchanging. There are other men who have been able to have communion directly with God, just as Christ did, and I think, possibly, through the same methods Christ used for His enlightenment."

He smiled. "Surely you don't mean yogis?"

"You may call them yogis if you like," she said quietly. "For that matter, I think it is conceivable that Christ may have been what is known as a yogi. From the age of twelve until He began His ministry, nothing is known of His life. Who knows that He was not a yogi? Who knows that He did not spend years acquiring His special gifts, perhaps even here in India?"

"I've heard the theory," he said. "It's interesting, but I don't consider it likely," he said. "I also don't believe there are men existing who have direct communion with God."

"I know there are," she said, quietly. She looked at him and her eyes were somber. "I understand your disbelief. It is difficult to forget things we have been taught. It is not easy to risk scorn or punishment and put aside beliefs that are authoritatively ordained. But God is beyond dogma. And so is true religion beyond ritual. In considering religion, we must not be deluded by things we prefer to believe. It is easy to hold fast to familiar ritual and beloved myths. That is the stage where most people always have halted. They are satisfied, semi-religious. They do not wish to unlock the mysteries. They feel no need to ask questions, to strive for higher things. Since it works, it is good, so why should they seek something better and truer? In every age they accept doctrine as it is pressed into molds by their churches and dispensed like sacrament wafers, never realizing that the molds constantly are being changed. But there is an absolute, unchanging truth. Believed or not believed, known or not known, it always is the same. For God does not change, only man does. That absolute truth is the reward awaiting those few who suffer until they claim it. They join a fellowship in the Kingdom of God. 'Strait is the gate, and narrow is the way . . . and few there be that find it.' " She studied his face for a long moment, then turned quickly. She pointed toward one of the niches. "That ugly figure with three eyes is the goddess Ellamma."

He muttered something appropriate. What an astounding

person she was. So knowledgeable about some things, so naïve about others. He did not feel in a mood to argue with her.

They circled the temple slowly and were moving toward the door when the fat robed attendant entered. He came directly to them, smiling, but his voice was low and serious as he spoke to her in Hindustani. She nodded and replied and he went away, still smiling.

She said, "He thought he should tell us that a R.S.S.S. procession is passing, and it would be best if we remained here until it is gone. He is right, of course. There probably would be no difficulty, but there is no point in taking a chance."

"What is this group?" he asked.

"It has quite an involved name and an involved history," she said. "It is called the Rashtriya Swayam Sevak Sangha, but most people refer to it as the R.S.S.S. It is a militant branch of the Hindu Mahasabha, which supposedly safeguards Hindu traditions and customs. Some well-meaning devout Hindus belong to it, but it also attracts a great number of hotheaded young fools and stupid reactionaries. They often provoke trouble. The young zealot who assassinated Gandhi belonged to it."

There were a few shouts and an irregular chant from the street outside.

"Come, we can watch from here," she said. He followed her to the pavilion in front of the temple.

A ragged procession of men, some of them carrying black flags, was making its way through the crowded street. For the most part, the marchers were walking along slowly and dispiritedly, but at intervals there were young dhoti-clad leaders who shouted slogans and waved their arms, and tried to get the marchers to join in. White-jacketed, red-turbaned Benares policemen, carrying long brass-bound lathis, walked along boredly on each side of the procession. The crowd in the street paid no attention to the marchers at all.

"They don't look very dangerous," he said.

The coldness of her voice surprised him. "Not when they are being watched."

Three *dhoti*-clad young men brought up the rear of the procession, shouting and waving their arms. As they passed, one of them, a lanky man with shoulder length hair, looked toward the temple and saw them on the pavilion. He said something to his companions and pointed to them. Then he stooped and picked up something from the street and threw it in their direction. Whatever it was, mud or cowdung, burst apart and fell yards short of where they stood. A short, squat policeman, slouching along at the end of the procession, saw it all. Without breaking his stride, almost casually, he raised his *lathi* and struck the young demonstrator across the side of the head. He fell as if he had been pole-axed. The policeman slouched past the fallen body without even glancing down.

He grunted approval. "Serves him right." She remained silent.

The demonstrator's two companions lifted him by the feet and shoulders and half carried, half dragged, him to a nearby doorway. Only a few people in the street stopped, looked on briefly, and moved on again.

As they made their way down the temple steps through the wailing beggars, he looked toward the doorway. The injured man was sitting up groggily, supported by his two companions. One of them stood up, rushed to the middle of the narrow street and waved his hand in a pointing gesture and shouted something angrily. Martine paused and looked at him coldly and answered. The man looked startled. Then he glowered, and turned and walked back to his friends.

As he followed Martine into the car, he noticed that Sixteen, who had heard the exchange, was grinning broadly.

After they were seated, he asked, "What did you say to him?"

"It is nothing," she said.

"I would like to know."

"He spoke Hindi. He said, 'Thou art a white-faced whore,' and I said, 'Thou wilt be reborn as a black worm in the intestine of a dog.'"

He grinned, but broke off when he saw the shadow across her face and eyes.

"I hate them," she said with deadly calm. "I hate people who try to force their beliefs on others." She sat silently for a long time. When she spoke again her voice was normal. "Indians have the reputation of being a docile people. They like to boast that they are nonviolent. Actually, some of the worst blood-letting in history has taken place here. People who were not here during the riots over partition have no idea of how dreadful it was. In the heart of New Delhi, bands of Sikhs would march into the homes of Westerners who had Muslim servants. They always knew where they were hiding. A few Sikhs would go and drag them out while the others waited politely. Then they would chop off the Muslims' heads, leave their bodies soaking blood over the drawing room carpet, bow, and march away.

"The Muslims were just as bad. Perhaps even worse, because they are warriors by nature. They would walk into a Hindu's shop and pick up his small child. 'How old is this son of yours?' they would ask. 'He is four, Huzzor,' the Hindu would say, trembling with fear. 'Very well, we will cut him into four parts,' they would say, and they would. Both groups stopped trains and systematically chopped all the Hindu or Muslim passengers to bits. Or they surrounded each other's shops, and as the frightened occupants ran out: men, women, little children—it did not matter—they would beat them to death with clubs.

"India gained a reputation for nonviolence because of the teachings of one man—Gandhi. He won a revolution by teaching the people to use nonviolence as a weapon. In doing so, he created the most fantastic of all Indian myths—the myth that Indians are not a violent people. The myth was not even destroyed when he died violently himself. The truth is, from the beginnings of Indian history, right on up to the present time, India has had an almost unsurpassed record of violence. There is scarcely a day that passes when Muslims and Hindus do not fight somewhere."

"But it's not so bad as it once was, is it?" he asked.

"The worst of it has ended, of course," she said. "But it still goes on. It probably always will as long as India has Muslims and Hindus—and the temperature reaches one hundred and twenty degrees. One does not hear about many of the incidents. They are too commonplace. A Hindu is stabbed to death on a train here, a Mussulman gets beaten to death in his shop there . . . it is a despicable thing. One is able to feel sympathy and outrage when a single group is persecuted. When two groups kill and persecute each other, one can only see the ugliness and beastliness of it, and not sympathize with either. The worst thing of all is the way extremists on both sides continually whip up hate against each other. The slightest incident leads to bloodshed. Maybe fewer people die today than ever before, but even one person is too many."

She took him to lunch at a small Indian restaurant she knew. It was barren and somewhat dingy; the waiter served them with his bare hands, and there was no cutlery. They each had a scrawny, long-legged Indian chicken which had been dipped in a red curry mixture and cooked in an oven, in the style called tandoori, served with a huge country chapati soaked with ghee and a fresh chutney of onions, chillies, and tomatoes. It was the first Indian food he had ever truly enjoyed. He told her so.

"It is because it is plain food," she said. "Most people who come to India and order Indian dishes at the hotels or better restaurants cannot understand how Indians can live on such a rich and spicy diet. The truth is, they don't; no more than Frenchmen live on the kind of dishes featured in four-star restaurants. It is only another one of the many misconceptions Westerners have about India, even after they have visited here. I believe it was Indira Nehru who said that no book about India written by a Westerner was wholly correct."

"I was reading a couple of remarkable books last night which I found on the counter in the hotel lobby," he said. "They were called *Karma Sutra* and *Ananga-Ranga*. Do you know them?"

There was a glint of amusement in her eyes. "Yes, everyone knows those books. Do you not find it surprising that they were written more than two thousand years ago?"

He smiled. "I find it surprising that they were written at all," he said.

"You are an American with a Puritan tradition," she said. "A good wicked Frenchman would not be surprised at all."

"Seriously, do you suppose they are considered part of India's literary heritage?"

"Yes, I should imagine so. At least, most Indians who can read have read them. And I should think they have their use as part of sex instructions. When they first were written I imagine many of the maharajahs and shahs found them invaluable. With so many wives it must have been helpful to have them catalogued so beautifully."

"They certainly are explicit enough," he said.

"One would never realize it from reading Indian mythology or seeing the number of Westernized oily haired Lotharios about," she said, "but ordinary Indians of the lower and middle classes are so straitlaced in their dealings with women that even the Victorians seem lascivious by comparison. There are almost no sex crimes and women seldom are molested on the streets, which is certainly strange considering the number of mental cases walking about. And yet rape is rampant whenever they fight. During the partition riots, hundreds of women killed themselves to keep from falling into the hands of their conquerors. Literally thousands of women were abducted. Ignorance and sexual laxity frequently go hand in hand in some countries, but it is not true here. One reason, of course, may be that women are aware that they must stay chaste if they wish to make a good marriage. As you know, even now practically all marriages are arranged by parents. I think there is a great deal to be said for the system. Parents who have their children's happiness and future in mind should be able to arrange a better marriage than the children themselves. Do you agree?"

He grinned. "In principle, yes. But I shouldn't have liked it if it had happened to me."

"Well, so far only the more Westernized young people seem inclined to revolt. Maybe others will in time, but there certainly is no evidence at present that they will. India has known for centuries what psychiatry is now publicizing in the West, that repression is harmful and corrupting. So marriages generally are arranged when couples are quite young. Puberty used to be considered the ideal time. Among enlightened parents the age gradually has crept up to, say nineteen or twenty for the man, and seventeen or eighteen for the woman. There still are a tremendous number of child marriages among the lower classes. Such marriages are not supposed to be consummated until puberty, but they often are. But the point I wanted to make was that marriage of the young is encouraged in India. One who runs away from marriage is considered to be shirking his duty. Yet celibacy seems to have a special fascination here. Gandhi used to say that his greatest regret was that he had experienced sex. He had almost an embarrassing obsession with the subject.

"Marriage is a sacrament, so divorce is practically unknown among Hindus. The perfectly ethical marriage is a monogamous one, but even today some rich Hindus make as many marriages as they like. Frequently, even poor sweepers have two or three wives. Husbands use their wives dreadfully, and this also is odd considering the poor diet and low vitality of most Indians. Yet there is considerable medical evidence that it is true. Perhaps it is because there is so little else to do in Indian villages."

"What about upper-class Indians?" he asked.

"From what I have been able to determine," she said, "they

are about like upper-classes anywhere—only more so." She smiled her small smile.

After luncheon she took him to see *Jnana-vapi*, the well of knowledge, in which all devout Hindus throw flowers when they make a pilgrimage to Benares. The jostling crowd was so thick, the beggars so worrisome and the stench so overpowering, that they left after a minute or two.

As they walked toward the car, sidestepping clamoring beggars and mendicant fakirs, she said, "It helps if you remember most of what you smell is only decaying flowers."

"Distance helps more," he muttered.

A small dirty girl, carrying a limp skinny baby on her hip, darted forward with outstretched hand. The baby's face was a mass of yellow pustules, and its eyes were glued shut with a heavy discharge. Martine stopped and spoke to the girl in Hindustani. She cowered and whined but kept darting her small outstretched hand toward them.

Martine took a rupee from her purse and spoke to her again, almost sharply. The girl answered, then sly amusement lighted her pinched face and she grabbed the rupee and dashed away.

"I told her to take the baby to a dispensary," she said, "but she will not, of course. She may have hired it for the day."

A chubby fakir with two brass weights hooked to his lower eyelids groped his way toward them. She looked at him absently and said, "*Jao*."

A flock of small boys had gathered around the car. When they saw them, they began chanting, "Watch car, *sahib!* Watch car, *memsahib!*" Sixteen alighted from the car and growled at them. They retreated a distance, but edged forward again like hungry sparrows. After he and Martine were seated in the car, he tossed them some change out the window. They scrambled for it, elbowing and shouting angrily.

"I can't understand why they are so dirty," he said. "Even animals keep themselves clean."

"Theoretically, they should be clean," she said. "Every Indian bathes at least once a day. The difficulty is they are not particular about the water they use, any puddle or stream will do. And their clothes, of course, are usually filthy. Indians who have the facilities and a change of clothing probably are the cleanest people on earth. Many of them bathe three times a day."

He looked at the dirty swarming crowd. "Do you suppose they realize how poor and miserable they are?"

"Certainly," she said

"It doesn't always follow, you know," he said. "Poverty, like everything else, is comparative. When I was a boy, my family was poor, and I never realized it."

"Were you always hungry?"

"Of course not."

"Did you have one ragged piece of cloth to cover yourself, and did you sleep in the street?"

"No, but what I meant was that most of us judge our own state by the state of the people about us. In the small town where I grew up, most families were exactly like mine. I didn't feel poor and I never heard my mother or father even discuss money. I was a grown man before it dawned on me how poor we were."

"But you weren't unhappy?"

"Quite the contrary, I was happy."

"Then you were not truly poor. You were rich—richer than you have ever been since you discovered the uses of money."

TWELVE . . .

She invited him to dinner again, and when the bearer admitted him, he was pleased and vaguely excited because he knew she had been thinking of him and was looking forward to seeing him. He could not have explained by what masculine intuitive process he knew. But it was unmistakable. Maybe the flowing but starkly simple Grecian-like white gown she wore was her favorite. Maybe she had applied an extra touch of cologne, or maybe her color was heightened and her eyes were softer. Whatever it was, he knew. It made everything seem warmer and brighter and happier.

They had a bottle of passably good Bordeaux with their dinter that Ram, her bearer, had bought from a bootlegger, who had smuggled it in from Pondicherry. They did not talk seriously. He told her about his boyhood in Indiana, of his parents, and his early days on a newspaper. She sat quietly, listening intently, her eyes bright with amusement or warm with understanding. There was an intimacy about the conversation and in the relaxed way in which they ate together. They no longer were strangers.

After they returned to the drawing room, she brought him a brandy and sat down beside the table and poured coffee. He told her anecdotes about his work in Hollywood and in the theater. Like everyone he had ever met, she was fascinated by the duplicity, the tricks and the problems of making films. She sat listening with a sort of bemused wonder, sometimes asking questions about various actors and actresses. He made a passing reference to Cynthia, and she said, "She is lovely. I have seen several of her films."

"She is very talented," he said.

She studied his face. "Are you in love with her?"

He sat thoughtfully. "No, I don't think so."

"You are not sure?"

"Yes, I'm sure," he said. "I hesitated because I'm terribly fond of her and I enjoy her company. I've thought of her often since I left London. Sometimes I've wondered if the way I feel about her is not what often passes for love."

"It is odd you have never married," she said.

He nodded. "Perhaps it is. When I was younger—if I thought about it consciously at all—I don't believe I intended to be a bachelor. Still, I suppose it is better not to have married at all than to have married a number of times like so many of my friends. Yet I realize I've missed something. I was thinking about it this afternoon when you said that Hindus consider a man who runs away from marriage to be shirking his duty."

"Do you feel you have run away?"

"I'm not sure. Maybe I have. I wanted to marry very much on one occasion. Since then perhaps I have been running. Maybe it's the business I'm in." He smiled. "I think I convinced myself that marriage was an unnatural state for a normal, sensibly aggressive male. Perhaps I even convinced myself that all married men simply were unfortunate enough to have been trapped."

She returned his smile. She was seated Indian fashion, legs crossed under her full skirt, her back very erect. Her beautiful face was calm and her enormous eyes seemed almost aglow with a light which could have been understanding or tenderness—or love. A sudden thought filled his mind. He would marry her, if he could. Yes, he would be proud of her beauty, her womanliness, comforted by her calm stability. He sat and thought about it, and he was not aware that his smile had faded, not conscious of how long they sat there studying each other before she lowered her eyes. With a single fluid movement, she rose to her feet. "Before I forget about it, I have

164 . . .

some books for you," she said. He sat staring into the fire until he heard her voice, her much too casual voice, saying, "I think you will find this one interesting."

He rose slowly. "I'm sure I will," he said. He crossed to where she stood by the book shelves. She was holding a small book which she held out. He took it, and without removing his eyes from her face, laid it aside on the shelf. He leaned forward and kissed her. It was a tentative kiss, tender, yet infinitely sweet. Suddenly, it was more than that, much, much more. He felt her tremble, and with a little cry she was in his arms. Her lips were startlingly hungry, demanding. His own response was more rackingly immediate, more shattering, than he had thought was any longer possible. *My God*, he thought, *how hot she is.*

"Wha . . ." His exclamation was an explosive grunt. He stood there momentarily stunned before he realized what had happened. She had suddenly thrust both hands against his chest and roughly broken away. It was more of a blow than a shove. He stared at her disbelievingly. Her dark eyes were expressionless, but her cheeks were flushed, and she was breathing rapidly. Unaccountably, he felt a slow embarrassment. It lasted only a moment. She turned away, and immediately he realized what he actually felt was anger. Not since he was a fumbling adolescent had he been repulsed so crudely. He was not accustomed to forcing his way with women. She had not acted like a woman. She had behaved like a schoolgirl . . . a goddamned silly schoolgirl.

She turned and her face was calm. "That was very foolish of me."

He ignored her meaning. His voice was icy. "Damned foolish."

She studied his face, then dropped her eyes. "Yes," she said, quietly. "I am sorry." After a short silence, she looked up. "I do have a husband, you know."

"You don't care for your husband," he said.

Something flickered in her eyes. For the first time since he had known her, she smiled a full smile. It did not suit her; it made her look artificial, gave her face a spurious brightness that was unattractive. "Why should you say that?" she asked. "What reason have I given you to say that?"

He looked at her silently. "Sorry," he said finally. "My mistake." He turned and walked toward the door. He was no longer angry, just tired, and . . . well, empty. No, it was more than that. As he crossed the foyer, he realized the emptiness was a hurt and he was lonely and stricken. He should have known better.

"Paul."

He turned. She was standing in the middle of the room. Her face was composed but her eyes looked tragic and beseeching. "Please come back, Paul," she said. "There is something . . . something I should like to tell you."

There was tension, an awkwardness. If she had come rushing to his arms, it could have been resolved instantly. If he had been guilty of making a casual pass, perhaps it could have been laughed off. But that hot and hungry kiss could not be brushed aside. He stood with his back to the fire, waiting. She stood looking at him, as if uncertain what to say. Finally, she asked, politely, "May I fix you a drink?"

"No thanks."

"I think I will have a sherry," she said.

"Let me get it," he said. "I'll have a drink, after all." He went to the table and poured her a sherry and mixed himself a scotch and water. She was seated in a chair near the fireplace. He handed her the sherry and took a seat on the sofa. There was a long silence. She toyed with her sherry glass and, suddenly, came over and sat at his feet beside the coffee table.

"I am sorry, Paul," she said, earnestly. "I behaved like a fool. A woman of my age should knew better than to provoke such a situation. But I wanted you to kiss me. All evening I have been wanting you to take me in your arms . . . to hold me . . . touch me." She placed her hand on his knee and gave him one of her small smiles. "I have been attracted to you ever since we first met. You know that." She paused, and looked down at her hands. "I have built up defenses for so long that I suppose I felt a panic when they crumbled all at once."

He smiled at her. "I didn't know I was so frightening."

She did not appear to hear, but sat looking at her hands thoughtfully. Then, as if she had made up her mind about something, she looked up and asked, "Have you ever heard of a man named Bhaiji, Paul?"

"Yes—yes, I think so," he said slowly, puzzled. "He's a Holy Man of some sort."

"Yes," she said. "He is a Holy Man. He also is my husband."

"But his name . . . it sounds Czech or Polish."

"No, it is Indian. *Bhai* means brother, and *ji* is a suffix of respect, meaning honorable or esteemed. His real name is André: André Valois." She paused. "We were married in Paris during the war . . . during the German occupation. I was eighteen and he was twenty-eight. He was one of my lecturers at the Sorbonne. He was handsome, witty, brilliant—and also very rich and spoiled. His father had been one of the most distinguished surgeons in France. I do not know what attracted André to me, but I loved him . . . well, I loved him more than I thought it was possible to love. But it was not a happy marriage and, perhaps, it was largely my fault. I was young and terribly immature, and frightfully serious and idealistic, as only the young can be idealistic. I had never really known any man very well except my father, and I suppose I thought all men were supposed to be exactly like him. Most people in France were slightly insane in those days, anyway, I think—especially young men of André's age. He had been wounded at the beginning of the war. By the time he had recovered, France had fallen. Perhaps he and his friends felt they had to flaunt their masculinity and recklessness to compensate for France's humiliation. Besides, André had received a terrible blow. He adored his father, and he had been interned by the Germans and had died in prison. We always have thought they killed him.

"Before we had been married a year, André was having affairs with other women. I simply did not know what to do. I was crushed and angry and humiliated. I also was very much in love. There was one woman in particular. Her name no longer matters, but she was beautiful and gay—and apparently had all the things André wanted and I could not give. Perhaps, eventually, he would have left me for her. There is no way of knowing because . . . of something horrible that happened.

"On the night Paris was liberated, we went to a party with André's wild young friends. It was on the seventh floor of an apartment house on Avenue Foch. There was a large balcony off the drawing room. There was still some fighting going on in Paris that night and from time to time tracer bullets lit up the sky. There were great glowing fires all over the city where the Germans were burning equipment and blowing up ammunition depots. Everyone crowded out on the balcony as if it were Bastille Day and they were there to watch the fireworks display. We were drinking champagne—a great deal of champagne, some of it bottles that we had hoarded just for a victory celebration. I did not join the crowd on the balcony. André's girl friend was there and, as usual, he was at her side. I sat in the drawing room alone, hurt and angry, listening to the laughter and shouts. There was one other couple in the kitchen. They had gone there to open more champagne.

"Then—then, suddenly, the balcony fell, tore loose from its moorings and plunged down seven floors to the ground. It was frightful. Fourteen people were on the balcony. Only André survived the fall.

"They thought he was dead at first, too. They had moved him and placed him with the other bodies when a gendarme saw him stir. They carried him to the hospital. His arms were broken and his skull was fractured—considering the fall, not a very serious fracture. The doctors were dumbfounded. They expected internal injuries, as a matter of course, but there were none.

"I had collapsed completely, absolutely frozen with horror,

168 . . .

and a doctor had given me a needle to put me to sleep. It was the next morning before I learned André was alive.

"He was unconscious for three days. When he recovered, he was not the same person. He returned home from the hospital after three weeks. We never lived together again."

"How had he changed?" he asked.

"He was ... well, he was a complete stranger; kind and quiet, but unsmiling and withdrawn. I assumed that it simply was the shock and he would recover and become himself again in time. But he never did.

"One day, about a month after he had returned home, he told me that he was leaving. He could not tell we where he was going; he did not seem to know. I begged him not to go. I wept, and, finally, I stormed at him. His mother pleaded with him. It did no good. He left that night. It was months before his mother and I could trace him. Then some agents Maman Valois had employed learned that he was living in Simla. We sent him money and flew out. He was living in a single room in the native quarter. He did not seem surprised to see us. He was terribly thin, and although he was gentle and polite, we simply could not reach him. He was not in our world. He had not even bothered to collect the money we had sent. We alternated in pleading with him to return home with us, but he refused. He would sit for hours, simply staring into space. One day we went to his room and he was not there. We began the search again. We hired agents and notified the British and French authorities. Maman Valois' health was bad and after several months the worry and the climate almost were too much for her. I made her return to Paris with me.

"The next winter I returned to India alone. That was in 1946. The authorities still did not have a clue as to his whereabouts, so I wandered aimlessly, hoping by chance to find him, or find somebody who had seen him. I came back every year. I traveled from Madras to Gilgit and from Kalimpong to Karachi, but I did not find him and I never found anyone who had seen him. In the spring of 1952—seven years after he had disappeared in Simla, Maman Valois died. She was a wonderfully dear woman, and I loved her as I would have my own mother. Ironically, a month after she died I received word that André had reappeared and was living here in Benares. I flew out immediately.

"I really did not know what to expect. I assumed that the years would have changed him; but he was utterly and completely different. He had become a Holy Man . . . well, the change in him just defies all description. I cannot even begin to explain it. He is not the same man in any respect. I cannot think of him as the same man. I asked him where he had been, of course, but he said he had been seeking truth, and that is as much as I know to this day. I told him about his mother's death, and he merely said, 'I know'—and I knew that he did know.

"He had attracted followers and was living in a grove on the banks of the Ganges. It is impossible to talk to such a man about money, but I had to tell him we were quite well off. He told me to see an old Pandit named Coomaraswamy, who was his chief disciple, and ask him if anything was needed. I did that, and the Pandit and I established a fund, and eventually bought land and his followers built an ashram. I stayed around a while, feeling confused and unnecessary and, finally, returned to Paris.

"I left thinking that a chapter in my life had been closed. I made up my mind that I would never return. After all the hopeless years, I decided I would cut myself free and try to make a new life. It has not worked out that way. I have returned here in the winters, and until my father died three years ago, we lived together in Paris. The years have gone somehow. I have managed to keep busy. Over the years I have made a study of India and Hinduism and, of course, I have learned to speak several Indian dialects. I go to London at least once a year, principally because of the Indian library there. It is the best in the world."

He sat silently. Finally, he said, "It's a fantastic story."

"Yes," she said. She sat with downcast eyes, brooding. Suddenly, she looked up. "I should like to tell you the rest of it, Paul. I never even told it to Maman Valois. Only my father knew. André did not fall with that balcony. He jumped."

"I don't understand," he said.

"I mean he had stepped inside the room when the balcony fell," she said. "He turned and jumped out the door."

He thought about it. "Are you positive? Perhaps you saw him near the door."

She shook her head slowly. "My father also found it difficult to believe. It is so fantastic that I suppose that is one reason I always have hesitated to tell it."

"Can you remember exactly how it happened?" he asked.

"How can I ever forget anything so horrible? I remember every second, every minor detail, as if it were a film in slow motion. André was coming in from the balcony, smiling. He had one foot in the room and the other was still on the balcony. There was an awful tearing sound, a woman's frightened scream, and a scraping noise. André threw himself into the room, face downward on the carpet. There were more screams and shouts, and then, seemingly a long time afterward, a far away crash. I knew what had happened immediately. Even in that moment when I was frozen with horror, I remember thinking, Thank God, he is safe. I had my eyes on him as he slowly raised himself on his hands and knees. His face was white and strained. Then, suddenly, it was convulsed by the most agonizing, grief-stricken expression I have ever seen in my life. It seemed to show more despair than a human being is capable of feeling. It lasted only a few seconds. With one bound, he was on his feet and had turned and thrown himself through the doorway. I remember my own almost unbearable agony when I heard the awful sound his body made when it struck the ground." She shook her head slowly. "No, I was not mistaken. I told you he had champagne glasses in his hand. When he drew himself to his hands and knees, I saw the glasses had broken and he had cut his right hand on the splinters. When I saw him in the hospital the next day, I looked, and there was a small cut at the base of his thumb."

"Did you ever discuss this with him?"

"Yes, I told him I had seen it. He said, 'I could not have lived with myself if I had not done it.' "

He sat silently, mulling it over. "It's an almost unbelievable story," he said. He studied his glass. "Why haven't you divorced him? It seems slightly ridiculous that a person of your intelligence wouldn't have. You are a lovely woman, and there must have been men . . ."

"Yes, there were men," she said. "A woman can always find men who wish to be attentive. But I have always avoided them. It has not been too difficult. Men never truly understand the desire of a woman, Paul. Oh, I do not mean sexual desire, though I was not made for a nunnery and I have suffered that also. I sometimes have been tempted to choose some handsome young boulevardier with broad shoulders for a lover. But I could never bring myself to do it. Perhaps I know it would not work anyway. My desire is deeper, Paul. Like any woman, my desire is to be wanted, to be needed, and to love and comfort someone who loves me in return."

He was startled. "You mean all these years . . ." He looked at her incredulously. "My God, you don't mean you've been a . . . a celibate for all this time?"

His astonishment amused her. She studied him, smiling slightly. "No, not a celibate," she corrected. "I am married."

"Well, whatever you call it," he said. "It's criminal. It's the silliest thing I've ever heard. It's . . . it's stupid."

She looked at him, still smiling slightly, then shrugged. "Perhaps it has been," she said. "But it hasn't been as difficult as you may think. For one thing, Paul, I have never met a man who has tempted me as you did. I did consider divorce once. I debated whether I should marry for devotion and kindness. There was a man I knew in Paris. He was a good man, a widower with two children. But there were other things I wanted. It probably sounds foolish. All my life I have wanted to have sons. I want them to have long legs and broad shoulders . . . and walk the earth as if they had bought it. His sons would not have been like that. It is something only a woman can understand."

"No," he said, "I can understand it."

They sat in silence. Finally, he asked, "Have you gone into the legal difficulties of all this?"

"Do you mean about a divorce?"

"Yes—that, and also about putting your husband some place where he can get proper psychiatric care. Even forcibly, if necessary. It often . . . He stopped because her large eyes were incredulous. "You don't think that is necessary?" he asked.

She shook her head slowly, and her voice was gentle. "No, Paul, you will have to meet him to realize how strange that sounds."

He did not say what he thought. Instead, he asked, "When may I meet him?"

"We can go to the ashram tomorrow if you like," she said. "It is less than an hour by car."

THIRTEEN . . .

He had no clear idea of what an ashram would be like, but he had imagined that it would be similar to a religious retreat or monastery. When the car turned off a dusty road and entered a narrow well-kept lane leading to a cluster of low buildings, he was surprised.

"It looks like a farm," he said.

Martine said, "It is a farm." She smiled. "And a textile plant . . . and a dairy. A good ashram always is as self-sustaining as possible. This one is nearly so."

"I had assumed they only prayed, and meditated, and read holy books."

"They do all those things," she said. "But they work also. It is one of the teachings of Gandhi—one of the fine things he taught India: the dignity of labor. For centuries high-born Indians have thought that to work with one's hands is degrading."

He asked, "Does André speak English, or will I have to limp along in my French?"

"He speaks English perfectly," she said. "He had an English nanny as a child." She paused. "He always has had a gift for languages. He speaks seven or eight fluently. He used to be very proud of it."

The car drew up into the courtyard formed by the buildings. The first thing that struck him was how well kept and immaculately clean everything was. There were a dozen or so medium-sized huts surrounding a sizeable low-roofed house, built on a small rise, that had a verandah running its entire length. The mud walls of all the buildings were whitewashed and gleamed under the bright and cloudless sky. About fifty yards in the distance there were a number of other large buildings. Through the open front of one he saw cows and water buffaloes feeding at a trough. In the other direction and about the same distance from the house there was an amphitheater of some sort with a small platform in the center. As they stepped from the car, he noticed the ground was packed hard and swept clean. A half-dozen or so small children were playing in the shade of an immense banyan tree. Shrieking with excitement, they came dashing toward the car. They halted and put their hands together in the traditional Indian greeting and said, "Salaam, sahib! Salaam, memsahib." Martine returned the greeting and said something to them in one or another of the languages which he always had assumed before was Hindustani. A tall elderly Indian wearing a white cloth jacket and a Gandhi cap, but with a *dhoti* flapping around his spindly legs, emerged from the nearest hut. His steel-rimmed spectacles and white teeth gleamed, as he rushed forward, smiling, to greet them. "Pandit Coomaraswamy," Martine said.

The Pandit gave them the Indian greeting, and Martine introduced them. He was surprised when the Pandit gave him a strong handshake and said in a ripe upper-class English accent, "It is a pleasure to meet you, Mr. Fraser." He smiled at Martine. "I hope you intend spending some time with us, Madame Valois."

She said, "No, I have brought Mr. Fraser to meet Bhaiji."

The Pandit nodded. "Certainly, I will announce you."

As the Pandit left them and walked toward the large house, he was amused to see he was wearing blue sneakers. Martine was looking after him fondly. "He is a dear old man, and a strange one also. He is a Brahman and for many years was a professor at a Hindu college outside Poona. After he retired, he became a wandering mendicant, visiting Holy Men and temples all over India, searching for someone to serve. He met André in Patna when he first emerged from seclusion. The

Pandit says the moment he saw him he knew his search had ended. He has told me he knelt and said, 'I am your *chela*.' One must know India to realize how strange that seems. A *chela* is a pupil and an attendant to a Holy Man, and usually he is a boy or young man."

He watched as the Pandit paused outside a door on the verandah and slipped out of his sneakers. He entered, and in a few moments emerged and beckoned to them, smiling. He followed Martine up the steps to the verandah. In one corner a wrinkled and toothless old woman and a dark-skinned young girl in a white sari sat before whirling spinning wheels, holding the lengthening threads in their bare toes. Both flashed smiles of greeting.

At the door, the Pandit said, "The Master is awaiting you. He knew you were here, of course." He felt a flash of amusement that the old Pandit would use such a corny carnival trick, particularly with Martine, but he kept his face straight.

Martine was removing her sandals, and he stepped out of his loafers. She said, "That is not necessary, Paul," but they were already off and he did not replace them.

They stepped into a large barren, but bright and airy, room. Just as he had no clear preconceived notion about an ashram, he could not have told what he expected André Valois to be like. At the best, he probably expected an erratic religious fanatic in a robe. At the worst, he would have expected an ash-smeared ascetic who obviously was insane. But when he first saw André Valois, his first thought was, *Why, I know him. I know him well.*

Then, with a profound shock, he realized why this was so. From the time he was a child, he had carried an image of God in his mind. Where it came from he did not know. It was somewhat similar, yet not the same as Michelangelo's portrait of the Creator in the Sistine Chapel. Probably the image first took form and grew from some cheap lithograph he had been given in Sunday school, or maybe it was from some Old Testament engraving he had once seen in a book in his father's study. Until he saw André Valois, he never had encountered a face quite like it; he probably had not thought about it for years. But here was the same broad and serene forehead, the long strong nose, a mouth that was wide and rather thin-lipped, but touched with kindness and strength. But the eyes made the face unique. They were deeply set, the color as clear blue as the heavens on a quiet day; calm and gentle, but literally depthless with so much wisdom that one felt there were no secrets they had not seen and solved. Except that this man's beard was short and not flowing, the face was the same as his image. After he recovered from his first jolting shock, he felt annoyed, almost angry with himself, because he honestly could not tell himself he was mistaken.

André Valois sat Indian fashion, his long legs crossed and drawn close to his body, on a small cloth-covered dais near the window. All he wore was a pure white *dhoti*, pulled up about his loins. His long body was thin, almost alarmingly thin, but his pale olive skin had a healthy glow. He did not rise or speak as they entered the room.

He looked at the serene figure and it was several seconds before he realized that there was no smile on the remarkable face. Only something in the depthless blue eyes made it seem that there was. He became aware that two *dhoti*-clad young Indians were seated crosslegged before a low writing desk in the corner near the dais. They smiled a greeting.

Martine said, "André, this is Paul Fraser, a friend."

The quiet figure still had not moved a muscle, but he felt that he had been given a warm and affectionate greeting.

"You are welcome here, Mr. Fraser." His voice was low, almost flat, but it had strength.

"Shall I send for a chair for you, Paul?" Martine asked.

"No, I can manage," he said. He and Marine sat on the floor which was covered from wall to wall with a white cloth. He looked at the figure and again felt the full force of those strangely wonderful eyes. They held his attention.

There was a long silence, and the calm voice said, "No, I am not the stranger you are seeking, Mr. Fraser."

He felt another shock, for it was as if his mind had been read. But it lasted for only a moment or two, because, automatically, he assessed the stage effect of such an opening remark. He smiled and kept his voice unimpressed, light. "Then perhaps you can tell me where to find this stranger?"

"I can," the voice said. "The stranger is yourself."

He thought that over. The deep eyes were gentle and receptive, but there was no expression on the serene face. He was strongly, oddly, impressed, but he was determined not to show it. He forced a laugh. "I can understand that," he said. "I see the value of getting to know one's self, but isn't that something all men are continually trying to do?"

"No, Mr. Fraser. Man's first true instinct is to know himself, but in the pursuit of other knowledge he begins to concentrate on objects which are distant and alien. Only on rare and fortunate occasions does he return to contemplate that which is his own and near. Then he suffers and asks why he wandered from himself. Yet his wanderings have served a purpose. Because he cannot ever know himself while he knows only himself. It is always so. Man cannot know God above unless he knows the world below." It was strange what a lulling effect the voice had. He had to exert himself to resist it.

"Is that always the answer?" he asked. "Is religion the only way to know one's self?"

"It is the most direct path. The way of man is known only so far as the way of God is known. To learn the identity of the two ways is the supreme lesson of life."

"But there are many religions," he said. "May I ask what is your belief?"

"I am a child of God."

"Is any religion good, then, if one believes in God?"

"It need not always be so. Religion is not necessarily good. It may be evil. Some of mankind's most degrading customs, hysteria, bigotry, can be attributed to religion. It often is a

178 . . .

popular refuge of human indifference. It is not religions which go unto God, but men who use them as a means of salvation. Religion is good only when it leads to truth. For once man has learned truth he cannot be sustained by any power which is separate from truth."

"Ah!" he said brightly, a bit too brightly. "That brings up an old question. How is one to know truth? It means different things to different people. What is truth?"

The voice did not change, but he sensed a reprimand. "That is an excuse man perpetually uses when he wishes to escape the effects of his evil or indifference. For he knows truth is vulnerable only when one tries to explain or defend it. Truth is absolute. Truth is righteousness. You recognize untruth. Why do you not know truth?"

He could not be sure whether it was a question or a statement. There was no change on the serene face, no quirking of the mouth, no lifting of the eyebrows; no gestures of his beautifully molded hands—none of the signs which one depends on to interpret meaning. He had never heard such a voice. It never lost its softness, was absolutely devoid of emphasis or dramatic effects. It never faltered. He realized he was being childish with his trite, carping questions. "I am not certain I always do recognize untruth," he said sincerely.

"Whatever is worthless, unclean, unjust, unholy, and evil is above all else untrue. The pursuit of it is the pursuit of delusion."

"Is that why you came to India? Is it the best place to find the meaning of truth?"

"No, Mr. Fraser, truth is everywhere, just as God is everywhere. Men are misled because their kindred appetites for speaking only what is new and hearing only what is new has replaced the old passion for searching into what is true. In India the path merely is made smoother for those who seek truth."

Did he detect more benevolence in that apparently unchanging voice? More understanding? For the first time he forgot the presence of Martine and the two young men. He said earnestly, "I am interested in that. Very interested. In what way is it made smoother?"

"Renunciation and meditation are made easier for the novice. There are fewer temptations. There is wisdom for those who seek diligently. There are many teachers. India allows those who search to walk in peace. You do not place your writing table on a busy avenue, Mr. Fraser. You find a proper place to do your writing. So it is with those who seek truth. They must find conditions under which to purify the body, life, and mind. For only when the frame is perfected does the light shine through without obstruction."

"But aren't there some mysteries hidden here, some secrets which belong to India alone?"

"There are no mysteries anywhere. They exist only in the minds of those blinded by the disease of ignorance. The wireless is a mystery to the child who does not understand its workings."

He thought about that. "But only the Divine understands everything," he said. It was not an argument, but a question.

"The mind is an instrument of the Divine. With it we comprehend what we behold. Supreme happiness comes to those whose minds are peaceful, who have quenched their passions, who have abandoned all selfish desires, and who have become one with God."

"Some men have the ability or vocation for that," he said. "But how does an ordinary man go about suppressing natural desires and becoming indifferent to doubts and worries?"

"One begins by discovering oneself so that ego can be effaced and contact made with the Eternal. When that is done, as the *Gita* says, one becomes as undisturbed as a lamp placed in a windless place. One achieves humility, integrity, and becomes nonviolent, patient, upright, pure of body and mind, steadfast, and self-controlled. God bears the burdens and cares of those who worship Him. If we love God as we should, we do not have leisure to do evil or question His will."

"Yes, I can see that," he said slowly. "But if one withdraws completely from the world, aren't many good and precious things lost also?"

"There is no life worthy to be called life entirely separate from joy and gladness. As a man learns the pleasures of childhood were often superficial and meaningless, so does he learn that pleasures he experienced before he achieved union with God were but poor substitutes for true happiness."

He was aware now only of that calm figure, that magnificent voice. "Will you define God for me?"

"God is not a subject for explanation or dialectic, Mr. Fraser —a possibility, an inspiration, or a nebulous hope. God's light dwells in the self and nowhere else. It shines alike in every living being and one can truly see it only when one's mind is steadied. God is a living and vivid reality in which we are in constant touch, and Whose presence we can feel if we are willing to pay the price in self-control and discipline. Some do not have the urge to seek Him. Others are hindered by their doubts and weaknesses. Some are frightened away by the difficulties. But for those who are willing to make the sacrifice, He is always there. Many are the men who have found His illuminating grace, Hindus and Buddhists, Christians and Muslims."

He sat silently, looking directly at the peaceful face. He felt something—some indefinable something he had not felt for years. "I think I know about that illuminating grace," he said, slowly. "I knew it when I was young. But I lost it somehow. Tell me how I can go about regaining it?"

"You will return tomorrow, Mr. Fraser."

Again, he could not decide whether it was a question or a statement. The deep and compelling eyes seemingly were unchanged, but once more he felt as if he had been given an affectionate smile. He knew he was being dismissed, and he felt a deep regret. There were so many things he wanted to ask. "I should like to return if I may," he said.

He was pleased . . . no, relieved, when the voice said, "You are always welcome here." There was a brief silence, and then the calm voice said, "In each man there are two natures, the good and the evil. But every man does not gravitate to one or the other and become divinely good or diabolically evil. Some men choose the path of damnable indifference. They believe that life is a time to satisfy all their foolish and vain desires, for death is the end of all existence and nothing lies beyond. They are not cursed, nor are they saved. They suffer more than most men."

He sat silently. He knew this remarkable man somehow knew him perfectly.

After they were back in the car, it was a long time before he spoke. He felt he should make some quip, say something light to hide how he felt. But what he finally said was, "I was impressed. I must confess I never have met anyone quite like him."

"I knew you would be," she said.

He made a helpless little gesture. "It was not so much what he said, though I thought it was wise and perceptive. It was the way he said it. He spoke as if he had some deep and sure knowledge. I felt that he knew what I was going to ask even before I found the words."

"That is one of his characteristics," she said. "Another is that he never speaks only to make conversation. He never asks questions. One somehow has the feeling that they are unnecessary. He does not observe even the ordinary social amenities."

"He did say something pleasant when I arrived," he said.

"He said that you were welcome. It was a statement of fact and he does not use it with all visitors. He did not ask you how you were, or how you liked India, or how long you would remain. I often think about him when I am forced to carry on small talk. He has taught me how banal and useless most conversations really are. We spend most of our lives, even with people we know best, discussing things which are frivolous or inconsequential."

After a silence, she said, "It was the first noticeable change

182 . . .

in him after his accident. He always had a captivating insouciance. People smiled and brightened when he entered a room. He loved to drink and argue with his friends. His students were wild about him because he used to say ridiculous things to provoke them into arguments. Like all men with great charm, he relied on his charm heavily, perhaps too heavily. He had a marvelously expressive voice and he used it skillfully. I used to think that he would have been a great actor."

"He still has one of the most unusual voices I have ever heard," he said.

"Yes, but now it is unusual for a different reason. I have never heard it lose its calmness. One knows that he has completely erased all passion, any anxiety to please, a wish to impress. Perhaps you noticed that he never pauses to reflect; he never uses qualifying phrases. It is almost as if his words follow an open channel directly from his mind. One knows that he could not lie or deceive. Before, one could never be sure."

"Tell me more about what he was like before."

"What would you like to know?"

"Was he a passionate man?"

"As a lover or in other ways?"

"In all ways."

She sat silently, thinking, before she spoke. "Yes, I suppose one would call him passionate. He was easily upset and moody when we were alone, and he had a violent temper when he was aroused. He could hate blindly. Even the sight of German soldiers in news films made him grow rigid with anger. He also had what the English like to call a social conscience, though he was never directly interested in politics and had a contempt for politicians. He was a sensuous and sensitive lover—perhaps too much so, if that is possible. It was as—well, as if he could never give himself completely because he took too much pride in his skill and virtuosity. But perhaps I am doing him an injustice. For I cannot forget he had an unerring instinct, almost a feminine instinct, for knowing how to wound a woman. Once, after we had been married for only a short time, we went to a country place we had outside Paris. He became enraged over some trifle, and for once I was not as contrite as he had expected me to be. He waited until we were in bed and then casually told me that I was the third woman he had brought there. I cannot tell you how much it hurt me."

"That makes him sound pretty unsavory."

"Does it? Then I am sorry I said it, because he was not an unsavory person. Over the years, I have come to realize that compared with most men, he fundamentally was good and extraordinarily sensitive. He was only thoughtless and spoiled, never evil."

He looked at her somber face, the shadow in her dark eyes, and placed his hand on hers. "I understand a lot of things now, Martine. I . . . well, I understand about last night." He smiled. "I may not altogether approve, but I understand." They rode in silence for a while, and he sighed. "I can see how impossible it would be simply to walk away from such a man and pretend he doesn't exist. Somehow it seems pretty ridiculous to talk about divorcing him. In some vague way, I even know why he would inhibit you . . . why you haven't been able to find somebody else." He turned, meaning to give her a wry smile, but when he looked into her lovely face, had an awareness of the full womanliness of her, he felt a flash of indignation. "But it's still damned unfair. You didn't renounce the world. He did. You're not a recluse in an ashram. He is. You have a right to your own life."

She studied his face, and her small smile was both amused and tender. "Are you now trying to help me, Paul?" she asked.

He shrugged, and then he saw the humor of it. He smiled. "Why not?"

"I'm not unhappy, Paul," she said. "On the contrary, I am grateful that I have such a good life. There was a time when it wasn't so, but now I have a peaceful life." There was a touch of laughter in her voice. "My life has not become less happy because I have grown fond of you. You must not feel sorry for

184 . . .

me because you tempted me, and I did not succumb completely."

He grinned. "I don't. I even forgive you." They sat smiling at each other, and he said, "Someday I really must remember to sit down and decide exactly how I do feel about sex—try to sort out fact from fancy. I know I wouldn't care to live a life of celibacy. God forbid. I'm all in favor of sex. I'm afraid I'm not up on the latest psychology on the subject, but I stick to the old-fashioned and trite notion that you really can't overrate sex when two people are in love. A good sexual relationship may not preserve love, but a bad one certainly can destroy it. Even so, now that I'm forty-six, my ideas about sex aren't quite the same as they were when I was younger. For one thing, I've learned that it's only in bad novels and arty Scandinavian movies that lusty males stalk about covering panting females and cause fireworks to explode in the sky." He smiled. "Maybe I shouldn't admit it, but all the commotion about sex bores me silly. Oh, I don't mean just the dirty books and plays, and the nudie shows and the girlie magazines. They just offend my taste. I mean the whole simpering or earnest preoccupation with eroticism nowadays—the stupid, false mystique. It makes me wonder if most people really know what sex is all about. I find people who make such a thing of it a little suspect. Most of my adult life has been spent in a business where there's a lot of bed-hopping, and I do know for a fact that the people who indulge in it the most have the least appreciation of it. When you reach a point where you enjoy a little sex as casually as taking a drink, or eating a meal, there's something wrong—and I don't mean morally."

She smiled. "I think you are right. But I seldom equate ordinary sexual behavior with morality."

That surprised him. "What do you equate it with?"

She shrugged. "I'm not quite sure. With customs, perhaps. Or cultural mores." She smiled. "Perhaps only with biology."

He laughed. "That's what most of us equate it with, but I thought you . . ."

"I am married," she said, quietly. "I took vows before God that I would remain faithful to my husband. And I did so without reservation. I was not merely following a ritual. Being an adultress is not the same as merely being unchaste." She paused. "Most of the great religions have commandments against adultery. Few of them agree, or are too specific, about sexual behavior otherwise." She gave him her small smile, but her eyes were serious. "That's what I have been contriving to tell you. I want you to understand."

"I thought I did understand," he said. "But I guess I didn't. Are you telling me that your primary concern is with some pact you made with God, instead of some inhibitions you feel because of your husband?"

"Essentially that is what I mean," she said.

He felt a stab of annoyance that was close to anger, but he made his voice amused. "Then essentially you're as superstitious as a Neapolitan peasant woman, aren't you? Maybe you should deck yourself out in a stiff black dress and black stockings."

When she did not answer, but continued to look at him calmly, he said impatiently, "Do you really believe that God cares, or even knows, about your marriage vows?"

"He knows and cares what we all do," she said quietly.

He barely restrained an angry snort. Instead, he looked out the window. He thought about that strange figure back at the ashram. It irritated him now to remember how he had fallen under the spell of those penetrating blue eyes and that compelling voice. He turned. "What does André do, anyway?"

"I don't understand," she said.

He sensed amusement in her voice. It nettled him. "Well, he doesn't just sit in the lotus position all the times, does he? He must teach or preach, or walk around, impressing the natives. Doesn't he ever eat or sleep—or go to the toilet?"

She smiled slightly. "I do not know all the things he does. But, no, he is not a teacher or a preacher. He sometimes sees visitors, as he saw you today; but not very often. He leaves the ashram only for a month each year when he goes to Muza-puram, a small town, about thirty miles away. He maintains another ashram there, an old house in the poorest district of the town." She paused. "I am not certain why André feels it is his duty to go to Muzapuram. He makes the journey on foot, and it has turned into a kind of pilgrimage. I suppose he chose Muzapuram because it is such an ugly town—perhaps the ugliest in India."

He grunted. "That's saying quite a lot."

Her face remained serious. "I do not mean ugly in appearance. It looks like an ordinary small town, except that it is predominantly Muslim. It is ugly because it is the home of a fanatical sect of Muslims who call themselves the Seed of Husain. They have a long history of violence. André goes there during a religious festival they hold each year. There is often trouble between the Hindus and Muslims, and I suppose he feels his presence in Muzapuram is beneficial."

She turned, and made a helpless gesture. "I cannot tell you a great deal about his daily schedule. Members of the ashram say he never sleeps. Perhaps he does not in the ordinary way, or in the ordinary sense. He eats so little that it is a wonder he remains alive: a small cup of milk with a spoonful of honey in it in the mornings, a cup of curds, or a few spoonfuls of rice or greens, in the evenings. He is, of course, a strict vegetarian, as are all members of the ashram. Most of them will not even use products made of leather. They went barefoot until I ordered a supply of canvas shoes. You may have noticed Pandit Coomaraswamy was wearing a pair today. I think André follows a regimen of yoga exercises for physical fitness. But I am not sure it is entirely separate from jnana yoga which he practices for all except a few hours of each day." She looked at him. "Jnana yoga, as you may know, is the yogi discipline of meditation and knowledge. He uses its power so he can spend most of his time in union with God. When he is in this state, called samdhi, he appears to be in a trance. He simply leaves the world until he chooses to return."

He looked at her serious face and shook his head. "No, Martine," he said gently, "he is a remarkable man, and somehow . . . in some way, he has found an extraordinary peace of mind and soul. But he doesn't have supernatural powers. He doesn't actually commune directly with God. He's still only a man."

She accepted this rebuff without a change of expression. "You do not yet understand, Paul," she said. "Genuine sannyasins, or holy men, are comparatively rare here, but they are not unique. There are several, besides André, who are recognized at the present time. No one knows how many there are who are unknown."

"But I think I do understand," he said. "I understand how mystics often become unusual and impressive people. I told you I was impressed by André. I sensed that he had somehow acquired remarkable powers." He smiled. "But I still do not believe that men communicate directly with God. Perhaps because of certain practices or austerities they sometimes honestly think they do, feel they do. When I was a young man, a student, one of the things drilled into me was that religious truth is developed from knowledge acquired when our ordinary senses and intellects are under the highest discipline. To move one step away from this, to go blundering off into the dark areas of abnormal psychology, is actually to abandon any real foundation for religious belief."

"I believe that also," she said. "Where we differ is that there are rare and wondrous ways of disciplining the senses and intellect that only a few men acquire." She shrugged. "At any rate, there is always one sure way of telling genuine sannyasins."

"What is that?"

"Well, besides showing unusual gifts, they change completely. Religious fanatics, or poor sick people who suffer hallucinations or delusions, seldom change, except perhaps to become more fanatical or addled. But anyone who has ever known a genuine sannyasin can tell you that his character has been transformed miraculously. A sannyasin acquires a strange and wonderful serenity which comes from purity and goodness, a composure that comes from wisdom. And you can tell, you simply know, that his compassion is limitless."

He looked at her smiling, as she sat looking down at her hands, apparently in deep thought. Finally, she looked up, and when she saw his face she smiled back. She placed her hand on his. "Paul, why don't you go to the ashram for a visit? Spend some time with André. Sit with him, and talk with him. I think there are many things you will find that are interesting and worthwhile."

"You mean stay there?" he asked, surprised.

She smiled. "Why not? For a few days—a week. It will be another fortnight before André goes to Muzapuram."

"But I don't . . ." he began.

"Pandit Coomaraswamy will arrange a hut for you," she said. "You will find everything very plain, even primitive, but you shouldn't find it unbearable for a few days. You can take your own food along, if you wish. Everything is quite clean, really. There is no danger."

He was half-amused, half-annoyed. "Oh, for Heaven's sake, I'm not so effete I can't rough it for a few days." He thought about it for a moment or two. "But what about the other people—won't I get in the way, interfere with their routine?"

"Certainly not," she said, surprised. "They are also there only temporarily."

"You mean they haven't taken vows, or something? They aren't permanent members of the ashram?"

She smiled. "No. Only Pandit Coomaraswamy, and Munoo, the sweeper, and his family, remain all the time. The others come and go."

"Where do they all come from?"

She shrugged. "It is difficult to say. The young men with André today probably were students from Benares University. There are always a few of them around. "The others?" She shrugged. "Who knows? There are thousands, perhaps, even millions, of them constantly drifting around India, looking for a *guru* or master. All of them are intensely religious, and except for an occasional eccentric, they are serious and hardworking and probably above the average in intelligence."

"No one is turned away?"

"Never," she said.

"But why isn't the ashram swamped by beggars and ne'er-do-wells?"

"I don't know," she said. "It just doesn't happen. Rarely does anyone even beg for food. I suppose it is a holdover from the days when it was considered a sin to ask charity from Brahmans. Maybe it is for the same reason ne'er-do-wells are not a problem at religious retreats in European countries." She paused thoughtfully. "You know, originally there was only a single mud hut where the ashram now stands. Old Pandit Coomaraswamy brought André there. It was where I first found them more than seven years after André's disappearance."

"Where do you suppose he went for all that time?"

She shook her head. "I don't know. In the wilderness . . . somewhere in the Himalayas, I suppose." After a short silence, she said, "News that a new Holy Man, a European, had arrived caused tremendous excitement that first year. On some days thousands were camped around the hut, waiting to catch a glimpse of him. One young Brahman insisted on being his sweeper. A young Hindu girl appeared with a notebook and took down every word he uttered."

"How did he react to all that?"

She shrugged. "As he reacts now—kind and gentle and, somehow, untouched by it all. I was still unaccustomed to . . . to the way he had become. I suppose my main concern still was to try and persuade him to return home. I . . . I—well, I simply did not understand. One day when the crowd was especially heavy, I said to him, 'Why don't you speak to them and send them away?' He said, 'They are my children.' I said, 'But they think you are a god or something.' I shall never forget how softly and sweetly he answered, 'A father does not tell his children how unworthy he is. He tries to merit their respect.'"

He sat silently, thinking that over, toying with the possibility of staying at the ashram for a few days. Why not? It would be a novel experience, and though he did not like to admit it even to himself, he was utterly fascinated by that strange man. He knew he had to learn more about him. Finally, he said, "Maybe I will try to stay at the ashram for a day or two. I'll ask Bhaiji about it tomorrow."

She smiled. "I am glad. I know he will welcome you." She studied his face and her dark eyes were bright with amusement. "There are some rules at the ashram, of course," she said. "By custom, visitors are expected to observe *Bramachari*."

"What on earth is that?"

She laughed. "Strictly speaking, it means keeping one's sexual desires under control. In actual practice, it means observing celibacy."

He grinned. "It seems a harsh rule, but I'll try not to break it. Anyway, it's just for a day or two."

FOURTEEN . . .

As Sixteen drove him out to the ashram, he was preoccupied, almost grumpy. He was strangely excited
by the prospect of seeing Bhaiji again—and it annoyed, even angered, him. Twice during the night, he had
awakened and each time he had thought about that calm, sure
voice and those depthless blue eyes. In some way he had felt
oddly reassured, almost as if he had found the solution to a
problem that was bothering him. Now as he sat in the front
seat of the car on a sunshiny morning, idly looking at the passing fields of cane, noting the old men placidly sitting in the
shade of banyan trees with their hookahs and grandchildren,
watching the young men trudging away on water wheels, he
thought about how preposterous his feelings were. Finally, as
usual, he tried to find refuge in levity. He turned to Sixteen
and smiled, "Bhaiji puts on quite a performance, Sixteen. Did
you ever see him?"

Sixteen shook his head. "No, sir. He very good man, sir.
Very holy."

He laughed. "How do you know, Sixteen?"

He was a bit disappointed when the loyal Sixteen said firmly,
"All people know, sir. Bhaiji do much good. He no fake like
bad mans at temple. Very holy man, sir."

When the car stopped in the compound, the children ran
squealing toward it. When they saw Martine had not come
they halted at a distance and stood regarding him solemnly.
But Pandit Coomaraswamy was as cheerfully brisk as he had
been the day before. He came bustling from his hut with a big

smile and greeted him in his rich English accent. "You are to go right in, sir," he said. "Bhaiji is expecting you." He smiled, wondering if the old Pandit never varied this old gimmick. As he removed his shoes on the verandah, he reminded himself firmly that he would not be as impressed as he had been the first time. But when he stepped into that large, bright room and saw Bhaiji's straight and serene figure, again felt the indescribable power and gentleness in his penetrating eyes, he suddenly felt humble as a child.

It was a long time before Bhaiji spoke, but as before, he felt that he had received an affectionate greeting. "I am glad you have resisted doubts and selfish desires and have returned," the voice said. "There is love and understanding for you here." Without moving or shifting his gaze, Bhaiji said something in Hindi. The two young Indians arose and quietly left the room.

Again there was a long silence. As he looked into those deep, unwavering eyes, he felt they were seeking out all his secrets. Automatically, he forced himself to resist. *He's only a Frenchman*, he said to himself firmly—*only a Frenchman in a dhoti*.

Bhaiji's eyes closed and the almost flat, unhurried voice said, "When one has become disabled for unlearning, one also is disabled for learning. Disbelief in the possibility of wisdom and a belief in the limitation of knowledge is a blindness which afflicts men who do not wish to improve themselves. The chasm between the human question and the divine answer is never bridged by one who says it cannot be done. It requires an unskeptical and dedicated mind. For the answer is never given to satisfy idle curiosity, but to raise man's thoughts."

He suddenly felt contrite. How could he any longer doubt that this strange man knew what he was thinking? He said quietly, apologetically, "I do wish to learn. That is why I have come."

After a short silence, the eyes opened and once again he felt that he had received a kindly smile though the serene face remained unchanged. The lulling voice said, "We are all brothers, Mr. Fraser, so I will call you brother. I will speak to you first of man's relation to the world. If you do not at the beginning comprehend fully, do not despair. Truth always sends forth a feeble light, but as a man advances the light grows in illumination. At each stage, he sees a little beyond what he has attained, but never much more. Fresh insight comes only as a result of fresh attainment. Knowledge like righteousness always grows slowly.

"The world as man now knows it is only an effect of God. For God is the cause, and the cause always is more real than the effect. To the extent that man fails to perceive the Divine cause, the world becomes unrelated to God and is a source of delusion. To achieve full reality, man must never forget the Divine essence in everything which exists.

"Reality is absolute, infinite, and possessed of its own unity and bliss. Few mortals achieve reality because of dualities and oppositions which arise in their nature and shut them off from the truth. But it can be attained by those who strive for it and acquire the necessary qualities for success.

"The order God has created is unalterable, unchanging. The entire cosmic process is divided into five stages. First there is matter, then life, then mind, then intelligence, and, finally, bliss. Mankind as a whole has reached the fourth stage in this process, that of intelligence. But man still is not in full control of his acts. He is propelled by an inner direction given to things because they are but a part of the creative onrush of life. Man has learned to know matter, life and mind during the comparatively short period he has existed. He has gained control to a large extent of the material world. He understands dimly the vitality hidden within his mentality, but he has not yet reached the stage where he can achieve easily the next stage, the completely illumined higher and divine life. As matter has been succeeded by life, life by mind, and mind by intelligence, he eventually will do so because progression is an impulse of nature. It is God's purpose that he should do so.

"Mankind, in general, still does not realize it possesses the ability to break forth from its bondage and realize a Oneness with the Divine. Man still is shackled by his ignorance, his desire to live in a world which is only illusion, and which will remain an illusion as long as he sees only the effect and not the Cause. It is only through struggle and sacrifice that man can give his nature the ability to strike off the enslavement of the object world and reach enlightenment by seeing the Cause. Nothing forces this process on man. Even God seldom compels man to remove the scales from his eyes. He does not interfere with man's development because the aim of His creation is the production of selves who will by their own volition freely carry out His will. God merely endows man with an instinct to control his base impulses, to quell his lustful appetites, to stop his wanderings and shake off his confusion. Yet the very imperfections of the human soul belong to it as a necessity if man perpetually is to seek the truth.

"Final perfection is a task that must be accomplished with conscious endeavor and sacrifice. Again God gives man guidance by producing in him a sense of insufficiency, by making him realize the impermanence and precariousness of human happiness. There are those who become hardened or indifferent to the laceration of spirit. They choose to live on the surface of life. They do not always realize that by doing so they renounce the true dignity of the human spirit. They are born, they enjoy or suffer as is given to them because of their abilities, and they die. They do not answer the promptings in their nature to cleanse the soul of its defilement and kindle the spiritual vision. They ignore their natures by indulging in more pleasures, by throwing themselves more fully into the world of illusion."

The lulling voice stopped. Bhaiji sat motionless. After a long silence, he resumed. "Yours is not the way of a yogi, brother. Your destiny is not total renunciation. Your need is to shake off cynical compromise and become a man of settled goodness. If a man falls victim to his impulses, his life becomes aimless and devoid of intelligence. So long as he acts in certain ways merely because they give him pleasure, and abstains from others merely because he dislikes them, he is bound by his actions to an illusory course. A man must overcome these impulses and act from a sense of duty. The duly rendered service of truth is discipline. Human freedom is only conditioned, it is not lost because of a sense of duty. One has to understand what duty is. Likewise one has to learn what inaction is, before one can put it aside. Plotinus said, 'Out of discussion we call to vision, to those desiring to see we point the path, our teaching is a guiding in the way, the seeing must be the very act of him who has made the choice.' It is man's duty to make his outward life reflect his inward being, to follow the good and pure, to be content with simple things, to cast away selfishness and pride, to have a mind at peace.

"It is harmful for a man to work beyond the level of his nature. But within the power of his nature, he must live up fully to his duty. Swine are not evil beasts, but when men behave like swine we call them evil. It is not because their actions are more evil than those of swine. The evil of the degradation lies in the comparison of what is with what might have been.

"It is not given to some men to withdraw from the world or seek a destruction of the senses of the world. The Gita tells us that to hate the senses is as wrong as to love them. The horses of senses are not to be unyoked from the chariot but controlled by the reins of the mind. The Gita also tells us, 'He unto whom all desires enter as waters into the sea, which, though ever being filled is ever motionless, attains to peace and not he who hugs his desires.'"

There was a long silence. The face remained serene, but he felt that strange inward glow, as if he had been given a warm smile.

"You will return, brother."

"Yes, I will return," he said. He paused. "I wish to return and live at the ashram for a while, if I may."

Was he mistaken, or was there more warmth in the voice?

"Come and depart as you wish. Our love and understanding will abide with you. You are a follower of Jesus Christ. Heed

His teachings and you shall meet God. But remember, my brother, that religion is merely a system of general truths which becomes a force of belief. What emerges from religion is individual worth of character. Such worth may be good or bad. In your religious belief take heed that the God with whom you make terms is not a God of destruction, a God who leaves in His wake the loss of a greater reality. Do not be beguiled by the enthusiasms or trappings of religions in their passing forms. Accept Jesus Christ alone as your Teacher. Regard with caution ambitious or fanatical men who profess to speak in His name. Devote a part of each day to reading the words of Jesus, study His words, live with His words, absorb His words until they become part of your being. If you do this, brother, then surely you will realize His promise: 'Ask, and it shall be given you: seek and ye shall find: knock and it shall be opened to you. For every one that asketh receiveth: and he that seeketh findeth: and to him that knocketh it shall be opened.' "

"I will do that," he said.

But he was not certain whether Bhaiji heard. He sat silent and motionless, and his eyes were closed.

PART
3

FIFTEEN . . .

He was awakened by the tinkling of a bell. He heard
the rattle of a lantern, the soft shuffling of bare feet
on packed earth, and then the slow clapping of hands.
Old Pandit Coomaraswamy's voice, wavery and reedy, utterly
devoid of its usual polished accents, began the refrain, *"Ram,
Ram Sri, Sri, Hari . . ."* The other voices picked it up rag-
gedly, *"Narayan, Narayan, Sri Krishna, Sri Krishna . . ."*
He opened his eyes and stared into the darkness, listening.
*". . . Hey Hanuman jodah, Kali Mai, Om, Om, Shanti De-
va . . ."* They were chanting the names of the Hindu deities.
It would soon be four o'clock. If Panditji did not feel particularly devout and decide to praise the lesser gods, morning prayers were coming to an end.

He became aware that one of the heavy cords of the *charpoy*
was biting into his shoulder. He winced and shifted his weight,
and then smiled. Every morning when he first awakened, he
always had a feeling of amused disbelief to find himself here,
living in a mud hut, sleeping on a rope bed. But it was worth
it—yes, definitely worth it. He stretched his muscles and closed
his eyes, luxuriating in peaceful lassitude, listening while the
chanting reached a crescendo and abruptly halted.

He could not explain what had happened to him during the
last eleven—no, twelve days. It bothered him when he thought
about it, as he did now, lying half-asleep, again hearing the soft
pad of feet and the flap of sandals as the prayer meeting broke
up. Nobody spoke, for the ashram observed silence until sun-
rise. How could he ever make sense out of all this to his

friends? He could see their slow, wise smiles, imagine their clever quips. And he couldn't blame them . . . not really. Once he would have reacted the same way.

Most of all, how could he explain Bhaiji? What would Cynthia say if he told her that each morning he removed his shoes, sat crosslegged at the feet of a half-naked Frenchman, and came away feeling . . . well, exalted. Feeling as though his soul had been freshly laundered and starched. For the first time in his life he now knew what his father had meant when he used to say that religion was a force of belief cleansing the inward parts. How could he possibly explain? He did not really understand himself. He only knew that Bhaiji affected him in a way no other human being ever had. When he was in Bhaiji's presence he seemed to absorb some of his unbelievably radiant peace and goodness. He had tried to rationalize it— God knows, he had tried. He had thought about it for hours. Several times he had tried to put it down on paper. But words were more than futile; they looked ridiculous, either corny or embarrassingly overblown.

How could he say that being with Bhaiji gave him a feeling that was similar, but not quite the same, as the stilly awe he had sometimes felt when he walked through a deserted cathedral; only magnified a hundredfold. No, that not only was corny, but not even right. In his gropings, he had wondered if what he felt could be explained in terms of the *Numinous*. Maybe when he had a chance to do some reading on the subject, he would discover that it could. It was odd—the things a man could dredge up out of his memory. He was positive he had not so much as heard the word *Numinous* for nearly thirty years. Yet, one night when it suddenly did crop up in his mind, there had been an almost dizzying onrush of memories. It was almost as if he was actually back in Lecture Hall A in Martha McDowell Memorial Annex; lolling back, stupid with boredom, listening to old Dr. Lokey droning away, his Adam's apple bobbing up and down over the edge of his stiff collar, a patch of toilet paper sticking to a razor cut on his chin. "Gentlemen, if I told you there was an insane murderer roaming the corridors of this building, you would feel endangered and undoubtedly feel fear. But suppose I told you this building was haunted and you believed it. You would also feel fear, but of a different kind, for nobody is normally afraid of what ghosts may do to him, but only of the fact that ghosts do exist and are present. This particular kind of fear which is devoid of a sense of actual danger might be described as Dread. Now, if you understand Dread, you are in a position to understand the experience of the *Numinous*. For suppose I told you that there was a mighty supernatural spirit in this building, and you believed me. You would not have a fear of danger, nor would you feel Dread. Yet you would be profoundly disturbed; filled with a sense of wonder for the visitant, perhaps even worshipful wonder, and, at the same time, feel a shrinking, an inability to cope with it. Gentlemen, that feeling is known as awe, and the phenomenon which arouses it is the *Numinous*."

But could a man cause another to experience the *Numinous*? He didn't think so. Besides, the awe he felt in Bhaiji's presence wasn't entirely from without. It was something he felt inside —something that ignored all the prickly defenses he had built over the years to protect his ego. When he was with Bhaiji, he was overwhelmed by the depth of his own unselfconscious, simple . . . well, sincerity. Sincerity was the primary religious virtue, wasn't it? He simply hadn't dreamt he was capable of such a penetrating sincerity. But he was, and perhaps it was because he hadn't realized it for so long that he had felt so utterly forsaken, even by God.

He lay thinking about that. It was not what Bhaiji said that had caused him . . . that had brought him this marvelous quietude. His calm discourses helped—they helped immeasurably. Everything Bhaiji said was wise and satisfying, and often impressively revealing. But he gradually had come to realize that what Bhaiji said only helped dispel his doubts; Bhaiji really strengthened his basic beliefs, confirmed things he had felt all along but forgotten or ignored. Each morning when he left

Bhaiji he returned to the hut and wrote down in a journal he was keeping the things Bhaiji had said that impressed him most. He had already filled the pages in his memo book, and had nearly half filled a cheap composition book that Munoo, the sweeper, had bought for him in the village. He was always astounded how easily he transcribed Bhaiji's words. He had only to settle himself, think of that serene face, and the words seemed to flow almost automatically from his pencil. But even more astounding, he had discovered how little he even wanted to write down. Questions that had been bothering him before he went in to see Bhaiji, doubts that had accumulated, had somehow already been answered and swept away. Bhaiji had spoken; he had accepted and absorbed. Problems that only an hour ago had seemed so puzzling were no longer even worth recording. He no longer questioned, or even found it odd, that Bhaiji knew fully what he was thinking. But that was only a small part of Bhaiji's mysterious power. When he was in Bhaiji's presence, he—well, his soul was quickened and his intuitions were confirmed.

Bhaiji dispelled his doubts, and . . . he smiled . . . well, Pandit Coomaraswamy kindled them. It seemed inconceivable that he could ever have so stupidly underestimated Panditji —that dear old man with his urbanity, his understanding, his sharp and well-decorated mind. He had begun to appreciate Panditji on his first morning at the ashram. He had been seated in the barren dining room, politely picking at a bowl of cracked rice, glumly berating himself for not packing a supply of powdered coffee, when Panditji bustled in, teeth and spectacles gleaming. Panditji greeted him, and glanced down at his bowl of rice. He leaned forward confidentially. "Mr. Fraser, I have a confession to make. I am a weak and frail vessel. I cannot always practice the austerities imposed here at the ashram. I have an especial weakness for tea, and I keep a secret cache in the kichen. May I offer you a cup?" He grinned at Panditji. "I would love it." So every morning since, plump little Lakshmi, the Untouchable girl who waited table in the dining room, had served him a cup of strong, black and hot Indian tea with his breakfast. But Panditji had never joined him in having a cup.

Panditji had also come to his rescue about the matter of baths. For his first two days at the ashram, he simply did not bathe. He settled for shaving, washing his face and hands, and brushing his teeth, with water from a small earthenware jug in his hut. Going unbathed seemed preferable to joining other members for their communal ablutions. Besides little Lakshmi, Munoo, the sweeper, and Janki, his wife, and their six children, there were more than a half-dozen other people at the ashram whom he had not yet sorted out. Each morning, shortly after sunup, all of them, young and old, gathered at the well in the center of the courtyard for a bath. It was not a festive occasion. Solemnly, effortlessly, they unwound and shifted their *dhotis* and saris, keeping themselves modestly covered, while pouring water over their heads from small copper pots. He shrank at the thought of joining them. He felt he couldn't manage it; besides, he didn't have a *dhoti*. Pride prevented him from asking Munoo to bring water to his hut. As the only Westerner, he was not going to seek special privileges. He was annoyed with himself for sending Sixteen back to Benares with Martine. At least, Sixteen could have driven him somewhere for a bath.

Finally, on the third morning, after the others had left, he strode down to the well, a towel girding his loins under his terry robe. He was splashing himself vigorously, if unsatisfactorily, when he looked up and discovered he had an audience. Nearly everybody, from Munoo's small children to Sher Singh, the aged and toothless old cowherd, were watching him with the frankest and most solemn interest. Panditji was not in the crowd, but he must have heard about it. That afternoon he found a large wooden tub in his hut; each morning since then Munoo had been bringing him two pails of hot water.

Actually, living at the ashram had not been nearly as rigorous as he had expected. The food was plain, but surprisingly appetizing, though unvarying. For breakfast he had his tea and a bowl of cracked rice, topped with a gob of sticky palm molasses, called *gur*. At luncheon was also rice, two vegetables, generally cauliflower and a soupy lentil, called *dal*, as well as buckwheat *chapatis* dripping with *ghee*, and usually a tartly delicious concoction of lemons and ginger mixed with strained butter and the juice of aloe. There was also a tray of fruit—small finger-sized Indian bananas, oranges and, sometimes, fresh lechee nuts or sweet lemons—from which members of the ashram helped themselves. Martine had told him that only two meals a day would be served, but this turned out not to be altogether correct. After evening prayers, everybody drifted back to the dining room where Lakshmi had laid out more fruit and *chapatis*. They were also free to help themselves from a large container of *curds*, a kind of clabbered milk tasting like a mixture of yoghurt and buttermilk, which he had grown to love. Food simply was not a problem; even, oddly enough, the lack of meat in his diet. Except for breaking out half a dozen chocolate bars for the children, he had not touched the musette bag which Sixteen had packed with canned goods and other edibles before he left Benares.

The thing he missed most was chairs. He had discovered long before that it took a special set of muscles to sit on the floor Indian-style. He still had not developed them fully, but he was making progress. For the first week he was stiff and sore. Fortunately, there was a single table with benches in the dining room—put there especially for Westerners, he supposed —so he did have his meals in comfort.

It amused him now that he had felt some hesitancy about coming to the ashram. The only time he had felt ill at ease, or even slightly put out, was the afternoon he arrived. One by one, all the helpers and employees at the ashram kept popping through the curtained doors of his hut without warning. Munoo came first, salaaming deeply, and ceremoniously presented him with a roll of the kind of slick, nonabsorbent toilet paper found in British railway stations. He knew Indians used pots of water instead of toilet paper, so he tried to let Munoo know how much he appreciated this mark of special solicitude. A cheerful Bengali girl, who was then helping Lakshmi in the kitchen, barged in next, bringing him a bowl of fruit. Little Hari, the eldest son of Sher, the cowherd, came in to check the fuel in his kerosene lantern, and silently and solemnly demonstrated how to light it again and again, until apparently satisfied the stupid foreigner had grasped how it worked. Acha and Tulsi, two Hindu University students who were visiting the ashram, came in for no reason at all, except to welcome him in their chirruping English. People shuttled in and out all afternoon.

Finally, strangest of all, just before dark Lakshmi appeared and beckoned him to follow her. She led him across the courtyard and down a slight rise to a small wooden building. Suddenly, to his surprise, he realized it was a latrine. Lakshmi stood at the door, and smilingly motioned him inside. It was an ordinary four-holer ditch latrine, similar to the kind he had known in the army. Lakshmi made a sweeping gesture and stood smiling at him expectantly. For a bewildered moment or two, he wondered if she was inviting him to try it. Then he realized she merely wanted him to comment, that to Lakshmi, a village Untouchable girl, it must have seemed the grandest, most modern toilet imaginable. He said it was great—very fine indeed, and she beamed with pleasure. He never thought to inquire why Lakshmi was assigned the task of showing newcomers the latrine; she obviously considered it an honor.

His worries that impromptu visits were a part of ashram living turned out to be needless. After that first afternoon, no one except Munoo ever came to his hut. It was amazing how quickly the quiet days passed. He arose at five, and after he had bathed and dressed, it was time for breakfast. Then it was time for his visit with Bhaiji, which lasted about forty-five minutes to an hour. Afterwards he returned to his hut and wrote and read the badly printed Bible he had acquired in Benares, or, often, merely lay on his charpoy and thought. He usually looked up with surprise when he heard the lunchtime bell. Lunch was a long meal because he and Panditji sat talking endlessly about everything, and the others at the ashram joined them at the table in relays. After lunch, a drowsy lull fell over the ashram; it was Indian siesta time, the hottest time of the day, and he found the silence almost eerie. He never heard so much as the buzzing of an insect. He usually fell asleep, gently, happily. At three o'clock, he awakened, had a washup, and read, took a meandering walk, or, infrequently, sat with other visitors to the ashram in their endless discussions on a corner of the verandah of the main house. He liked to save his serious talk for Panditji. After the evening snack, they usually sat together in the dining room for hours.

He turned on the charpoy and sighed. It had proved to be an unbelievably pleasant and rewarding experience. Each unhurried day seemed to have just the right number of hours. He had never felt so . . . well, so relaxed, so fit. The diet had even dissolved the surplus pounds around his waist. One night as he sat with Panditji he slapped his new belly and said, "This simple life agrees with me."

Panditji's eyes glinted behind his spectacles. "Simple, Mr. Fraser?" he asked. "By whose standards? The concept that it is normal to have a full stomach and a snug roof over one's head arose in Central Europe only a comparatively few years ago. Most of humanity would not call this a simple life, but a bountiful one. I do myself. When Gandhi was still alive, it was sometimes jokingly said that it cost a fortune to keep him living in poverty. I can assure you it also costs Madame Valois a great deal of money to keep us beggars."

He had to watch himself with Panditji. He grinned, thinking about it. Panditji might live in an ashram, but he was the eternal professor: aggressively Socratic, beaming more delightedly when he was refuted than when he scored a point. On the first day, Panditji had let him know that while Bhaiji would be his teacher, he intended being his goading tutor. "I blush to tell you, Mr. Fraser," he said, in his beautifully precise English, "that two decades after we Indians won our Independence, there still are two kinds of facilities in our public buildings. One is marked 'Officers,' and the other is marked 'Other Classes.' Unfortunately, religion is equally undemocratic. There is one grade of religion for the uneducated and semi-civilized who are satisfied with established ritual and easy belief. This religion works; we must be tolerant of it. But there is another religion reserved for civilized persons who seek God on a higher level. I consider you, sir, a civilized man. I hope you don't become cross with me if I treat you accordingly."

Panditji had been a man of his word. He badgered him incessantly, testing his faith, making him think, laying traps. On the surface, some of his endless questions seemed naïve. "I simply cannot understand this furor in the West over whether God is dead, Mr. Fraser," he said blandly. "If Christians profess to believe that God created man in His image, isn't such speculation warranted? Surely, if man has God's image, it is logical that a wholly honest God also has man's characteristics. Tell me, as a Christian, how do you envision God? Does God eat? Drink? Defecate?"

Sometimes he served up warmed-over theological chestnuts. "Christianity rejects the doctrine that souls suffer transmigration, doesn't it, Mr. Fraser? Could you tell me, please, when Christians believe souls are created? Does God create a reserve supply from time to time, and keep them on hand in a state of preexistence? Or is He put to the pains of creating a new soul every time a couple casually conceives?"

Whenever he defended any of his positions on the grounds that it was accepted dogma, Panditji would pounce triumphantly. "Dogma? Ah, don't try to confound me with dogma, Mr. Fraser. The boneyards of time are filled with religions that committed suicide because they found their inspirations in dogma. Admit that many things are unknowable, if you must. Confess you have beliefs, which you can't explain, but are elicited by faith. But do not derive your inspirations from theological pedantry. Until you develop intuitive responses that go beyond dogma, Mr. Fraser, you have not found the well-springs of religious expression."

Panditji delighted in catching him off-guard. When they were discussing the efficacy of prayer, he said casually, "Have you ever considered, Mr. Fraser, that man may be more concerned with God than God is with man? A sentimental God, Who is eager to dry the tears of small children and halt the natural process of death if beseeched piteously enough, is, after all, a purely Western concept. Only a few years ago, in Victorian times, I understand God was thought of differently: vengeful and unsparing in his punishment of sinners. Must God either be a kind of benign Father Christmas or an unrelenting Lord High Executioner? Isn't it possible He is supracosmic, spaceless, eternal, timeless, and entirely impersonal?"

He had never, even at first, really been fooled by the old man's baiting. Panditji was too transparent for that; eyes and face shining, looking so pleased with himself, when he thought he had said something particularly outrageous; wiggling with glee, almost literally chortling, when he could needle him into a spirited argument. But the old man's methods did work; he wondered if Panditji really knew how effective they were. For as Panditji had provoked him into arguing, explaining and defending his faith, he had been astonished to find how much of it remained intact. Over the years he had often thought how wonderful it would have been if he could have retained the simple, uncomplicated faith of his boyhood. Then God was in Heaven, and Hell was below, and Jesus was the Redeemer, and everything else was unimportant. The few doubts that did arise were easily resolved. He still remembered the time when he was six or seven and had questioned something in the Bible. He had been surprised when his father smiled and said, "You don't have to believe the stories in the Bible, son, as long as you believe the lessons they teach."

He lay mulling that over, feeling a pang as he recalled that boy's innocence. Considering the time and place and his father's simple orthodoxy, it was an amazingly enlightened answer. Or was it so amazing? What did he really know about the quality of his father's faith? He loved his father, but as he grew up and his doubts about religion multiplied and became more sophisticated, the fact that his father was a minister had created a gulf between them. He had always avoided admitting it to himself, but in his college years, secretly, he was ashamed of his father's calling. Cocky, superior, his head filled with all sorts of doctrinal blasphemies he had found in books on comparative religion, he had decided the ministry attracted greaseballs and jerks. He was half-pitying, half-scornful of the ministerial students who surrounded him in college: their bony, half-finished young faces always so earnest, always decked out in cheap neckties tied in hard, tight knots and stiff black jackets that hiked up in the back, always pressing flesh and twanging away in their countrified voices about The Fellowship of Christ.

That little boy had grown up and forgotten that believing the stories was not important. He perhaps never had fully grasped that religion is not a social fact; that its purpose is beyond myths and institutions and, frequently, even codes of behavior. Looking back, he could not explain why he had not realized such an obvious truth. But maybe at one time he had. One night when he had been arguing with Panditji, he discovered to his surprise that he recalled great chunks of Whitehead. When he was in college he had been tremendously impressed by Whitehead's thesis that religion is what the individual does with his solitariness, that a man who is never solitary is never truly religious. He found himself becoming more and more eloquent as he told Panditji that all the great religious conceptions which haunted mankind were scenes of solitariness: Prometheus chained to his rock, Mohammed brooding in a desert cave, Buddha meditating alone under a Bo tree, the deserted Man on the Cross.

Panditji had been impressed. Because of Bhaiji, he . . . He paused. Back to Bhaiji again. His ruminations always began and ran full circle to Bhaiji. Even Panditji could not help him in his gropings for some way to explain that beneficent figure. When he first questioned the old man about Bhaiji, he had a vague feeling that he was being evasive. Now he realized he probably was only bewildered by his naïveté. "He is a very Holy Man, Mr. Fraser," Panditji said. "Through discipline and suffering he has reached the abyss of pure subjectivity." He made a helpless little gesture. "When one is in his presence, one senses his wisdom and love and purity. Many religious leaders and mystics have had this quality. Many people thought Gandhi, who was a politician, had it.

"But why does he still go into a . . . a trance for all but a few hours every day?"

"When he is in *samdhi* he dwells in the Godhead, Mr. Fraser." Panditji paused. "You do understand that the word *yoga* is derived from a root meaning to yoke up, and that . . ."

"Yes, yes, I understand that," he said almost impatiently. "But what is the nature of his state? Does he ever speak of it?"

Panditji said quietly, "No, Mr. Fraser."

"Has anyone ever asked him what it is like?"

Panditji hesitated. "When we first . . . when Madame Valois was new to India, she inquired one day, Mr. Fraser."

"What did Bhaiji say?"

Panditji sighed. "He said nothing, Mr. Fraser. He remained silent." He studied his wrinkled but graceful hands for a long time, then looked up with a smile. "Did I ever tell you, Mr. Fraser, that when I was a small lad and simultaneously saw my first motor car and first Englishman, I was so terrified I fled to a ditch and hid. Afterwards, I simply couldn't find the words in our district dialect to convey to my mother and brothers the frightening sight of a redfaced gentleman in a topee riding in a noisy motor car. Even if I were unaware of the long religious tradition, I probably shouldn't find it strange that there are spiritual experiences which defy our halting descriptions." He paused, then said quietly, "But let us examine the tradition, Mr. Fraser. Buddha remained silent when he was questioned about the nature of reality and *Nirvana*. Your

Christ kept a similar silence when the Roman Pontius Pilate questioned him as to the nature of truth. Lao Tze said simply that the Tao—the Ultimate Reality—that can be named is not Tao. Our Hindu holy books teach us that the Supreme is so infinitely real that we dare not try to call it by a name since a name itself is an idea derived from worldly experience.

"What could Bhaiji answer, Mr. Fraser? The reality of what ordinary men find Unknowable, and the unreality of trying to make it knowable is accepted by all religions. All religions likewise acknowledge that only personal spiritual attainment can overcome this duality between the knowing and the unknowing. Utter silence by those who have achieved the supreme spiritual experience is actually the telling proof of the inadequacy of our fumbling descriptions and imperfect standards."

He lay pondering on that. He did not dispute it; he had always accepted that there were religious geniuses, men and women—saints, mystics, sannyasins, yogis, sufis—who had advanced far beyond ordinary men in their search for God. One of the odd fragments of information he had retained since college, possibly because he doubted it, was that, for opposite reasons, only ancient Greeks and Jews did not produce mystics who sought actual communion with the Highest; the Greeks supposedly because of their bright and translucent naturalism, and the Jews supposedly because of their rigid monotheism and hallowed statutory observances. But whether he accepted this or not, the important question was whether he believed some few of the untold thousands, perhaps millions, of God-obsessed seekers who had come along over the ages truly had established a union with that divine essence, outside the objective world, which men called God. Only a few days ago he had not believed they had. Sometimes when he meditated on it, when his doubts and cynical appraisals made Bhaiji seem remote, he still denied it; it was mostly a myth, a delusion, sometimes flickering hallucinations in sick or overtaxed minds. Yet, when he was in Bhaiji's presence, he accepted it as simple fact.

Somehow it stirred in him vague yearnings. He had no illusions about his spiritual attainments. Finding he still believed in God as strongly as he did was immensely consoling. Still, outwardly it probably would not change his life too much. He was more firmly resolved than ever to give up the unreflecting, stupid life he had led whose only goal was his own satisfaction; but he would not go around wearing his faith like a gaudy lodge button, proselytizing, trying to reform his friends; he doubted if his own particular brand of rationalism would ever permit him to join a church and accept its rites and rituals.

Wasn't there more to it than that? He cherished his newly found peace of mind, but wasn't he capable of going further? Often when he was sitting with Bhaiji, basking in his indescribable serenity, he had the feeling that he was on the verge of some wondrous discovery. It was almost as if he had received a promise, unspoken but felt. Did this strange man have some rare gift for him? At the proper time would he, even momentarily, give him a glimpse of mysteries he could not even imagine? His common sense told him this wasn't so. Bhaiji was surrounded by people who were more unselfishly devout and richer in spiritual values than he was. The secrets he possessed had never been shared with them. Bhaiji himself had told him that his own spiritual abilities were limited. Yet, the yearnings he felt, or the promise he thought he sometimes felt, had kept him lingering on here at the ashram. He would stay a while longer, continue sitting with Bhaiji, even though Martine . . .

He stopped, with a qualm. His relationship with Martine had changed in some undefinable way, and it disturbed him. He had discovered it during the two trips she had made to the ashram. He had felt a tinge of annoyance when he saw her—and this had made him feel guilty. It wasn't that he really wasn't glad to see her. As silly and unreasoning as it was, what he had felt was a sense of intrusion—the kind of irritable impatience he felt if interrupted while he was working and preoccupied. He had not shown it, of course. On her first visit, he had allowed her and the smiling Sixteen to inspect his hut, had assured them that he was getting enough to eat, and had entertained them with the story of his troubles in getting a bath. Martine had joined him and Panditji for lunch and it had all been very pleasant. Nevertheless he was glad to see her leave.

Her second visit, two days before, had not gone so well. She and Sixteen had arrived early in the afternoon and she was obviously disappointed, surprisingly so, it seemed to him, when she learned Bhaiji was in *samdhi* and she could not see him. She had also obviously taken it for granted that he would be leaving the ashram at the end of the week. When he said he would like to remain a while longer, she seemed startled. "But that is impossible," she said. "The ashram moves to Muzapuram on Monday."

"I thought perhaps I could go along," he said.

At first he thought she was going to object; but she continued to look at him silently, a shadow in her eyes. Finally, she gave a small shrug. "If you wish," she said.

He was both embarrassed and annoyed at her response. He made himself smile. "If I'm not welcome, I . . ."

"No, no," she said, quickly. "Of course, you are welcome." She gave him a small smile, but her eyes still looked troubled.

He grinned. "Maybe you think I'm not up to the walk?"

"It is not difficult," she said. "In some ways, I have always found it enjoyable."

He looked at her in surprise. "You mean you'll be going?"

"I always go," she said.

"What on earth for?"

"André has asked that I go," she said.

"Oh." He was at a complete loss. It had never occurred to him that she still had any kind of personal relationship with Bhaiji. He had assumed that it was the same as the relationship Bhaiji had with everyone else. He simply couldn't imagine Bhaiji making a purely private request of anyone.

They had been walking slowly across the courtyard as they talked, and now, automatically, he led her onto the path toward the river that he took on his afternoon walks. After a long silence, she said, "You will need stout shoes."

"Yes, I know," he said absently. He had suddenly become conscious of the delicate fragrance of her cologne, and it had struck him with a jolt that he seemed to have lost all awareness of her as a woman. He looked at her from the corners of his eyes—a marvelously desirable woman, her beautiful lips so full and inviting, her unusual skin so glowing, her lush figure provocatively rustling the soft green linen sheath she wore. Yet his admiration was purely abstract. He felt a flash of anger with himself. What the hell was wrong, anyway? Was he so fickle or jaded that no woman could hold his interest for more than a couple of weeks? No, it wasn't that. What then? Had he mentally castrated himself in his pursuit of religion—just as old Origen actually castrated himself so he wouldn't be tempted while instructing female catechumens? But that was silly because . . . He stopped, for, suddenly, he had a deeply disturbing thought. Was it because of Bhaiji? Without consciously realizing it, had he made Martine taboo because she still was Bhaiji's wife? Did he shrink from the thought of facing that calm, all-knowing gaze, realizing that Bhaiji would know all there was to know about Martine and him? He told himself it was foolish, but he brooded on it all afternoon while he and Martine talked desultorily about almost everything— except the fact that they were supposed to love each other.

He brooded on it now. It no longer seemed incredible or ridiculous that Martine had remained continent all these years. He didn't in the least doubt that her deep—and to him, unreasoning—feelings about her marriage vows had inhibited her. But he knew now that the real reason was that she saw Bhaiji regularly for six months of each year. He knew the real reason, for he knew that he would not, perhaps could not, make love to Martine as long as he had to face those depthless, all-knowing blue eyes. Maybe it was unfair, but there—

A glimmer of light appeared in the doorway. Munoo entered slowly, hunkered down on his haunches, carrying his two pails of bath water. "*Salaam,* Munoo," he said. "*Salaam, sahib,*" Munoo answered, and crept out again. He lay still a moment longer, sighed, and threw back the cotton coverlet and arose. He was wearing only pajama pants; he untied the cord, let them drop, and stepped out of them. Then, before lighting the lantern, he knelt, naked, on the dirt floor and said his simple morning prayers.

SIXTEEN...

"Man often does not understand that God has no limitations except His goodness," Bhaiji said. "Since the world dwells in God, and God is Himself a synthesis of the total universe, they ask why good and evil exist in the world if both do not partake of His nature. Their confusion begins with the erroneous assumption that since good is positive and creative, evil must likewise be positive though destructive. Evil is never positive. It cannot be because it is in disharmony with God's design. Evil always is a result of the stupidity, blindness, or rebellion of man. God does not fight evil. He has no cause to fight because evil is not a challenge to His order in the universe. Evil is a negation of His order and so is self-destroying and always has in itself a purpose toward self-elimination. A species whose members are always in pain will either cease to exist, or lose the perception which results in the pain, or develop a better relationship of its bodily parts. The instability of evil is a triumph of God's order. Physical suffering, mental suffering, loss of the higher experience in favor of the low experience—all such manifestations of evil, are problems man creates for himself, and God has furnished the means by which they may be overcome if man only avails himself of them. People who suffer are not necessarily evil; the ignorance which allows pain is evil. Young theologians often ask if God did not intend evil to exist in the world why, then, is there cancer in fish? The problem is not related to evil. It is God's design that at this stage of development all lives shall have passing phases and the termination of those lives are brought about by methods which also are part of His design. They will remain part of His design until the next stage of development is reached."

"Proselytizers would do well to leave alone the vast multitudes of devout simple people who have found a means to worship God which they understand, and who know no difficulties, nor need know none," Bhaiji said. "Evangelism should be directed toward the multitudes who have an unthinking disbelief, or who stand suspended in easy acquiescence between belief and disbelief."

"No, brother," Bhaiji said, "God is outside metaphysical rationalization. Metaphysics is a description and therefore its basic analysis has been concerned with the actual world passing in time, and the elements which go into its formation. Some metaphysics are confined to relatively simple concepts. Descartes saw the world as composed of God, minds, and organic and inorganic matter. Kant saw the necessity for God in the moral order but rejected the argument from the Cosmos. Other descriptions have found the foundation of the world in an aesthetic or moral order. Some have omitted God and retained only mind and matter, or omitted God and minds and retained matter, or have omitted all but God.

"None is true because God is not met and realized with men's minds, but with their imperishable souls. Souls are distinct from men's minds and as man progresses he will be made aware of the distinction. God is. The fact of His existence lies beyond the vulgarities of description."

Bhaiji said, "Man suffers final degradation when he scoffs at God, but he also suffers degradation when he becomes so narrow and unfeeling in his egotistical goodness that he attacks those who do not worship God with the same prayers and rituals he uses."

"There is no evil passion cherished, no evil practice followed which does not cloud our vision when we look toward God," Bhaiji said. "Every flaw and scar of our nature will go to distort His true image."

Bhaiji said, "Every religion which exists, or has ever existed, has had to subvert the old order of things and therefore is built on the ashes and ruins of what earlier men believed to be a true and confirmed knowledge of God."

"Whether God has bestowed a truth beyond discovery of men is a question which has been debated by theologians for centuries. God has no secrets; neither is any revelation to be considered a discovery. Truth merely remains inert until it finally is perceived by a human working of recognition."

"To dwell in the presence of God calls not for the development of a unique power," Bhaiji said. "It calls for the purification and cooperation of every power God has given man."

"Infatuation with miracles is evidence of man's spiritual immaturity. Christians reject the great promise of their own Faith when they exult over the miracles of the raising of the dead. For bringing the dead to life again is only the undoing of a more complete mastery exercised by death. Of the daughter announced to be dead, it is promised that 'she shall be saved': the father of the dying boy is told simply 'Thy son liveth.' "

"Man is always slow to learn that truth is never what he chooses, but always that which he is under a necessity to believe."

"The desire to abolish evil and live in harmony with God is the reason men heed the promptings of their souls and seek

God. The wisdom the search brings would be sufficient reward if God did not exist."

"True religion can never be subversive to a government which seeks the welfare of its citizens. Love of God is loyalty to mankind."

"The power by which God sustains the world is the power of Himself as the Ideal. What God does not know is not a fact."

"The better heathenisms were religions of life; that was the source of their power. But they fell and they were false because they were limited by that life which they upheld and expressed."

"The growth of character demands an independent life."

SEVENTEEN...

He had forgotten that it could be so dark; there was an unreality about it. The sky was black, absolutely starless. Only when he occasionally caught a flicker from the lantern bobbing along at the head of the column was he sure where the sky left off and the earth began: he felt he was groping his way through a void. A figure on his left, who made snuffling noises through his or her nose and smelled faintly of cocoanut oil, kept bumping into him, knocking him off balance. His suede chukkar boots were too tight across the instep and the right one was rubbing his heel. He stepped high, bringing his feet down cautiously in case he encountered a rut or pothole, trying not to step on the heels of the person ahead of him, hoping that the person behind would not step on his. He strained his eyes trying to detect a glow from the lantern. He was not even certain he still was on the dirt road.

He had really not troubled to examine the way he felt about making the walk to Muzapuram. Now he knew; he felt uncomfortable, irritable, and faintly comic. What in hell was he doing walking down a dirt road in the middle of India on a dark night? Next to a glimmer of daylight, the thing he wanted more than anything was a cup of good strong coffee. He felt resentful because he had missed his usual tea. The whole thing was badly planned. He had been miles deep in sleep when Munoo awakened him at three o'clock. He had taken his time bathing and dressing, thinking when the morning prayers started that he had at least a half hour left. How could he know they were starting earlier?

When he emerged from his hut the only light he saw came from the doorway of the main house. Silhouetted against it, gathered around the verandah, were members of the ashram, chanting and softly clapping their hands. Even while he adjusted his eyes, Bhaiji had come through the doorway, a long white shawl draped over his head and wrapped around the upper part of his body. It was the first time he had ever seen Bhaiji standing; it gave him a jolt of surprise to see how tall he was, and how quickly he moved. The crowd opened a path for Bhaiji, and without looking right or left, he walked briskly down the steps and disappeared into the darkness. The crowd jostled into formation behind him, still chanting and clapping hands, a single dim lantern flickering in its midst. A shadowy figure broke from the crowd and came up to him. By the dim light, he could barely make out Martine's face; she smiled and pointed to her lips to indicate she was observing silence, and hurried away. He had dashed back into his hut for his musette bag, and was coming out again, when he almost collided with Sixteen.

"You not change mind and ride, sir?" Sixteen asked.

"No, Sixteen," he said, impatiently.

"I follow you in car," Sixteen said.

He felt a touch of exasperation; they had been all through this. "No, Sixteen. I'll expect you day after tomorrow, as we planned." Leaving Sixteen standing there dolefully, he ran to catch up to the others.

How long ago had that been? He had already discovered it was a waste of time to look at his wristwatch; in the total darkness, its luminous dial was a faint, uncipherable glow. He set his jaw and cautiously planted one foot after another in the dampish void. The figure on his left bumped into him again; his right heel was beginning to feel tender. He sighed and plodded along—left, right; left, right . . .

Suddenly, as startling as a clash of cymbals, the sky was a soft rose color, then salmon pink. Dawn had arrived in a mighty rush. He had seen this phenomenon before, but he looked up, marveling at it. A rustling sigh ran through the column. It was straggled out along the road, in tadpole formation, for twenty or twenty-five yards, and he was in the slender tail. At the head he saw Panditji's Congress cap rising and falling; right behind it was Bhaiji's shawl-covered head. He could not spot Martine. He looked at his watch—4:30. They had been on the road about an hour. He looked to his left and met the smiling face of one of the half-dozen students who had arrived by truck from Benares the afternoon before, especially to make the walk. She was the tiny vivacious one, the one who bounced when she sang. Martine, Panditji and he had sat in the dining room almost to ten o'clock, listening to the students sing *ragas* in their nasal, high-pitched, but somehow melodious voices. He started to speak to her, but she placed her finger over her lips, and he grinned instead.

Now that he could see, he felt better. Still a little foolish, perhaps, but more cheerful. He plodded along, gradually catching up to the others, rather enjoying the exercise. The dirt road was smooth and hard, the fields on either side flat and blackly rich, shimmering with a greenish stubble of some crop that he supposed was cane. Looking around, he made a perfunctory head count; there were twenty-eight of them, give or take one or . . . He spotted Martine. He had missed her before because she was wearing a sari, plain white cotton with a red border. It surprised him a bit. With her full figure, her black hair hanging in a single braid down her back, she looked exactly like an Indian from the rear.

The sun had barely leaped into the sky, a glowing red ball high above the rim of the earth, when Panditji's long arm shot up, waving a handkerchief. The column halted, then scattered to both sides of the road with a rising murmur of voices. It was five o'clock. He looked at the small Indian girl by his side. Her eyes were glowing, brimming with youthful fervor. "Doesn't it . . . isn't it thrilling to know one is following in the tradition of the great saints?" she said.

He smiled, wondering what she would say if he told her how he truly felt.

"My name is Sutra," she said. There was the tiniest cast in her right eye.

"I enjoyed your singing last night," he said. "I'm Paul Fraser."

She was looking at him with open admiration. "Yes, I know, Mr. Fraser. You are a famous literary person, I believe."

He laughed. "I am a person who is about to get a blister." He went to the side of the road and sat down and began removing his right shoe. She followed and sat beside him, watching solicitously while he placed a folded pocket tissue inside his sock over his tender heel and replaced his shoe. He stood up, tested his shoe, and grinned at Sutra.

"Do you know the poetry of Rabindranath Tagore, Mr. Fraser?" she asked.

"Only slightly, I'm afraid," he said.

Sutra began telling him about Tagore, but he was only half-listening. He saw that Bhaiji alone had not sat down to rest. Still swathed in his long white shawl, he stood at the edge of the road absolutely motionless, gazing across the level fields. In the soft and silvery morning light, he looked like an Old Testament patriarch, noble, wise, holy. Looking at him, he forgot his annoyances of the morning. He decided that he was, after all, glad that he had come.

As they took to the road again, he discovered that Sutra was both a delight and a bore. She chattered away incessantly. Some of her girlish talk was amusing, but after a while he began to feel as if he were being pestered by a lively chirruping cricket. He was relieved when, finally, she left him to join her friends. His heel no longer bothered him, the morning freshness felt good on his face. He trudged along at the end of the column, sunk deeply in his own thoughts.

Martine had obviously been walking beside him for some time before he turned and saw her. She smiled at his look of surprise. "I was beginning to feel deserted," he said. "The day is only beginning," she said. "We have miles to go." He grinned, thinking how lovely she looked in her simple sari. It was pleasant having her beside him; it seemed to put a new swing into his walk.

It was almost seven o'clock when they reached the first village. It was tiny; about a dozen mud-walled houses, dingy and crumbling. He saw a long well sweep weighed with stones, got a jumbled impression of mud and piles of cowdung cakes, poverty and neglect, a scum-covered pond. Mud and more mud. A crude and rickety wooden archway, hung with wilted mango leaves looking like green rags, had been erected over the road. Probably fifty ragged villagers and their naked children were scattered around its base. When they saw Bhaiji, they scrambled into lines along the road and began a ragged chant, "*Bhaiji ki-jai, Bhaiji kai-jai.*" A frail old woman in a limp and dingy white sari tottered out of line, toothless mouth working convulsively, and tried to kneel and touch Bhaiji's feet. He stopped and lifted her and said something quietly. She placed her palms together, bowed deeply, and backed away.

The headman, scrawny and stooped, wearing a dirty orange turban and a long threadbare coat, stepped forward, bowed low, and offered Bhaiji a garland made of tinsel and red twine. Bhaiji accepted the garland and bowed low in return. He had slipped the shawl from his head, and his composed face seemed to glow with gentleness. He said something in his low, unhurried voice.

"He is asking if there are any Muslims in the village," Martine whispered.

There was a good-natured murmur from the crowd. A single half-naked little man with a stream of red betel juice running down his chin was pushed forward. Bhaiji bowed to him, then reached out and placed his hand on his shoulder. The little Mussulman's *salaam* was so low that his hands almost touched the ground.

Bhaiji spoke again. "He's asking about the Harijans," Martine said.

226 . . .

There was another good-natured murmur from the crowd. Grinning broadly, the headman turned and indicated several families at the end of the line. Bhaiji moved down to them and bowed. The Untouchables pressed their palms together and bent low. Several of the women dropped to their knees. Bhaiji stooped and placed the garland over the head of a small naked boy with wide eyes and a runny nose.

Bhaiji placed his palms together and bowed to the assembled crowd, turned and walked away at his brisk pace.

"Bhaiji ki-jai!" the stooped headman yelled joyously.

"Bhaiji ki-jai! Bhaiji ki-jai!" the crowd responded.

As they left the cheering villagers behind, he asked Martine, "Do they always turn out like this?"

She nodded. "Yes, and it is the same in all villages." After they had walked for a while, she said, "It annoys me that everything Indians do must always be attributed to religion. Perhaps it is true that those poor people believe they receive darshan, a kind of grace, when André passes through here twice each year. But it is foolish to pretend that they also are not delighted to have an excuse for a celebration. It adds some excitement to their wretched lives."

He smiled. "Better Bhaiji than a TV cowboy or a rock 'n' roll singer."

"Yes," she said, not smiling, "I suppose that is some consolation."

Before eleven o'clock they had paused briefly at two more villages. He found them indistinguishable from the first one: a jumble of sunbaked clay and cow dung. In each, the ceremony was the same. There was the same rickety arch hung with drooping mango leaves; a crowd of ragged, half-naked villagers, eyes shining with excitement as well as with the peculiar, almost visionary brightness that comes from perpetual starvation. The only minor difference was that the headmen placed garlands made of a flower that looked like marigold around Bhaiji's neck. He removed the garlands quickly, almost impatiently, and as he moved along, broke them into pieces which he handed to children in the crowd. At the third village, some of the marchers broke for a nearby well to get a drink. He and Martine joined them. He felt thirsty, but after Martine had drunk and handed him a mugful of grayish, cloudy water, he hesitated. "Do you suppose it's safe?" he asked.

She shrugged, and he realized it was an inane question. He drank, trusting in God and his inoculations. The water tasted much better than it looked.

As the morning wore on, he had discovered a pattern to the countryside. The fields on both sides of the road were flat and monotonous, but every half mile or so, they passed through a small grove of trees. Some of the trees were magnificent; towering, and so thickly foliaged that they formed a green canopy over the road. Often troops of monkeys lived in the groves. Except for one or two glowering old males that made menacing barking sounds, most of the monkeys looked at them with only interest as they walked past. The parakeets that filled the trees were more inquisitive. Sometimes he would look up into the branches and see dozens of them peering down, cocking their heads excitedly. Occasionally there was a great hollow rustling sound as flocks of a hundred or more took off in wheeling flights. He enjoyed walking through the groves, welcomed the brief respite that they offered from the monotony of the open road. He mentioned it to Martine.

"They are *neem* trees," she said. "They have all been planted, of course. It is necessary to have rest areas, especially in the summer when the glare and heat are too awful." Her tone changed. "Like almost everything else in India, *neem* trees are supposed to be sacred. I am not sure why. I suppose the Brahmans decreed it so poor ignorant villagers would not cut them down for fuel."

He looked at her. It was the second time that morning, she had spoken slightingly, almost sarcastically, of Indian religious customs. It was unlike her. Her face was composed, imperturbable, but he had a vague feeling that somehow she resented this entire journey. Was it because he had come along? She

228 . . .

had certainly been less than happy when he asked to come. Still, she had seemed cordial enough since then. She probably was only tired— Then he remembered something else that seemed odd. Back at the well when she served him water, he had noticed she was wearing her wedding ring. He had become distracted before he had a chance to think about it. He let his eyes drop to her left hand; it was there, all right, a heavy gold band. Now, why would she suddenly don a wedding band? She had never worn one before, either in Benares or during her visits to the ashram. It was strange . . . very strange.

It was well past noon when they arrived in Durga, the large village, where they were scheduled to stop for lunch. Besides the usual shaky triumphal arch, there were pennants strung along the street, and garlands for the leading marchers as well as for Bhaiji. He was in no mood to watch the welcoming ceremony. Threading his way through a crush of eager-eyed, straining villagers, he headed directly for the well. He was hot, thirsty, beginning to be footsore, and tense with annoyance. For almost an hour and a half they had not stopped to rest; for the last thirty minutes Bhaiji's effortless, relentless pace had been so rapid that a few marchers had straggled behind. He had found it difficult to keep up himself.

"Why so fast?" he asked Martine.

She shrugged. If she found the pace grueling, she showed no signs of it. "His mind is on other things," she said.

He grunted. "Why doesn't Panditji remind him we're along?"

"Durga is only a short distance now," she said. "We will have two hours to rest."

Well, he had kept up. But the last hour had exhausted him more than all the rest of the march. Ignoring a black pie-dog puppy that came bounding up to sniff his feet, he stepped around a tethered goat that eyed him speculatively, and crossed the straw-strewn ground to the well. He let down the galvanized iron bucket and brought it up brimming full. He was about to drink directly from the bucket when he heard a soft hissing sound. A slim young girl with a gold stud in her left nostril, wearing a spotless white sari, stood there holding out a glass. He smiled and thanked her in sign language, and he was surprised when she said in perfect English, "Please leave it on the ledge for the others, sir." As she walked away, he saw that a dozen or so more other little girls were watching them from a grove about thirty yards away. Others were flitting about steaming cauldrons. He remembered that either Martine or Panditji had told him that their lunch would be served by students from a Hindu school.

He drank three full glassfuls of the water, and had a quick splashy washup. He was combing his hair when he heard the crowd break into a rhythmical chant, *Bhaiji ki-jai, Bhaiji ki-jai.* He looked up and saw an officious little man ushering Bhaiji into a hut. Panditji and Martine were close behind, in earnest conversation with a mustached man in a Congress cap.

Feeling refreshed, and somehow superior to the other marchers who were now rushing toward the well, he walked into the grove and found a sturdy tree that looked as if the sunlight never penetrated its shade. He sat down and leaned back against it, and with a sigh, stretched out his weary feet. Without willing it, or even realizing it, he was soon fast asleep.

They took to the road again at three o'clock. He felt slightly stiff, but the nap and an enjoyable lunch had restored his good humor. He had awakened after a half hour to find both Martine and Panditji sitting nearby, smiling at him. The little Hindu students had dished them up a surprisingly good meal —*chapatis*, rice, a curried mixture of peas and cauliflower and a slice of mango pickle—served on round, purple-green lotus leaves instead of plates. He was pleased that Martine seemed to have shaken off her melancholy mood of the morning; her eyes had been bright with amusement as she listened to the usual good-natured raillery between Panditji and himself. Only once, when Panditji mentioned that Bhaiji had refused his usual small cup of milk laced with honey, did her eyes cloud over.

"But he always fasts on the walk to Muzapuram," she said.

"I know he does, Madame," Panditji said, "but he should have some nourishment."

She shrugged impatiently. "Why should you worry? He always does as he wishes."

As soon as they left the village, he was startled to hear a vigorous rolling of drums from the head of the column. He craned his neck and saw that two villagers in frowsy, faded red jackets, carrying snare drums, were leading the march.

"What's that all about?" he asked.

Martine smiled slightly. "They are protecting us from lions."

"Lions!" he said, surprised. "There are no lions around here."

"No," she said, "but apparently there were at one time. Once—perhaps a few hundred years ago—a visitor leaving this village was eaten by lions. Since then, all important visitors have been given a drummer escort for protection."

He walked along smiling, not even minding that the drummers couldn't keep a marching beat. When they left the column after a couple of miles, he was sorry to see them go.

He had begun to notice a gradual change in the landscape. The farther they moved away from the course of the Ganges, the poorer the land become. The fields beside the road were now brownish instead of black, sunbaked, often flinty looking. Occasionally they passed stretches that were obviously too unfertile to cultivate, burnt looking, covered with straggly bushes and tufts of bristly weeds. It was not inspiring country, and during the long afternoon he saw only two things of interest. Once he heard a low murmur sweep the column, and looked up just in time to see a flock of perhaps a dozen peacocks crossing the road ahead. On another ocassion Martine touched his arm and pointed to the field on his right. In the distance, standing in knee-high undergrowth, he saw a skinny youth watching them gravely. He was surprised to see that he was carrying a bow and had a quiver of arrows slung around his shoulder.

"That is a Harijan boy out for his dinner," Martine said. "In this region Harijans often are better fed than anybody else. They will eat anything."

It was late afternoon, and darkness was almost on them, when they finally reached the small village where they were stopping for the night. Of all the squalid little settlements they had seen that day, it was by far the worst: a couple of dozen mud-walled, reed-roofed hovels strung out along a single muddy street. Yet, there was the inevitable archway, a garland for Bhaiji, and the ragged cheers. Fortunately, across the road from the village, gradually falling to musty ruin, was an old *dak* bungalow that had been used in British times. The villagers had cleared it out and strung lanterns along the edge of the buckling verandah. Although he was almost paralyzed with awe, the emaciated, pockmarked headman made a ceremony of leading Bhaiji, Pandijti and Martine to their rooms in the bungalow. The others were expected to sleep on the verandah or in straw-filled stalls in a shed adjoining the village well.

He saw Panditji in close conversation with the headman, and shortly afterward, bowing and bobbing shyly, the headman had taken him to one of the stalls and indicated that it was his alone. A platform running along one side was piled high with straw. He was simply too tired to protest that this special attention was unnecessary. He wanted to throw down his musette bag and sack out immediately. Instead, he joined the others at the well for a quick bath, and though numb with fatigue, sat with them on the verandah for a miserable meal of leathery *chapatis* and a few spoonfuls of curried potatoes. As tired as he was, he always remembered that meal. For, as he sat there in his stockinged feet, nibbling at the unappetizing food, he suddenly realized that his feet smelled. Not rankly, not overpoweringly, there was simply the unmistakable odor of socks that had been encased all day in hot shoes. He drew his feet close, hoping the others wouldn't notice. He looked around at their sockless, odorless, brown feet and thought that there was probably a worthwhile commentary to be made about the comparison somehow—but he was too weary to think of one.

As soon as he had eaten, he carefully threaded his way through the darkness and found his stall. He put on the cashmere pullover in his musette bag for extra warmth and snuggled down in the hay. He fell asleep almost instantly. But his adventures for the day had not ended. Sometime during that black night he was awakened by eager gasping, hungry sounds that could never be mistaken for anything except what they actually were. He raised his head and looked into the next stall. There was a lantern, wick no brighter than a glowing ember, hanging from a beam at the entrance. By its dim light, he could make out half a dozen figures scattered about in the hay. All lay perfectly still, except two figures near the farthermost wall. He could not recognize them, could barely make out their outline, but as he watched they reached the plunging, panting climax in a struggle of love. He lay back, shaking his head with wonder. Were they villagers or two of his fellow travelers? He knew he probably would never know, but as he drifted off to sleep again, he knew that of all the sights he had seen in India, this was one he would always remember.

EIGHTEEN...

It was almost eight o'clock, and the sun already had turned warm enough to make him shed his pullover, when they reached the asphalt road. A rustle of relief ran along the column. Martine turned to him with a small smile. "It is only a mile or so farther. How do you feel?"

"Fine—I feel fine," he said. It was almost true. The stiffness he had felt when he turned out in the predawn darkness was almost gone. His feet felt tender and abused but still serviceable. It gave him a sense of pride to realize that he had walked almost thirty miles. The only other time he had ever walked so far was during basic training in the Army. He had never forgotten the moaning and griping on that forced march. An Army six-by-six with medics aboard had followed along, picking up the stragglers and lancing blisters. Now, well over twenty years later, he had repeated the feat—and with far less trouble.

He swung along the road almost jauntily, pleased with himself and glad that Martine had smiled. All morning long, she had been somber-faced, hardly speaking. Somebody in the middle of the column began singing in a nasal, wobbly voice, and the others joined in. When the song ended, there was a burst of laughter. Anytime Indians laughed it was a happy occasion indeed. He looked at Martine and was disappointed to see that she was staring straight ahead, apparently as glum as ever.

At last, as they rounded a slight curve, he saw sunlight reflecting off the dome of a mosque in the distance. As they drew nearer, he saw a flurry of flags and pennants on buildings surrounding the mosque. He smiled at Martine. "They're planning quite a reception."

"No," she said, "the town is decorated for the Husain festival. It began at sundown last evening, though it . . ." She broke off.

A Land Rover was pulled across the road dead ahead. Two khaki-clad policemen, wearing fancy conical turbans, lolled against the hood. Without breaking stride, Bhaiji led the column past the vehicle. As he passed, one of the policemen stood up straight and touched his forehead. The other, still slumped back against the front fender, eyed him indolently. It seemed that they were going on past without stopping, when, suddenly, Panditji's arm shot up waving a handkerchief. *Dhoti* flapping, spectacles glinting in the sunlight, Panditji hurried back to speak to the policemen. Without a word, Martine left the column and went forward to join them.

It was soon obvious that Panditji was agitated about something. He gestured emphatically and seemed to be bawling out the policeman, who stood almost at attention, waggling his turbaned head from side to side. Martine spoke and the other policeman unbent his knobbly knees and stood up straight. A whisper spread down the column, "Trouble in the town . . . trouble in the town . . . trouble in the town."

Only Bhaiji seemed oblivious to the discussion. He stood exactly where he had halted, erect and motionless, looking neither right nor left. Panditji was now shaking his long forefinger at both policemen. Abruptly, he turned and took his place near the head of the column and waved his handkerchief. The march resumed.

As he drew abreast of the policemen, Martine stepped into place beside him. Her face was composed, but her eyes looked stricken.

"You heard?" she asked.

"Only that there is some kind of trouble," he said.

"I knew this was going to happen," she said. "It was the reason I felt you should not come with us."

There was something almost accusatory in her tone. He felt a touch of annoyance, but he kept his voice level. "Just what has happened?"

"We are not quite sure. The Husains burned some Hindu shops last evening. There were also probably beatings, maybe killings." Her voice hardened. "Those . . . those cowards we saw are members of the district constabulary. They claim they are on guard to keep troublemakers out of Muzapuram. They should be in the town, protecting the people. The local police are worthless."

"You mentioned these Husains once before," he said. "Tell me about them."

"They are bigoted and contemptible," she said, fiercely. "They are beastly when . . ." She stopped and made a helpless gesture. When she spoke again, her voice was calm. "Are you acquainted with the two major divisions among Muslims?"

"Do you mean the Shia and Sunni?"

She nodded. "Yes. As you probably know, the schism occurred after the death of Mohammed. The Shias believed that Mohammed's chosen successor was his son-in-law, Ali, and after him, Ali's two sons, Hasan and Husain. Orthodox Shias believe that Ali and his sons were murdered by usurpers. One of their major religious observances each year is a period of mourning for their martyrdom. But the Seed of Husain—the full name of the Husains—maintain that Husain did not die. They said that he mounted his horse and, with a sword in one hand and Koran in the other, fought his way through an army that had been sent to kill him. After all kinds of incredible hardships, the Husains say he made his way to Muzapuram.

"But that was back in six-hundred-something," he said.

"Yes, even the Husains themselves are vague about when Husain was supposed to have arrived. They simply claim it was a long time ago. Many people believe the sect probably is no more than a hundred years old." She shrugged. "At any rate, a man who claimed to be Husain did come to Muzapuram. He persuaded some Muslims that he was the true Imam, and he had many wives and many children. His tomb is in Muzapuram, and the Husains preserve what they claim was his Koran and a hair from his beard in their mosque. They also say he would have lived forever if he had not been poisoned by Brahmans who supposedly tricked him into attending a feast by pretending they wanted to be converted. As he was dying, he commanded his followers to kill Hindus on sight or else he would have his grandfather, the Holy Prophet, bar them from Paradise."

He grunted. "Charming old man."

"Fortunately, there have never been many Husains. Orthodox Muslims—both Shias and Sunnis—abhor them. There probably are not more than two thousand now, and most of them live in Muzapuram. They are clannish and live to themselves, and strangely enough, seldom cause any trouble until this time of year when they observe a four-day period of mourning commemorating the death of Husain, or the man they called Husain. Then their *mullahs* whip them up into a frenzy. They parade through the streets carrying replicas of Husain's tomb, called *tazias*, and many of them lacerate themselves with chains and knives. And, of course, after their *mullahs* tell them again and again of Husain's dying wish, some of them look for any pretext to attack Hindus."

"Why don't the police keep them under control?"

"The police!" she said scornfully. "The police are not able to prevent communal riots in the center of New Delhi. In a forgotten, miserable little rural town like Muzapuram, they do not even try. The local police run away and hide when trouble starts, and you saw those gallant constables back there. Who cares about a few dead Hindu storekeepers?"

He had never seen her so upset; did not think it possible. But when she spoke again her voice was calm. "André has more influence than the police, but he can only do so much."

"Do you really think there is danger?" he asked.

She looked at him, and her eyes were dark and brooding. "Yes, there is danger," she said quietly.

Partly to show he was not afraid, partly to try and reassure her, he smiled and nodded to the marchers ahead. Since the halt where they had encountered the policemen, they had been plodding ahead as calmly and quietly as ever. "Nobody seems to be worried."

She turned away. Her voice sounded weary. "You do not understand the nature of Indians, especially devout Indians. They would march along like this if they knew they were going to be torn to pieces in the next minute."

It did not seem to be a dangerous town; only dingy and dilapidated and smelly. They had walked for some minutes along a narrow, twisting street, paved with large worn slabs of stone and reeking from an open drain running along its edge, before he realized that they had not met a single person. Neither had he heard a sound except the hollow clop-clop of their feet on the paving stones. He looked up at the crumbling, pitted buildings enclosing the street like an unbroken wall. The shutters in the upper stories were closed tight. For the first time, he felt a slight unease. He had long since learned that Indians are a noisy people, and whenever they are crowded together there was a frenetic hum and clamor. Maybe the shops were closed, but why hadn't he heard so much as the tinkle of a bicycle bell in the distance, the clack of a loom, or the cry of a child? The others must have felt as he did; since they had entered the town, not a person had coughed or cleared his throat or spoken. He looked at Martine from the corners of his eyes. She was looking straight ahead.

He was relieved when, finally, they emerged from the narrow street and reached the center of the town. A narrow *maidan*, crisscrossed with paths and worn smooth of all but a few patches of brown grass, formed one side of a square lined with small stores and stalls. All were shuttered tight or cleared of merchandise. The square was deserted, but it was oddly reassuring to see that green banners hung outside all the shops and from poles planted at intervals along the *maidan*. The whole town obviously took the Husain celebration seriously; that accounted for the lack of activity. Everything seemed normal otherwise. He was amused to see that a gigantic and garish birth control billboard, showing three types of plastic hoops, dominated one end of the square. It looked like an advertisement for pretzels.

They had almost crossed the square when he caught the first whiff of burnt wood and cloth. It grew stronger as they walked along, and by the time they reached the street that led from the square it was a pervading fuggy stench. As soon as they entered the street, he saw the cause. All the shops along its upper end had been gutted by fire; all that remained was a soggy black mess of charred timbers and heat-twisted galvanized tin roofing. Bundles of half-burned merchandise littered the narrow sidewalk and spilled over into the street in front of the destroyed buildings. He was almost abreast the first shop before he realized one of the smaller bundles had moved. For a long moment what he saw didn't register; he clearly saw the ugly naked neck and scaly head, the curved yellow beak, but his mind simply wasn't conditioned to grasp such a sight immediately. The vulture spread its wings slightly for better balance and ripped at the bundle again. He saw a gelatinous red mass and a slender yellowish hand flop limply before he really comprehended. It still took him several seconds to realize that vultures were clustered on other greasy-looking bundles nearby, tearing and gorging. A dark shadow came gliding down from a rooftop. He looked up; vultures lined the rooftops and ledges of nearby buildings like ugly rustling gargoyles.

Instead of horror, the first thing he felt was numbing disbelief, then anger. How could such a thing be happening, in the middle of a town, on a quiet and sunshiny morning? It was . . . monstrous . . . It was— He turned his head away. They had passed the last of the tearing, sluggish shapes before he looked at Martine. She was staring stonily ahead. But she must have caught his glance. "This is India," she said grittingly.

The more he thought about what he had seen, the angrier he became. He looked at Bhaiji marching along erectly at the head of the column; he had not broken his brisk and rhythmical stride. Panditji was directly behind him, not looking right or left. The whole column was moving along quietly and passively, just as if nothing had happened. He suddenly felt furious with all of them. He burst out angrily, not trying to keep his voice down, "Well, for God's sake, aren't we going to do something?"

Not a head turned in his direction, nobody stirred or gave a sign that they had heard him. He looked at Martine. Her face was now calm. "What would you have us do?" she asked, quietly.

"We can scare the buzzards off those . . . those corpses for a start," he said.

"Does it really matter?" she asked. He was about to reply angrily that it damned well did matter, that civilized people didn't leave bodies in the street like garbage, but he stopped when he saw her eyes. She placed her hand on his arm. "They will be taken care of, Paul," she said. "Their friends have been afraid to come out. Now that André is here they will feel safer." She made a small sweeping motion with her head. "Look around you."

He looked at the squalid, ramshackle little stores, bristling with garish signs, lining both sides of the deserted street, and as the number of shops and stalls increased, sometimes lined three deep with barely enough room to pass between them, the signs of activity increased. More and more heads popped from doorways or from behind shutters. Sometimes he caught the sound of running feet, low glad cries. "This is the Hindu bazaar," Martine said. "Usually it is crowded."

The shops had begun to thin out when, about five minutes later, Bhaiji turned into a gate in a high whitewashed wall that ran along the edge of the street. "We have arrived." Martine said. He had barely caught a glimpse of a flat roof towering up close behind the wall, when he heard the thump of feet on a wooden floor. A grossly fat little man, naked except for a loin cloth, forehead daubed with a vermillion caste mark, had run out onto the platform fronting a dilapidated store across the street. He threw himself to his knees and began rocking back and forth, thumping his head against the floor, chanting something in a shrill voice. His waddling wife and three wide-eyed children, their foreheads also smeared with caste marks, appeared in the curtained doorway of the store and stood watching dumbly.

He looked at the wailing fat man with annoyance. "What's he saying?" he asked Martine.

She did not turn her head. "He is saying, 'Saint Bhaiji—Saint Bhaiji. May he live forever.'"

He hated the massive, gloomy old house. Once it obviously had been imposingly palatial, an extravagance of some rich old Muslim or Hindu merchant who lived with feudal pomp, surrounded by wives, children, and servants. Now it was a stagnant pile of crumbling masonry and cracked marble. The walls had been freshly whitewashed, but it smelled of mildew, decay, and ever so faintly, of long eaten curries. The ground floor was completely bare of furnishings, a vast expanse of discolored marble and chipped columns, except for a single small room at the rear of the house. Bhaiji went there as soon as they arrived.

Martine turned him over to the ashram's caretaker, a rabbity, pockmarked little man named Lal, who led him up a broken marble staircase, through a maze of corridors and past a profusion of doors, to his room on the second floor. It contained only a charpoy and a wooden shelf that ran along one wall. He was more exasperated than pleased when he cautiously looked through an open door leading to an adjoining room and discovered it was his own private bath. The toilet was a rectangular hole in the marble floor, the only source of water a faucet placed about four feet high in one wall. As he bathed, seething with annoyance because the faucet periodically gurgled and threatened to go dry, he reflected that at least the primitive conditions at the home ashram had a dignified simplicity. Here he felt like a guest in an incredibly bad hotel. No . . . the atmosphere was more funereal than that. What the whole place reminded him of was a decaying mortuary.

While he dressed, he thought about the vultures and the bodies, especially the sight of that limp disembodied hand. He supposed he should feel some horror, but he simply couldn't; not even the uneasy nudge of horror he sometimes had felt when he drove past an accident on a highway and saw sheet-shrouded figures beside the smashed cars. Was that the answer? He could identify with victims of an automobile crackup, but those mangled, ragged bodies being attacked by vultures were completely alien to him Maybe his sense of outrage was not because they had been murdered, but simply because they had the bad grace to lie out in the street like carrion? He thought about that and, finally, sighed heavily, because he honestly wasn't sure. No matter what Martine said, he knew he wasn't afraid. He damned well couldn't be frightened by a ragtag mob of liquid-eyed Indians. He smiled wryly, realizing how silly that sounded. Well, what would he do—tell them how brave he was? How about the time at Maxim's when he sent back five bottles of Haut Brion '47 in a row because it was corky? He sighed again and slipped on his shirt.

It was shortly after noon when he first saw the Husains. He was on the front portico awaiting Sixteen's arrival, back against a scarred column, soaking up the sun and half dozing, when he heard a thin melancholy cry like a mu'adhdhin's call to prayers. It was echoed by a mournful chorus of reedy instruments, followed by the slow, steady beat of a drum. Then he heard the drone of voices growing louder and he realized a procession was coming up the street. At first he thought it was probably a funeral cortege for the dead they had seen that morning, but after a moment, it was obvious it was approaching from the opposite direction.

A half dozen or so members of the ashram who had been seated in the shade of the courtyard wall stood up and drifted toward the gate. He saw little Sutra spring up from a group of students who had gathered in one corner and beckon excitedly for them to follow her.

He sat back, undecided whether the procession was worth moving for, until he saw the top of a huge ornate, brightly painted structure swaying along behind the wall. It obviously was one of the tazias Martine had said the Husains carried. He stood up and walked toward the gate.

He arrived just as the last line of green-jacketed musicians straggled past, piping a mournful ragged elegy on instruments that looked like snake charmers' flutes. After a long interval, a double row of half-naked men appeared, struggling, straining, barely moving under the weight of a tazia hoisted on poles over their shoulders. It was a towering pagoda-like structure, apparently made of heavy wood, elaborately carved and gilded at the corners, and covered all over with swirling designs in purple, green, and crimson. It looked hideously garish in the bright sunlight, but as it slowly moved past he saw that every inch of its shiny surface was covered with tiny intricate designs within designs, and he marveled at the craftsmanship.

Perhaps a dozen bearded men followed the tazia, and he realized at once that they were mullahs. They were either bald or shaven headed, clothed only in white sheets, tied at one shoulder and leaving the other bare. They walked in a kind of hesitant lock-step, eyes straight ahead, chanting a dirge in flat, droning voices. At every second or third step, they raised their right hands and in unison brought their palms flat against their breasts in a hard slap. He kept his eyes on a frail old man whose hennaed beard showed he had made a haj to Mecca; his butter-colored face looked bloodless and strained, but his eyes burned fiercely. There was an ugly swollen red welt extending beyond the sheet draped near his bony left shoulder. But, as he watched, the old man slapped it resoundingly again and again without wincing.

Then, suddenly, the slow and sedate, rhythmic march changed into a whirling, jerky dance of red-clothed figures. The *mullahs* had been replaced by thin and muscular young men whose white undershirts and *dhotis* were drenched with blood. They pranced and shuffled aimlessly, lashing themselves with chains of tinkling blades and long slender swords that were as flexible as buggy whips. Their shoulders spurted with blood; they raised their hands and smeared it over their faces —a fine mist of blood flew from their long hair when they spun in dizzy circles; great dribbles of it ran down their backs. One wiry boy of fifteen or sixteen twirled in a flat-footed two-step, crooning hoarsely, whipping himself across the back with a knout of blades fastened to a wooden handle; his face was unmarked but the rest of his body was a scarlet dripping dabble. A tall gaunt figure stumbled along at the edge of the street, striking at his head with a sword; his hair was a sticky red mass, gouts of blood ran down his face; his eyes were fixed, unseeing.

He stood unmoving, a dozen feet away, as they jerked past in the sunlight, smelling the sweet hot odor of blood. When the last of them had disappeared and another *tazia* appeared, he turned and walked away. He had seen enough. Almost idly, he noticed that the entrance had a heavy solid iron gate, and he thought, *Thank God for that.*

Martine and Panditji were standing on the portico. She looked at him soberly, inquiringly. He kept his voice casual. "Those flagellists are drugged."

"We know," she said, quietly. "They smoke Indian hemp. That is why they are so dangerous.

Sixteen arrived shortly before dark. When he saw the heavy old Buick come through the gate, he felt an immense relief. As the afternoon wore on, he had become increasingly worried that Sixteen might have been barred from the town by the police or, worse still, blundered into a Husain procession. Sixteen alighted and gave him his most punctilious military salute.

His face was grave. "This very bad town, sir. There much trouble. You leave now."

He smiled. "No, Sixteen. We know about the trouble. We saw the shops this morning."

"Not this morning, sir," Sixteen said, grimly. "In town now, much trouble. Look, sir." He led him around to the back of the car and indignantly pointed out several small dents and nicks in its shiny surface. "They . . . they—" Sixteen struggled with his inadequate English— "shoot stones at car. Like this, sir." He made a throwing motion. "I have to come back way. They try to stop me." He rubbed his hand over the dents in his beloved car and scowled. "Bloody *goondas!*"

He placed his hand on Sixteen's shoulder. He found he was not in the least surprised at what had happened. "I'll have the car fixed, Sixteen," he said. "Let's unload my gear, and we'll go and tell Madame Valois about it."

They found Martine and Panditji in the whitewashed barren dining room in the basement. He told them what Sixteen had reported. Martine nodded. "Yes, we had already heard."

"But how could you have heard?" he asked.

"Lal has friends who bring him news," she said. "Apparently one of the *tazias* brushed against a telegraph wire and a piece of it fell to the ground. Somebody screamed that the Hindus were throwing stones." She shrugged wearily. "Now they are looking for Hindus to kill."

Panditji spoke briskly. "I have taken the liberty of sending a letter by messenger to Pir Chand, the district magistrate, Mr. Fraser. I have informed him of what is happening. He is a most able man, and I am sure he will see that police reinforcements are sent here immediately."

"After enough people are killed," Martine said.

Panditji's voice was gently chiding. "Now, Madame Valois, we are all upset that such things occur. It is tragic. But the state police have always coped in the past, and they will cope now. At any rate, we are quite safe here." He nodded emphatically. "Quite safe, Mr. Fraser. If there was danger of further violence, Bhaiji would not be in *samdhi*. In the past when things have threatened to get out of hand, he has walked through the streets for hours. Is that not true, Madame Valois?"

Martine did not answer. She turned away, her eyes dark and brooding. He was not certain how reassuring he found the old man's words, but he was touched, as usual, to realize how completely Panditji's world revolved around Bhaiji.

Yet . . . there was tension, a kind of general unease. He sensed it in the way members of the ashram gathered in small subdued groups, and especially by the unnatural silence in the diningroom during dinner. There was none of the usual chatter, no spirited arguments. Even Sutra and her friends had lost their exuberance. There were no chairs or tables, so he sat on the muslin-covered floor with Martine and Panditji while eating. Soon his already aching muscles were a torment. He was glad when he could excuse himself and go to his room.

He chanced another bath under the spitting faucet, and sighed with relief as he slipped into a terry cloth robe Sixteen had brought. Was it only this morning that they had arrived? It seemed days ago. And London? That seemed remote and blurred, belonging to another age and another life. He was so weary that he fully expected to fall asleep as soon as he lay down. Yet he was strangely restless. He stared into the darkness, smelling the dampness and decay of the old house, then, for no good reason, got up and snapped on the light again. That was better. He lay back staring at the dim overhead bulb, thinking what an improvement it was over a lantern. He was on the verge of sleep when he heard the knock. It was almost as if he had been expecting it.

It was Sixteen. "*Memsahib* say you come, sir," he said.

"What is it, Sixteen?"

"Policeman dead, I think, sir," Sixteen said.

He did not ask any more questions, but dressed quickly. He had already started down the hall when Sixteen called to him.

"This way, sir. On top of house." He turned and followed Sixteen down a series of poorly lit corridors and was surprised when they came to a broad staircase leading to the roof. It was one of those Indian nights when the sky literally exploded with stars. He saw that *charpoys* were scattered all over the flat roof and he felt envious of the people who used them. Martine and Panditji were in a group of silent figures clustered along the waist-high parapet facing the town. He saw a small fire flickering at the far end of the street, probably in the same vicinity where they had seen the burned shops. As he joined them, it flared briefly, then died to a bright red glow. Martine said quietly, "That is the vehicle those constables were using this morning. One of them has been killed."

He looked at the red glow, now flecked with black and slowly diminishing. He did not know what to say; was not entirely sure how he felt.

Panditji sighed and his tone was apologetic. "I wish now I had not been so . . . so impassioned when I spoke to them."

"They had a duty to perform," Martine said, tonelessly. She turned and her eyes seemed almost luminous in the dim light. "We also were told that the mob was coming to the Hindu bazaar."

"How long ago?" he asked.

She shrugged. "Ten minutes . . . fifteen minutes."

He thought about that. Except for the red glow, now looking no bigger than the end of a lighted cigar, he could not see a glimmer of light in the town. Despite the bright stars, the shops up and down the street were irregular black shadows. He turned to Sixteen. "Go down and close the front gate, Sixteen. Lock it, if possible."

"Sir!" Sixteen said, springing to attention.

"That is not necessary," Martine said.

Sixteen hesitated.

"Go ahead, Sixteen," he said.

"Sir!" Sixteen said again, and marched off.

They stood silently, attention riveted on the red glow which was fading slowly. He strained trying to detect shouts, perhaps the sound of breaking glass. Mobs were always noisy. At least, movie mobs were . . . He felt a touch of irritation. Actually, he didn't know a great deal even about movie mobs. He had shot a movie with a mob scene once, but he had hired a specialist to handle it—a big, scholarly man who plotted shooting angles as— He heard the clang of the front gate. He looked over the parapet and could barely make out Sixteen's figure in the light from the house.

"I think we should cut off the lights in the house," he said. "Is there a master switch?"

This time there was no protest.

"I'll attend to it, Mr. Fraser," Panditji said, and hurried away.

They stood waiting silently for what seemed a long time. Sixteen returned, and so did Panditji. The last, lingering glow from the burned Land Rover faded. He began to become aware of his overworked feet. He slid, first one foot, then the other, out of his loafers.

Ever so faintly, he heard a confused murmur. The others had heard too. There was a rustling along the parapet. "Silence!" Panditji said, sternly. The distant murmur became a babble, then grew louder and louder, and, suddenly, with shouts and an angry humming sound, the mob streamed out from between a row of shops about two blocks away. At first there didn't seem to be many of them, but he realized that was because he could only see those who were carrying torches. Soon the torches were distributed among a solid wiggling mass that clogged the street. The shouts were more pronounced now, but the dominant sound still was an angry humming.

Martine was tense beside him, but he felt neither afraid nor angry. The mob simply had no identity; it was a mass of shouting humanity. Small blobs of flame began showering out from the mob like spluttering roman candles, and he realized they were lighting sticks of wood or rolls of paper and throwing them at the shops. Several waving torches congregated near the front of one and, suddenly, it was a solid sheet of fire. A roof flared up on the other side of the street. Almost before he could single out individual fires, the shops on both sides of the street were burning fiercely.

A loud angry roar rose from the crowd, and by the light of the fires, he could see it surging back and forth along one side of the street. He heard a hissing intake of breath from around him before he realized someone had run out of one of the shops and was being flailed to death. He felt the first surge of anger. But could he be sure? The street was brightly lit now, but at this distance it still was difficult to make out individual figures.

That soon changed. Small flickering fires began appearing all along the street far in advance of the main body. Apparently a few in the mob took a special delight in being the first to set a shop afire. Before one blaze caught well, they dashed on to start another. The flimsy stalls near the edge of the street were the most flammable. As one was enveloped in a single gust of fire in the next block, he saw a half dozen or so little boys running along the street carrying torches, leaping with glee. His anger suddenly spilled over, not only at the prancing brats, but at the indignity of having to stand by while a shoeless, ignorant rabble ran amuck.

A solid block of shops were now burning brightly. Some burned slowly, sending off clouds of smoke. Others almost exploded, shooting red flames high in the air. Individual members of the mob were now clearly discernible, running, gesticulating, jumping up and down. His jaw was set so tightly it ached. At least the brats served one purpose. Only a halfwit or someone too old to run would stay in a shop after it was set fire. The mob was giving them ample time to run out, the back way. Only once had there been that fullthroated cry, and the jostling rush to get in on the kill. But maybe the mob was aware of what was happening. It was moving down the street rapidly now, passing up the stalls and small shops. Gaps had appeared in the solid wall of flame, though it was evident that whether they were set afire or not, all the close-packed shops were doomed.

There was a sodden explosive *poof* and flames leaped from the roof of a building not a hundred yards away. In seconds it was a raging, crackling torrent. Instinctively, they all stepped back. He could feel the blast of heat. Except for a few fitful black shadows, the street around the ashram could have been lit by a noonday sun. The mob was pouring down the street at a half run. He could clearly make out faces, some contorted with wide-open screaming mouths, others with teeth set in ecstatic grins. He saw a sea of staves, poles, and swords. For a moment or two, it all seemed unreal, particularly the swords. Then he saw a shaven-headed, stern old man, wearing a caftan-like robe, darting around the edge of the mob, tugging at the arms of sword-carrying young men and shouting at them, and he knew it was real enough. For all the aimless, shouting confusion, the mob had leaders.

For the first time he felt a chilly edge of fear. He forgot the nine- and ten-year-olds dancing at the edge of the mob, the skinny youths with long greasy hair aimlessly waving staves. That old man had a disciplined cadre under his command. If he decided in his fanatical mind to attack the ashram, it would be done in a minute. His mind was filled with the thought that he needed a weapon. He must be prepared to defend himself and the others. He wondered if there were knives in the kitchen. Yes, if the mob attacked, he would lead them all downstairs and set up barricades in the kitchen. If only he had a pistol or rifle . . . no, a tommygun. With a tommygun, he could— The thought was so utterly fanciful that, fortunately, it arrested his rising panic. He set his face and placed his arm protectively around Martine's shoulders. Her body was rigid.

The shops opposite the ashram wall were burning now. The mob had formed a rough semi-circle before them, but it was obvious they were empty. The occupants, if any, had been given more than enough time to slip away. For that matter, they could have clambered over the ashram wall. Despite its rickety appearance, the shop where he had seen the wailing fat man and his family was burning slowly. Then it happened so quickly that, as with the vultures, his mind refused for a second to believe what he saw. A skinny, completely naked man darted from the first shop, head low, feet and arms churning. The crowd screamed with triumph and he could see the rods and staves and swords rise and fall beyond the wall. That prepared him, so he saw perfectly what happened next. Three children scurried from the last shop like small frightened brown quail. He heard the shout and he saw the terrible flailing. He was aware that Martine turned slowly so that her back was to the street, plainly heard Panditji catch his breath and say, "Hai Rama." But he could not move. He watched as the waddling woman ran out, and, finally, the fat man, his mouth a squealing round O. He felt nauseous with horror, and he must have felt some anger. But the thing he felt most was rank fear; it clogged his throat and made it difficult to breathe, caused sweat to run in rivulets from his armpits. Perhaps he imagined it, but afterwards when he remembered those slow paralyzing moments, it seemed he could smell the musky odor of his fear. It soon passed; it was too wracking to endure. He found himself trembling with anger.

He blinked. A small boy, wearing a loin cloth and a lopsided turban, had appeared on the ashram wall. As he watched, another larger boy was catapulted up beside him, and stood teetering a moment to keep his balance. They ran nimbly along the top of the wall, swung over the side, and dropped into the courtyard near the gate. He watched numbly as the boys slid the bolt and the heavy iron doors slowly swung open with their own weight. For what seemed a long, long time nothing happened at all. He prayed that nothing would. He could see a jumble of swaying figures through the entrance. The boys were jumping with excitement and beckoning frantically. Finally, a few figures lurched through the gate. He knew that others would follow. They might be burned to death, but he already grimly had decided that he for one wouldn't be clubbed like a running rat. At least he could block the staircase long enough for them to throw themselves from the roof.

He felt strangely calm as he turned to Sixteen. "Let's get the *charpoys* and block the staircase. We can—" He heard Martine sigh or gasp, but it was old Panditji's agonized, "No! No!" that caused him to turn. Panditji knocked against him roughly as he turned and scurried toward the staircase. Martine was standing stock-still, staring into the courtyard. He looked over the parapet. Bhaiji had emerged from the house and was standing a few feet in front of the portico steps. His white shawl was draped over his head and clutched to his body by his folded arms. He stood completely motionless, erect, and looking straight ahead. In the flickering light of the fires, shrouded in his shawl, he made an awesome figure.

The crowd that had already spilled through the gate came to a milling halt in the middle of the courtyard when it saw Bhaiji. From the roof, he could see their rolling eyes and uneasy faces; they looked like misbehaving schoolboys in the presence of a teacher. As the trickle through the gate became a jostling, yelling crush and they were pushed closer to that shrouded, motionless figure, they dug in their bare toes and pressed backward. He was not certain how long that tableau lasted, but it was stamped indelibly on his memory: the great shadows cast by the flames dancing eerily across the courtyard, the desperate, frightened efforts of those in the front ranks not to be swept any closer to that solitary, erect figure, as the yelling, gesticulating mob continued to pour through the gate. Then there was a series of piercing yells from outside the wall. Instantly, the crowd coming through the gate turned and began moving back toward the street. He stared bewildered for a moment before he realized orders had been given to leave the ashram alone. He felt weak with relief.

As the pressure at their backs relaxed, the solid rows of figures in the courtyard began moving backward slowly, still facing Bhaiji. All but one—a wiry, bushy-haired youth who squeezed forward from the center of the crowd. He walked stiffly, carrying a sword waist high, one hand on the handle, the other grasping the blade perhaps a foot from the tip. From the way he approached Bhaiji, it seemed he was going to offer him the sword. Instead, he raised the sword, and using it like a prod, stabbed once, and—baring his teeth in a grimace—stabbed even more vigorously twice more. The blows jolted Bhaiji, but he remained standing. The youth turned and walked away stiffly before, ever so slowly, Bhaiji fell to his knees.

From the roof, he watched it all, frozen and almost disbelieving. Perhaps he did not fully grasp what had happened until he heard the long, frightened *ooohing* sound sweep the crowd below, the cries from those about him on the roof. But what he remembered most was Martine saying in a flat, toneless voice, "*Ça y est.*" Then she was gone. In the moment it took for him to follow her, he saw the crowd break and run toward the gate.

NINETEEN...

Old Panditji reached Bhaiji first. Without a glance toward the last of the crowd jostling to get through the gate, he stooped and gently lifted him in his arms. He staggered under the weight, but brushing past the hands that reached out to help, with tears streaming down his cheeks, he alone carried him to his room at the rear of the house. Panditji was seated on the floor with Bhaiji's head resting in his lap, the others gathered around numbly, when he and Martine elbowed their way into the room.

He did not need to look at Bhaiji's ashen pale face and limp body to know that he was dead. As he ran after Martine through the corridors and down the stairs, he had felt it with a cold certainty. It was not only the sight of those deliberate and deadly blows. He had grappled for several seconds with the little untranslatable phrase Martine had used before he remembered its meaning. Then it had run through his mind over and over again . . . ça y est . . . ça y est . . . until it had achieved a finality he could not doubt. Martine had said the preordained —the inevitable—had happened. Bhaiji had been killed and in some way she had known it would happen.

His heart went out to her as she knelt and touched Bhaiji's face and gently pressed his arm. How peaceful he looked, almost as if he were asleep. He saw Martine's body stiffen. Suddenly, roughly, she threw back the shawl over Bhaiji's chest. Three ugly wounds, like tiny gaping blue-lipped mouths, formed a rough triangle above his left nipple. At the sight, one of the women—fat little Lakshimi, he thought—began a high-pitched wailing. Martine turned and said coldly, "Stop that!" The wailing stopped. She reached out and gently spread one of the wounds apart. It was obviously quite deep, but there was no blood. Except for a single blotch on the underside of the shawl, he saw that there was no blood at all. Martine said quietly, "He is alive."

Panditji raised his strickened eyes and said sadly, "No, Madame, he has left us."

She said fiercely, "He is not dead, I tell you. He is in samdhi." A murmur swept the crowd. Someone in the rear started a hymn in a wavering voice. She turned angrily. "Stop that! All of you, get out!"

He marveled at how efficiently she took charge. The room was cleared and a charpoy was brought. As he helped Panditji lift Bhaiji on to it, he looked directly into the still face. He could not detect the slightest sign of life, no evidence that he was breathing, but somehow he knew that Martine was right and he was still alive. He placed his finger at the base of his throat, trying to find a pulse beat; the skin was warm but he could detect none. Martine said shortly, "That is useless. He has almost stopped his pulse." Someone brought a pan of warm water containing a strong smelling antiseptic and a large first aid kit. Martine tenderly washed the wounds, and, oddly enough, it was not until she began deftly applying a bandage that he even thought of a doctor.

He asked, "Someone has gone for a doctor?"

She shook her head. "No doctor."

He misunderstood. "Then where can I find one. Sixteen and I can go Benares if necessary."

"There will be no doctor," she said almost curtly.

He looked at her in astonishment. Panditji said gently, "The master would not allow it, Mr. Fraser."

He looked at them both disbelievingly. "But we must have a doctor," he said.

Old Panditji shook his head. She said in the same curt tone, "This is not London or New York, Paul."

He felt anger rising. "It certainly isn't," he said. "Why, this is barbarous. He might die without medical attention."

Panditji continued shaking his head. She applied a final strip of adhesive on the bandage and turned to face him. "He would not wish a doctor, Paul. Isn't that explanation enough? We know him best. Shouldn't you leave such decisions to us?"

He was more hurt than angered by the rebuff. "If you want to risk his life I can't stop you," he said stiffly. He stood up and walked toward the door. Almost immediately he was sorry he had acted so hastily, but pride kept him going. Outside the room, he was surrounded by members of the ashram who thronged the corridor. He could only tell them that there had been no change in Bhaiji's condition. As he looked at their anxious faces, some of them tear-stained, he was reminded that none of them had thought it odd that a doctor was not called. Feeling desolate and utterly exhausted, he left them and wandered out to the front verandah. The air was heavy with the smell of smoke. There was not a sound, and all the fires had burned out. All he could see across the wall was a dull reddish glow. He looked down the steps. Right down there, at that spot, a crazed bushy-haired youth had stabbed Bhaiji.

He heard the sound of her sandals as she crossed the marble floor. He pretended to be studying the starry sky until she spoke. "I wish to apologize, Paul."

"My fault," he said.

"No, I was distraught and I spoke hastily." She hesitated. "I . . . I know how you feel about a doctor. But we would be breaking faith with him if we summoned one. It is something we know he feels strongly about." She made a weary little gesture. "Anyway, it would not serve much purpose. If it is possible for a doctor to heal him, he will be able to heal himself."

"How bad is it, do you think?" he asked.

"It is quite serious," she said. "The wounds are very deep. He went into *samdhi* to prevent bleeding."

"How long can he remain in that state?"

"As long as he wishes." She paused. "Until he heals himself

—or if that is impossible, until he decides to slowly bleed to death."

"He won't die," he said firmly.

"We all die," she said. She looked up at the sky. "But do you realize what an incalculable loss we will suffer when he goes?"

"I realize very well," he said. "My loss will be greater because I've known him such a short time. There was so much I still had to learn."

She put her hand on his arm. "Yes," she said quietly. "Yes, you will suffer the greatest loss."

After she had gone, he sat down wearily with his back against one of the stone pillars. He looked up at the stars, trying to organize in orderly sequence all the many things that had happened that day. How strange it all was—and how utterly and completely he . . .

It could not have been very long, perhaps no more than an hour, when he felt her hand on his shoulder and heard her softly calling his name. He awakened and found her bending over him. "Come with me, Paul," she said quietly. He stared at her blankly, too exhausted and too sleepy to respond. She shook his shoulder. "Come quickly. There is not much time."

He clambered to his feet, instantly wide awake, wondering if the mob had returned. But the courtyard was dark and deserted. Through the gate he saw a patch of blinking embers where the fat man's shop had stood. As he watched, a charred timber fell with a shower of sparks. The old house was so quiet that he was conscious of the rustle of her sari, the sound of their footsteps, as he followed her through the bleak foyer and across the empty ground floor. The members of the ashram were still huddled in silent vigil along the walls of the darkened corridor outside Bhaiji's room. Most of them appeared to be asleep, and they stepped over several who were sprawled across the floor. She halted outside the door to Bhaiji's room and leaning close, spoke in a whisper. "He is conscious now. Go in to him. Ask him to tell you of the vision he had when he jumped from the balcony."

He looked at her half-surprised, half-bewildered. Through the open doorway he saw that someone had draped a cloth around the single bulb in the room. By the dim light he could barely make out Bhaiji's figure. He was propped up almost to a sitting position on the *charpoy*, swathed to his chin in blankets. His face was a white and disembodied blur. Old Panditji sat motionless on the floor beside the *charpoy*. "But I don't think . . ." he began.

"Please, Paul," she said. "You remember my telling you about the balcony. Simply ask him what happened." He could see that her face was set, but in the feeble light her eyes were unreadable.

He still hesitated. "Did he ask to see me?"

She did not answer but placed her hand on his arm and whispered urgently. "You must trust me. It is important."

Against his will, automatically, he obeyed then. Giving her a half nod, he stepped out of his shoes and entered the room. Panditji obviously was expecting him. He was barely past the threshold when, without turning, he rose quickly from beside the *charpoy*. His old face was drawn and as he hurried past, he whispered, "Please do not stay long, sir." He nodded, scarcely hearing. His eyes were fixed on Bhaiji's face. His eyes were closed and his body seemed unnaturally still beneath the shrouding blankets—yet somehow he knew that he was fully conscious. In some indescribable way, Bhaiji's starkly white face was lighted with that remarkable beneficent glow he always felt in his presence. He paused at the foot of the *charpoy* a moment, then dropped to his knees and sat in the place vacated by Panditji. Ever so briefly the blue eyes opened, and, as always, he felt he had been given a warm greeting. The voice was low, almost a whisper, but even and firm. "You have come reluctantly, brother."

"I didn't want to disturb you," he said. He was shocked to see the changes in the serene face. The eyes were dark and sunken, the lips bloodless, and two deep lines were etched beside the mouth. Had Martine been correct? Was his life slowly dripping away under the blankets? He felt a surge of sorrow and pity, and he asked, "Is there anything I can do?"

The voice said quietly, "Death is not an enemy, brother. Men fear it only when they do not understand it or prepare for it." The eyes opened suddenly and he was startled by their unwavering intensity. As he looked into their depths, he felt transfixed. It was an odd sensation—almost as if time itself was suspended. Finally, the eyes closed and the voice said, "There is not much time. Ask your question."

He found himself nodding obediently. "I am told you were once involved in an . . . an accident. A balcony fell and some of your friends were killed. Could you tell me about it?"

There was a long pause and the voice said, "I will withhold nothing from you. What you learn will depend on the force of your devotion. There is a gulf between the willingness to seek and the ability to comprehend. What the believer attributes to God has its origins in his own soul. You wish to know of the vision which was given me and which caused me to seek Reality. You must desire it fervently. Tell me your desire."

He hesitated, and the voice said, "Tell me your desire."

"I should like to know about the vision," he said.

"Even as a child I thirsted after God," said the soft voice, "but the undisciplined mind is like a nautical glass which is improperly focused. One can see but dimly and objects do not have their true form. I chose to waste my energies in meeting challenges that I encountered in the world of delusion. In my ignorance I believed that these transient and inconsequential challenges were the cause of my deep unrest and unhappiness. I was lustful and egotistical.

"Near the close of my twenty-eighth year I was on the balcony of a building in Paris with a group of my friends. One of them was a young woman with whom I imagined myself in love. We were drinking wine and toasting each other. 'I love you', I said. Laughing she held out her glass, 'Then get me more wine.'

"The image of her eyes and the column of her throat was in my mind as I turned to enter the room. I had one foot still on the balcony when I felt it tear loose and begin to fall. I threw myself headlong into the room. I heard the shouts and screams of my doomed friends. I felt a gripping and shuddering terror. It was the first emotion I had ever experienced which focused my undisciplined mind. For the first time my consciousness was erased of all but one thought and one thought alone.

"In that brief instant, for the power of complete concentration is not given longer to unsettled minds, I was at one with my friends. I felt them die, and I felt their sins strike my soul. Because of a frightful tragedy I was granted the privilege sought by many, but by God's will given to only a few—the privilege of atoning for the sins of others.

"I was not prepared to accept such a gift. Within moments I lost my brief contact with Reality. The agony was more than I could bear. I turned and sprang from the window, and I had my arms out longingly for the earth as I fell."

As the quiet voice spoke, he had sat entranced. He was not certain at what point the depthless blue eyes had opened, but he was looking directly into them, seeing nothing else. He was not sure how long the silence lasted, but when the voice began speaking again, he was overwhelmed with a feeling of inexpressible sadness. "I was not aware of any sensation as I fell. I did not feel the earth. There was only a final moment of gladness as darkness enveloped me. It was then that I had my vision."

Was there another long silence? It seemed so. It seemed he sat there with the silence growing thick and heavy, unmoving, staring into the unblinking, compelling eyes, before he recovered enough to whisper, "Could you tell me about it?"

The luminous eyes seemed to grow larger and more demanding.

"Tell me your desire."

"I should like to know about the vision."

The eyes were deep and bottomless. "Tell me your desire, my brother."

"I should like to know about the vision."

The eyes seemed to be drawing his body forward. He felt as if he could enter into their depths.

"Tell me your desire."

"I should . . ."

What he always recalled most clearly was his first feeling of stifling agony. It was as if his body was suddenly too tight to contain him. He clenched his teeth to keep from crying out. Tears were streaming down his cheeks. He blinked his eyes rapidly before he saw Bhaiji's pale face. He seemed to be asleep, eyes closed, features composed. He looked confusedly around the dimly lit room. He shook his head, and perhaps it was then that he said unbelievingly, "Why . . . you hypnotized me." Maybe he babbled it over and over again, for he did recall he seized on the thought gratefully. In his dazed, confused state, he groped desperately for some explanation of what had happened. He knew he was no longer in That Place, but the memory of what he had seen still lingered so powerfully that he could not relate to his surroundings. He felt an almost suffocating mixture of wonder, regret and melancholia.

Actually, he was never able to sort out exactly what happened next. He had a blurred impression that it was Panditji who came and touched his shoulder and led him from the room. He had a vague, jumbled memory of pausing at the foot of the charpoy and gazing down at Bhaiji, for he never forgot how his face seemed to be surrounded by a halo of mellow light. Perhaps Martine walked with him to his room. Or maybe she came later. He had a faint recollection of walking through the darkened corridors, not talking, stumbling along mechanically. He did remember sinking down gratefully on his charpoy and throwing his arm across his eyes. It seemed a long time before, gradually, the wonder and awe of it began to dissipate.

He opened his eyes and saw Martine standing quietly just inside the door.

He asked the question uppermost in his mind. "Are we . . . is this Hell?"

She studied him gravely before she answered. "No. I think not."

"But we are being punished?"

"Perhaps," she said quietly. "I do not know. Some men believe any separation from God is a punishment." She came and stood at the foot of the *charpoy*. "It will soon pass away," she said gently. "Tomorrow it will seem like a dream. After a while, there will be times when you forget it completely."

"I won't forget," he said. He thought about it and shook his head. "When . . . how long have you known?"

"For years," she said. "Since the second winter I visited the ashram."

"Why didn't you tell me?"

"What purpose would it have served? You would not have understood."

"But I would have," he said. He found his calmness disconcerting. He looked at her closely. "You do believe it really happened, don't you? I mean—it was real?"

She shrugged. "What can I say? Yes, I believe it was real. I believe a man named André Valois had such an experience. But it was his experience, not yours or mine. We were merely allowed to share what happened as onlookers—without his memories or knowledge. To that extent, it was simply a vision, a kind of hallucination."

He felt a tinge of resentment. He swung his feet over the edge of the *charpoy* and sat up. "But I saw it . . . I *felt* it," he said firmly. "It was not just because I was hypnotized."

She shrugged again. "Call it hypnosis if you like. Technically, I suppose it is something far more than that. He has acquired some means of transferring thought."

He thought about that, and the wonder of it all struck him anew. "You don't seem to realize what a stupendous thing this is," he said earnestly. "It shouldn't be kept a secret. It should be told to the whole world. Why, it could change . . ." He stopped because she was slowly shaking her head.

"It would not change anything, Paul," she said. "What you have learned is not new. Men have always known it—even the most primitive men." She made a weary little gesture. "The problem has never been that the majority of men deny the truth. Why should they bother? It is so much easier simply to forget it."

"But you don't understand," he said. "I am speaking of offering proof that will . . ."

"Proof," she interrupted quietly. "What proof, Paul? That you had a vision? That in some mysterious way a Holy Man in India offered you reaffirmation of an old belief?" He was about to frame a protest, when she said, "Oh, if you wished I suppose you could impress some few people. There are those who are always susceptible to old truths offered in a new way. I suppose it is true that sects, perhaps even new religions, have been founded on revelations no more substantial." She came close and placed her hand on his shoulder. "I know how you feel, Paul. Believe me, I do. When it first happened to me, I thought I would burst with the wonder of it. I wanted, just as you do, to shout it to the world. But, gradually, I learned to accept it for what it was."

"And what is that?" he asked.

"It is a gift," she said. "A personal gift. It has affected my life profoundly, and this is why I wanted you to have it, too."

"But that's unfair," he said. "It's . . . selfish. I know it was a gift, and I'm grateful for it. But it's a wonderful gift that should be shared."

"You cannot. Nobody can give it except André. You will find you will not be able to make people understand. It is not something—well, it cannot be explained with words."

"I can try," he said. "I believe it happened. I know it happened." He stood and faced her. "Don't you see how important this is. Suppose some people don't believe—suppose they think I'm a crank or nut. Others will believe it. Why, something like this could change our thinking about God . . . the universe."

She stood studying him silently, her eyes dark and unfathomable. Finally, she shrugged slightly and walked toward the door. "I must return to André," she said.

He watched her go, and because he wanted to say something, felt he had to say something, he said, "I think he's going to be all right, Martine."

She paused at the door for a moment, her face expressionless. "No," she said quietly, "he will die soon."

After she left, he lay on the *charpoy* and thought of the vision. The more he thought about it the more wondrous it became. It defied all description . . . it was—well, it was the most remarkable, the most awe-inspiring thing that had ever happened to him. It was . . . it was . . . He stood and slowly began to pace the floor. Martine was wrong, of course. It was such a moving, such a stunning experience that never for an instant would he be able to put it out of mind. He could remember every single thing, every nuance of what happened. And he could describe it perfectly. What did Martine mean when she said it could not be explained in words? Why, he could— With a sudden resolve, he went to his musette bag and rummaged around for his notebook and a pencil. He sat on the edge of the *charpoy* and held his pencil poised. No. No—that was not the way to do it. Don't try to compose it. Just write it down quickly . . . just exactly as it happened . . . everything that happened . . . let it speak for itself. He wrote:

Blessed release! Soaring . . . expanding . . . darting . . . spinning—exulting in the utter joy of being freed from those awful bonds. Shooting through the black and still darkness, faster and faster, feeling ecstasy as he felt the first faint vibrations of the pulsating whole. Closer and closer, absorbing the throbbing rhythmic beat, until gently and quietly he became united with the whole. Then, complete bliss, peaceful and secure, drifting along as an integral part of that mighty force. A chill . . . a sudden agonizing sense of loss, and he was adrift, passing through the strait and narrow passage into That Place, while the great pulsating tide of bliss receded farther and farther away. And he felt a sense of inconsolable loss because he knew he had failed again.

That Place was without form or substance; softly lit as a cloud at sunset. The others were there, huddled abjectly together, forlorn and fearful.

A quiet voice said, "I am the Recorder. The Executor comes."

And the Executor was there, without form or substance, but commanding all with his presence.

Asked the Executor, "It was involuntary?"

The quiet voice answered, "All save one, it was involuntary."

Asked the Executor, "There are witnesses summoned?"

The quiet voice answered, "They are here."

And a figure was there, humble and dejected, speaking in a low voice. "I was the man Mathieu Cavaignac. It was I who caused the building to be raised. I purchased the materials. I hired the workmen and paid fair wages to all, except one old mason, whom I cheated. I know no cause why it should have happened. I feel no guilt, though it might be that, unknowingly, I was at fault because I was an evil man."

He was gone.

And a figure was there, speaking slowly. "I was the man Emile Henry. It was I who built the balcony. I worked with care and I could find no fault with the materials I was furnished. I know no cause why it should fall. I feel no guilt, though it might be that, unwillingly, I was at fault, because at the time I was suffering from consumption and I was distracted because of the infidelity of my wife."

He was gone.

Said the Executor, "They are blameless."

The quiet voice answered, "It shall be recorded."

Said the Executor, "The deeds of those who have arrived shall be recorded."

The quiet voice answered, "All are at the fifth level, Executor, save Jacqueline Labori, an adultress; and André Valois, who came voluntarily."

Said the Executor, "Jacqueline Labori, you have been made aware of your sins. You may plead."

But the man who was André Valois spoke, "I will plead for her."

The quiet voice said, "Silence, André Valois. You have been made aware that there is only truth and justice here."

Said the man who was André Valois, "I bear the sins of those who came with me."

The quiet voice said, "It is not so recorded."

Said the Executor, "It is not possible to speak untruth here."

The quiet voice answered, "The claim of André Valois is not recorded."

Asked the Executor, "When did reason begin?"

The quiet voice answered, "In the fourth equinox."

Said the Executor, "I humbly beg for a decision."

A mighty voice spoke, soft, but with the echo and reecho of a thunderclap on a quiet day. "He has indeed gained a glimpse of The Cause. He has expiated all sins. Let him return for a period equal to the age of reason. And, then, let him be resummoned."

The quiet voice said, "It shall be so recorded."

Said the Executor, "There is no place for you here. You shall return until you are resummoned. You shall not remember."

The man who was André Valois said, "I shall remember. I must."

Said the Executor, "Go."

And there was darkness in That Place, and simultaneously, the wrenching agony of returning to the body.

He read what he had writtten with growing frustration and dismay. It was not what he had hoped to write at all. It was stilted, skimpy, even corny, and it failed completely to capture the wonder of what he had seen. He worked over the first few

266 . . .

sentences, crossing out some words, changing others. How could he convey that feeling of bliss beyond description he had experienced? It was as elusive as a dream. He could close his eyes and feel it perfectly. But words—well, words simply didn't do justice to what he felt. He stared glumly at other passages. Actually, what he had written was not even accurate. He had not really seen anything; he sensed it, felt it. And the voices? Did he really hear voices speak? No, it was something . . . something different from hearing.

He read it over slowly again and he sighed because he knew Martine was right. What he had experienced was a contact, a palpitation, something so wondrously fragile that it could not be reconstructed. He sat there holding the sheets in his hand for a long time. Finally, with a sigh he arose and walked into his bath. He tore the cheap paper into tiny bits and sadly dropped them down the hole in the floor.

Bhaiji died almost exactly at dawn. He marked the time precisely, because he was standing at his narrow window, staring into the night, when the first faint rosy wisps appeared in the sky—and, suddenly, the courtyard, the wall, and the landscape beyond came rushing at him out of the darkness and the brassy day was there. Just then he heard a woman's voice raised in a single wailing cry. As it died away, the voices of the others began an unmistakable lamenting chant. Perhaps he should have felt some sorrow or regret, but he could not. Instead, he stared unseeing out the window, and thought of that soul bursting forth. Rising, soaring, exulting—freed at last.

He stood there a long time before he became aware of the blackened, charred ruins beyond the wall. The memories of the night came welling up in a flood. But he was too weary to sort them out; too utterly, completely exhausted to cope. What he wanted more than anything was to sleep—a long, long blissful period of oblivion. He looked around the room. But not in this place—not on that rope bed. He stood there, conscious of the barrenness of the room, smelling the mildew, listening to the distant chanting, and he felt desolate and lonely and very, very old. He knew it could be avoided, but he dreaded having to go downstairs and facing the others in their grief and despair. He took his time shaving and bathing under the tap. He dawdled while he slipped into a clean bush shirt and slacks.

As he walked through the corridors, he noticed the chanting had stopped. All he heard was a single voice raised in a sing-song dirge. Only a few members of the ashram were clustered around the door to Bhaiji's room; all the rest had crowded inside. He made no attempt to enter. He looked over the heads of those at the door and saw that Bhaiji's body, covered with a muslin sheet, lay on the floor. That was the custom, he remembered. Hindus always lifted the dying out of bed and placed them as close as possible to the earth from whence they came. One of the young students sat near Bhaiji's covered head reciting holy scriptures in a nasal voice. Martine was close by his side, sitting Indian-style, her bowed head covered with the edge of her white sari. The others huddled close; some standing, others sitting, silent and motionless. The scene reminded him of an ancient Hindu print.

He stood there only briefly, then turned and wandered through the empty and silent ground floor out onto the verandah. The morning sun was bright and warm. He found his favorite seat near the column. It was only later that he realized what an excellent vantage point it made. During the next hour, it seemed he heard and saw everything. Sixteen brought him a cup of strong black tea, and told him that Martine had decided that Bhaiji's body would be cremated that morning. Later, when a loud and rhythmic chanting started indoors, he learned somehow that the body was being washed and anointed according to Hindu rites. He was stitting there when a Land Rover carrying three turbaned constables and a crisp and trim young constabulary officer came roaring through the gate. The officer alighted, and shot him a brief, curious glance, as he climbed the steps and went into the house. Shortly after he reemerged and again roared off in the waiting Land Rover, word spread quickly that the youth who stabbed Bhaiji had been surrendered by the Husain elders and was in custody. Oddly, he received the news almost disinterestedly. Last night he had hated the youth and the mob, but now, if he could summon up any feeling at all, it was one of pity. Punishing Bhaiji's crazed young assassin—hanging him, perhaps—would not bring him back.

Finally, he was seated there when the shaven-headed old Brahmin priest, wearing a long cinnamon robe, a huge caste mark covering his forehead, came out of the house and approached him. He looked at him with surprise. It wasn't until the old Brahmin spoke and, simultaneously, the sun glinted off his spectacles, that he realized it was Panditji. "Good morning, Mr. Fraser."

He couldn't suppress a smile. "Good morning, Panditji. I didn't recognize you."

Panditji's own smile was slight. "No, Mr. Fraser. Our relationship has always been on a different level."

He nodded. It was unbelievable how the robe and the caste mark had changed the cheerful old man. Or had he changed so much? It suddenly struck him how strange it was that he simply had never thought of Panditji as being a priest.

Panditji said, "Madame asked me to speak to you, sir. She wishes you to act as our master's nearest relation at his cremation."

He was completely taken aback. "Why, I . . . I . . ." He paused. "I couldn't do that."

Panditji's voice was chiding. "It is a great honor, sir."

"Yes, I know," he said slowly. He was still too dumbfounded to think clearly. He looked at Panditji silently until he recovered. Finally, he said, "I don't really think I should have the honor. Why can't someone else do it?"

Panditji said quietly, "Madame has chosen you."

He stood up slowly. "Maybe I should talk with her."

"She is in her room bathing, sir," Panditji said. "I will tell her you wish to see her when she comes down." He came closer and peered at him through his spectacles with the look he knew so well. "I also wish it, Mr. Fraser."

"But, why, Panditji? I . . . I . . . He broke off with a helpless gesture.

"Our master would have liked it," Panditji said, firmly.

"But I wouldn't know what to do," he said.

"I will show you," Panditji said. When he still hesitated, Panditji said, "It is your duty, sir."

He thought about it again. "All right," he said slowly, "I'll do it. But I still would like to speak with Madame Valois."

Panditji clutched his arm in a tight, affectionate squeeze. "You have made the right decision, Mr. Fraser. I'll tell Madame."

As Panditji hurried away, he found his seat again, mystified as to why Martine had chosen him for such a role. He was not certain whether he was pleased or displeased. He knew the chief duty of the nearest male relative at a cremation, of course. He was not squeamish about it . . . or was he? He thought about it and shrugged. He was still mulling it over when Panditji and Martine appeared in the doorway. Panditji was carrying an earthenware bowl filled with what appeared to be hot coals. He stepped out onto the verandah, but Martine remained in the doorway. When she saw him approaching, she stepped back into the shadows of the house.

It gave him a pang to see how drawn and pale she looked. Blue shadows circled her enormous eyes which seemed to be pure black and completely lusterless. Then he realized with surprise that she was not wearing a blouse under her white borderless sari. The trailing end was draped over her bare breasts. Her feet were also bare. It was the traditional mourning dress of a Hindu widow. "You will do it?" she asked, quietly.

"Yes," he said, "but why did you choose me?"

"You were his brother."

"All men were his brother," he said.

She shook her head. "No, they were his children. Most of them."

"You will not be coming?"

"No," she said. "It is not the custom. I will remain here."

Maybe it was because her bare feet and single winding garment made her look oddly like a penitent . . . or maybe it was something he saw in her face or eyes. But as he looked at her, in a single illuminating instant, he realized what it was about her that had always been so naggingly disturbing—the cause of her remoteness, her impenetrable reserve. Just as he had forgotten completely that old Panditji was a priest, it had never occurred to him until now that in her own fashion Martine actually was a nun. An odd nun, perhaps, but her dedication was the same . . . her chastity . . . He said slowly, "You'll always remain here now, won't you?"

She raised her eyes and looked at him somberly. It seemed she was about to speak, but at that moment, there was a rhythmic clapping of hands and a slow chanting from the rear of the house. She bowed her head and turned away. There was a burst of wailing from the women, and the procession appeared. Six men, three on each side, had shouldered the bamboo poles of the stretcher on which Bhaiji's body lay, bound tightly in a crimson and gold cloth. Panditji stepped through the doorway and handed him the earthenware bowl. "You will carry this, sir." The coals in the bowl were covered with a gray ash and looked dead but he could feel their heat on his face. He looked toward Martine, but she had her back to him, her smooth bare shoulders slumped dejectedly.

From somewhere Panditji had produced a small silk-covered book which he opened. Without looking at it, he began a rising and falling chant.

They walked out into the bright morning sunshine, down the steps, and started across the courtyard. He and Panditji were in the lead, the stretcher bearers right behind, and he presumed the men in the ashram were in the rear, but he did not turn around. The wailing and chanting from the women on the verandah increased in tempo, and when they passed through the gate and entered the street, it reached a final screeching crescendo. The men took up the chanting then, but softly, almost in a mumbling undertone. Occasionally, Panditji would raise his voice in a wavering half-cry, and they would respond.

As they passed through the gate, he had looked up the burned-out desolate street. The bodies had been removed, and he wondered who was responsible. If it had not been for the charred ruins, walking here in the sunshine, he could almost think that last night had been some horrible nightmare. But, no. That was not true. Bhaiji was dead—his cold and lifeless body right behind him. It was strange . . . strange how calmly and matter-of-factly he accepted Bhaiji's death. Was that the most important thing he had learned during these last few weeks: not to fear death? Could he still profess to be a Christian and not fear death? Christians were supposed to be afraid of dying. Theologians often made a great deal over the fact that Christ faced death with fear and trembling, while Socrates drank down his cup of hemlock calmly. It was their favorite argument when they claimed that all Christ had promised was resurrection for the godly, that the belief in immortality of all souls was a false doctrine absorbed by early Christians from the Greeks. St. Paul said death was God's enemy.

He walked along, feeling the heat of the bowl, listening to the soft chanting, thinking of that. No, Paul was wrong. Perhaps it was true, as some people claimed, that it was the only explanation Paul could think of when Christians kept dying after the crucifixion. How embarrassing and bewildering it must have been for Paul when people kept dying after he had promised those who accepted Jesus Christ would have Life Eternal. No, death was not an enemy. He knew how wrong Paul was now. He knew death was conquered by the mere act of dying.

He thought about the vision. It was already elusive and unreal. Martine had been right. It had not changed anything really; it had only strengthened what he had always believed: that there was a God and someday he must answer to Him. Yes, he believed devoutly enough. Why was it nonbelievers could never understand the covenant some men were fortunate enough to make with God? How unreasonable to think it was a sop, a pacifier, or—as Freud claimed—the extension of some childhood need for protection through love. God did not temper the icy blast of winter for believers or give them fewer miseries. Believers did not walk in perpetual sunshine. Pain and grief and troubles fall on believers and nonbelievers alike.

But what was he? He was not certain, but he was thankful that he was not one of those people who accepted religion like a family heirloom, dutifully accepted from one generation, dutifully handed on to another, without once being examined. How much they missed! Only lately had a few churchmen begun to appear who seemed to realize that organized religion with all its paraphernalia and pomp, by trying to show how it was the only true faith, actually blunted and mummified the love of God. He could never accept that the church denoted a morally superior people or embraced only those who were worthy of divine attention. God's goodness was a common goodness, and God's people were not necessarily those who had an ecclesiastical bent. When God was a failure, it was man's failure. Still, it was not necessary to believe in God to do His will. Perhaps—

Something showered against his trouser's leg. He looked down and saw several peppercorns in the dust. A wrinkled old woman in a faded sari, holding a bare-bottomed boy by the hand, stood at the edge of the street. She threw another handful of peppercorns. He was touched; her tribute probably cost her a day's food. For the first time, he realized that they had not encountered a single other person since leaving the ashram. That was strange. He could understand why the Husains and other Muslims had not turned out, but he would have thought the Hindus would have lined the streets. Perhaps they were still afraid. His arms were tiring from carrying the bowl. He looked at Panditji. He was still walking in his slow, measured pace, reciting his prayers in a sing-song chant.

It seemed they walked an interminable distance, down one dusty street and up another. Finally, the houses began to thin. Then, there were none at all, only sun-baked fields on each side of the road. He heard a distant murmuring. It grew louder as they trudged along. When they topped a small rise in the road, he saw a huge crowd of people gathered in a field near a small stream about a hundred yards away. Old Panditji stepped up the tempo of the prayers, and the chanting responses from the men behind grew louder. The crowd sent up a ragged cheer when they first appeared but fell silent almost immediately. It slowly parted to let them through.

Three shaven-pated, old funeral Brahmans, wearing limp and faded cinnamon robes, stood waiting on a crumbling ghat at the edge of the small stream. The low brick platform atop the ghat, looking hardly big enough to accommodate a body, had been freshly white-washed. He slowly followed Panditji up the worn steps, and when he reached the top of the ghat, he was startled to see the multitude of brown faces staring up at him. There must have been several thousand people packed into the field. Old Panditji turned to face the water, and so did he. The stretcher-bearers were carrying Bhaiji's body down the steps toward the stream. At the water's edge, they un-shouldered the stretcher and gently submerged it for a moment or two.

As they started back up the steps, Panditji came over and took the bowl from him and placed it near the white-washed platform. He said quietly, "Watch me, sir. When I nod, please walk around the pyre seven times. Light the fire near the head. When it is lit, do not look toward it. Either turn away—or leave, if you wish." He nodded, suddenly realizing that he felt both nervous and reluctant about what he had to do. He tried not to think about it.

When the stretcher-bearers reached the top of the ghat and tenderly placed Bhaiji's body on the platform, the oldest of the funeral Brahmans moved swiftly. Even before they had picked up their stretcher and departed, he had cut through the binding cords with a small circular blade and had whisked off the crimson and gold covering. Whining an incantation in a monotone, he began touching the body here and there.

He had watched until the Brahman removed the shroud. Now he let his eyes rest on that naked white form for only an instant or two. It did not seem like Bhaiji, but only a figure made of silky hair and wax. He saw a collar of cotton wool around the neck . . . rose petals clinging to the wet chest. Out of the corner of his eye, he saw that somebody was handing up wood from below. Panditji and the oldest of the funeral Brahmans were chanting loudly, while the other two Brahmans worked quickly. After a while, he looked again. Bhaiji's body was almost covered with thin, irregular slats of grayish-white wood. Sandalwood— This was an expensive ceremony. The Brahmans were now placing larger pieces of wood on the body, crisscross, Boy Scout fire-building-style. Then the massive pieces of wood were passed up, well-seasoned, thick as a man's leg. Next, came the earthenware pots of ghee. As they came in a seemingly endless chain, upturned and drained one after another, splotching the wood with greasy stains, he heard a murmur of wonder sweep the crowd. This was indeed a cremation fit for a rajah.

He looked toward Panditji. He had his eyes closed and was chanting loudly. One of the Brahmans, the fat, dull-faced one, came forward carrying a four-foot stave with greasy rags wrapped around one end. The Brahman knelt and blew on the coals in the bowl, placed the rags on the coals and blew again. The rags ignited with a slow, yellow flame. The Brahman handed him the torch, and he looked toward Panditji, who nodded.

As he began to walk around the pyre, he became aware that the crowd had now broken into a soft murmurous roar. It sounded for all the world like the roar of the surf on a beach on a quiet night. He used the fire bowl as a marker as he circled the pyre, walking stiffly, conscious of all the eyes watching, holding the torch carefully. After the fourth revolution, he wondered if he wasn't walking too quickly. He felt slightly dizzy, seeing Panditji and the Brahmans as indistinct blurs as he passed. It reminded him ... yes, it reminded him of riding the merry-go-round when he was a kid ... the roar had the same powerful hurdy-gurdy beat. *Six*. Only one more round to go, if he had counted right. Suppose he hadn't. Would they tell him? Were they counting? *Seven*. He stopped. He was standing at the head of the pyre. He lowered the torch and placed the flame under one of the larger pieces of wood dripping ghee. The *ghee* sizzled and ran off the wood faster, but nothing else happened. Suddenly, he realized that through the crevices he could see a portion of Bhaiji's white forehead and his hair. It gave him a cringing feeling. He tried to close off his mind. He switched the flame under a smaller piece of wood. It smoked and turned brownish, but still nothing happened. Somebody grabbed his wrist and thrust the torch deep into the pyre, near Bhaiji's head. He turned and looked directly into the grinning face of the fat Brahman. The wood caught with a loud crackling. The Brahman took the torch from his hand, and skipped around the pyre, thrusting it in deep every foot or so. Individual flames licked upward, then joined, and soon a solid sheet of fire climbed higher and higher. He watched fascinated, barely aware that the soft roar of the crowd had become a tumultuous screaming cheer.

He stepped back from the flames before he remembered he was supposed to turn his back. He turned quickly, and stood there feeling the heat on his back. Then, it slowly occurred to him that it was done. *Yes, it was done*. He suddenly felt the strain leave him, and he felt exhausted and drained, so utterly exhausted that it took an effort for him to move toward the steps. As he walked past Panditji, he was only dimly aware that he began chanting in English for his benefit:

> Fire! thou wast lighted by him; may he therefore be reproduced from thee that he may attain regions of celestial bliss. May this offering be auspicious!

He walked down the steps and the crowd parted to let him pass. He walked slowly, hearing the hiss of the flames behind him, the shouts from the crowd, the chanting, looking neither right nor left. It was some time before he became aware of the soft, furtive prodding. One hand after another reached out to touch him as he passed, an incessant nudging, timorous and delicate. They were seeking *darshan*. By touching him, they thought they could share in some of the grace and holiness that had been Bhaiji's. Well, perhaps it they believed they could, then it was possible.

He had passed through the last of the crowd and was trudging up the small hill before he realized Sixteen had fallen into step with him. He looked up and Sixteen said, "Car waiting, sir." The old Buick was parked just over the rise. He climbed in and Sixteen started the motor. "Back to ashram, sir?" he asked.

He hesitated for only a moment. "No, Sixteen," he said, "back to Benares to get my baggage. I'm going home."

AUTHOR'S NOTE

A bibliography for a novel is unusual, obviously incomplete, and probably unnecessary. Nevertheless, the author wishes to acknowledge his indebtedness to the following works which sometimes supplied—but more often suggested—ideas expressed in portions of this book:

S. Radhakrishnan, notes and introduction to *Mahabharata, Bhagavadgita* or *The Song Divine* (New York, Harper, 1948).

C. S. Lewis, *The Problem of Pain* (Toronto, Saunders, S. J. R., 1940).

Krister Stendahl, edited and with an introduction to *Immortality and Resurrection* (New York, Macmillan, 1965).

Romain Rolland, "The Life of Ramakrishna" in *Prophets of the New India*, translated from the French by E. F. Malcolm-Smith (New York, Boni, 1930; London, Cassell, 1930).

Bernard Murchland, *The Meaning of the Death of God* (New York, Random House, 1967).

Alfred North Whitehead, *Religion in the Making* (1926).

About the Author

Joe David Brown is a native of Birmingham, Alabama. He has been a newspaperman (Birmingham *Post*, *New York News*) and a foreign correspondent for *Time* (stationed in London, Paris, Moscow, and New Delhi). In addition to his novels—*Stars in My Crown*, *The Freeholder*, *Kings Go Forth*, and the present *Glimpse of a Stranger*—he is the author of *India* in the *Life* World Series and edited *The Hippies* for Time-Life Books. He now lives with his wife and daughter on an 84-acre farm in Orange County, New York.